QUEEN

of the

DEAD

SARAH
BROADWAY

ANGRY
ROBOT

ANGRY ROBOT
An imprint of Watkins Media Ltd

Unit 11, Shepperton House
89-93 Shepperton Road
London N1 3DF
UK

angryrobotbooks.com
Your queen to be

An Angry Robot paperback original, 2025

Edited by Desola Coker and Shona Kinsella
Cover by Alice Claire Coleman
Set in Meridien

ISBN 978 1 91599 892 7
Ebook ISBN 978 1 91599 893 4

Printed and bound in the United Kingdom by CPI Group (UK) Ltd, Croydon CR0 4YY

The manufacturer's authorised representative in the EU for product safety is eucomply OÜ - Pärnu mnt 139b-14, 11317 Tallinn, Estonia, hello@eucompliancepartner.com; www.eucompliancepartner.com

9 8 7 6 5 4 3 2 1

MIX
Paper | Supporting
responsible forestry
FSC® C013604

For the girl who didn't know she was writing inside the Veil the entire time. At least, not until she stepped out of it and found a world reborn – one full of life, warmth, and color.

CHAPTER 1

The sensation was like being pulled sideways, picked up in the air, and then dropped on the ground flat on your back. Once, when I was a little girl, I fell off the top of a playground set and got the breath knocked out of me. It felt just like that. Every time. Usually, it happened when I started to fall asleep at night, only to be woken up by the impact. As bad as that sounds, I rather preferred it. This time, I'd been wide awake, which made it a whole heck of a lot worse.

I rolled over, placed both hands open against the ground, and tried to reorient myself before the contents of my stomach could come up. *Take a deep breath... one more*, I repeated to myself over and over.

"Dammit, Mrs Hammond," I said when I was confident I wouldn't upchuck the microwave fettuccine alfredo I had during my lunch break. "We've talked about this before: not when I'm at work."

"Oh dear. I'm dreadfully sorry, but it is rather urgent."

I was pretty sure it wasn't since she always said that, and it never actually was.

I sat down on the ground and folded my legs in front of me, still taking deep, steadying breaths. I kept my palms open against the grass to remind myself that I was right-side up in the world like a normal human was supposed to be.

The only light in the cemetery was the occasional beam of moonlight filtering through the clouds and Mrs Hammond's glowing aura. Her perfectly pressed day dress barely swished as she paced – or rather floated – back and forth over the graves in front of me. This was new. Usually, she sat on a tombstone with a teacup and saucer on her lap, ready to yap my ears off.

"I didn't know what to do." She wrinkled up the hankie in her hands, then straightened it only to twist it up again.

I'd never seen her so nervous.

"He refuses to go back to sleep, and he keeps calling for you."

"Who does?" I looked around, but it seemed no one else was up and about except for Mrs Hammond. Everyone was tucked neatly in the ground, sleeping just like the dead were supposed to be doing. Mrs Hammond was usually the exception. Barring the chaos that is Halloween, she was the only ghost who refused to accept her eternal slumber, roaming around Magnolia Grove Cemetery at her leisure with her bouffant hair neatly coiffed and a string of pearls around her neck. The woman was a dead-ringer for June Cleaver in *Leave it to Beaver* – no pun intended.

Lately, she had the habit of summoning me whenever she got bored or lonely. I'd never come across another apparition with the ability to do that. It surprised Mrs Hammond, too, and when she found out she could call me at will whenever the need arose... Well, let's just say it's been teatime several times a week since then.

She twisted her hankie into a wad and nodded nervously in the direction of the stone angel at the edge of the cemetery. Big blue eyes peeked out from behind the angel's stone robes.

Well, blimey, it really was urgent after all.

I stood up and dusted off the loose grass clippings from my black tights. It's like the groundskeeper always knew I would be wearing tights to work when Mrs Hammond was likely to interrupt my night.

Instead of going to the stone angel, I headed toward the rusted iron bench under the nearby oak tree. I sat down, patted the empty spot next to me, and waited.

A blond head peeked all the way out from behind the angel.

"Hi there, Tom-Tom," I said, giving him my best smile.

The little boy looked around nervously.

While Mrs Hammond's aura was a warm white, Tom's was a flickering blue that matched the blue of his Victorian sailor boy outfit. He climbed up on the bench, his legs too short to touch the ground.

"I'm scared, Lou," he said to me, swinging his legs back and forth. "He woke up. He's been asleep, just waiting, but not anymore. Now he's awake, and he's looking for you. I think… I think he wants what you have."

The scary part wasn't exactly what Tom-Tom said but how he said it. He spoke in the impassive, oblivious voice of a toddler who had no idea the dangers the real world held for him. It was as if he'd held up three fingers and told me he was "this many" and that his favorite color was blue.

The key to successfully interacting with Tom was to pretend that none of that was creepy as hell, something Mrs Hammond was terrible at doing. The three-year-old boy with his doom-filled prophecies more than disturbed her and she made sure to keep as far away as politely possible, all the while trying to mask her horror by adjusting her pearls over and over again. Ironic that a ghost could be weirded out by another ghost, but that was Mrs Hammond for you… an enigma.

"Who's looking for me?" I asked.

"He wants what you have," he repeated instead of answering me.

The other key to dealing with Tom was to just let it ride. The less you said, the more he would. I simply nodded and waited for more than gibberish to come out of the kid's mouth.

"He won't stop until he takes it from you... until he takes it all from you."

Great, more gibberish. I waited a little while longer for any other tidbit of information, but it seemed that was all I was going to get.

"Who's looking for me, Tom-Tom?" I pressed him again.

He sucked in his bottom lip, his big blue eyes darting nervously about, and shook his head instead of answering me.

"Something's changing, Lou," he said, still looking around scared. "Can you feel it? The Veil is thinning. Soon, it'll tear, and then he's gonna break free. It's only a matter of time."

And just like that he was gone, disappearing in a burst of cold air that sent goosebumps rippling up my arm.

Mrs Hammond rushed toward me. "Whatever do you think he meant?"

"Haven't the foggiest, but I guess I'll have to be on the lookout. In the meantime, I really have to get back to work." I'd been gone too long as it was, and I still had to walk all the way back. Mrs Hammond could successfully yank me into the cemetery no matter where I was, but returning me seemed inconveniently beyond her limits.

"You'll come visit again soon I hope," she said, walking with me to the cemetery's great iron gate.

"Of course," I reassured her. I figured out pretty quickly that if I didn't respond in the positive, she'd summon me sooner than I'd like, probably while I was at work or even in the shower – *that* had been a fun night. Let's just say I learned to keep a backpack of spare clothes hidden under an overgrown rose bush at the back of the cemetery out of sight.

"It's always nice chatting with you, Mrs H."

"Oh, you're such a dear. Try not to work too hard." She smiled and waved goodbye behind the fence as I started out on the sidewalk back to work.

Someday, she and I were going to have a serious discussion about exactly what was keeping her in this earthly realm and not resting deep in the ground beside the dearly departed Mr Hammond.

The night was cold, and my jacket was back at work. Why couldn't Mrs Hammond have summoned that, too? Could ghosts summon inanimate objects? These were just some of the thoughts running through my head as I dug my fingers into the pockets of my jean skirt to keep them warm.

Lucky for me, I was just fifteen minutes walking distance from work. Unfortunately, I had to pass by the police station to get there. An off-duty officer came out of the building wearing sweats from working out in the station's gym. He tossed a duffle bag in the trunk of his patrol car and gave me a nod of recognition. I returned it and pressed on down the sidewalk, averting my gaze. It wasn't the cop that bothered me. In fact, he was super cute. Mrs Hammond had the habit of dumping me in the cemetery toward the end of his shift and it was the third time this week I'd seen Officer Super Cute coming out of work.

It was the dozens upon dozens of spirits swarming the building. These ghosts were nothing like the full apparition of Mrs Hammond. Instead, they were wispy, blurry vapors, fractions of souls left over from the echo of tormented human beings stuck in a loop of pain and sorrow. They tended to cling to places like the police station or the hospital, especially the emergency room entrance. I could do nothing for them. I tried once and it was a nightmare. Literally. It took months before I could get a good night's sleep without the horror of them seeping into my dreams.

Unlike Tom-Tom and Mrs H, these spirits were oblivious to me, focused solely on their pain and whatever past traumatic events in their human lives anchored them here. Every now and then, one floated close to me, its empty eye sockets looming over me, noting there was something different about me from the other normal living beings inside the station. They never got too close or stayed too long, always returning to the others floating around the building.

This time was different.

One of them brushed by me on the sidewalk, way closer than they usually got. I sped up, quickly putting my earbuds in and blasting music on the old Walkman I'd found at the thrift store. I never had a cell phone on me or any other new technology. Anything new seemed to get drained of power within seconds of being around a ghost. With the Walkman, I had a solid ten minutes before batteries with fresh juice were sucked dry.

I turned up the music on my earbuds and tried to ignore the spirit circling me on the sidewalk. I kept straight on, trying to keep my cool, sort of like when you're avoiding a fuzzy bumble bee buzzing around your head – keep calm and maybe you won't get stung. Well, it was just a theory anyway.

The wisp's hand reached out. A frozen scream distorted its blurry face. The vaporous limb passed over my skin, and the catchy tunes of Journey disappeared from my earbuds, replaced by the soft whisper of a woman's voice.

The Veil is thinning. He wants what you have. He'll take it all from you if he can, the voice repeated Tom-Tom's words. The Walkman batteries died out and silence filled my ears.

I sucked in a harsh breath, held it for a second, and then very calmly let it out. All my life I'd dealt with the dead, in one way or another. I was pretty much used to all sorts of scary stuff. Normally, that scary stuff was just on the surface and underneath it was something completely harmless. Normally.

Getting touched by one of these wispy spirit things forced me to remind myself of the general harmlessness of ghosts. The wisp's eye sockets looked at me one last time, checking to make sure I got the message, then floated back down to the station with the rest of the swarm. The spot where she touched my arm was ice-cold and covered with beads of moisture. My first instinct was to cover it with my hand to warm it up, but I knew better. The cold would only transfer to my palm and linger there for a few minutes. I kept my hands in my skirt pockets and picked up the pace back to work.

CHAPTER 2

Past the 24-hour pharmacy and across the street from the Italian restaurant was a vast sea of empty parking spots. A neon Piggly Wiggly sign lit up in the middle of it like a beacon marking safe harbor. I jogged around to the back loading entrance and slipped my dead Walkman into the front pocket of my work apron.

"For a girl who doesn't smoke, you sure take a lot of smoke breaks." The night floor-manager leaned against the back of the brick building working on his second cigarette, his black Piggly Wiggly apron slung over his shoulder. A soft breeze tugged at his comb-over, threatening to uncover the bald patch underneath. He was a sight for sore eyes after my cemetery jaunt, and I could have kissed that shining forehead.

"Hey, Cliff," I said. "Sorry about that."

He shrugged it off. He didn't care and that was the best kind of boss a girl like me could have. Cliff was there for a paycheck and that was it.

He crushed the cigarette butt with the tip of his tennis shoe. "There's an endcap of tomato soup that needs refilling. After that, let's start working on closing up. I know it's still early yet but maybe when it's time to lock up we can get out of here in record time."

Cliff wasn't much for doing anything beyond what was absolutely necessary, and I loved him for it.

"No problem-o," I said and got back to work.

No one haunted grocery stores. It was the perfect place to work. Getting groceries was just as mundane as taking out the trash – a necessity of life that everyone sort of forgets about until they run out of milk or need another loaf of bread. Grocery stores didn't tether you to the earth or make you bother stock girls who were just minding their own business.

I straightened the aisles and helped bag groceries for Marge at the checkout counter while Diego took a quick smoke break himself. Technically, he didn't smoke either, but he liked to go outside away from everyone and read for a little while.

We all managed to wrap up the end of shift chores ten minutes after closing. I waved to Marge as she got into her minivan and drove away, following Cliff's junker Trans Am out of the parking lot.

"See ya, Lou," Diego called out to me as he started his short walk to the apartment complex around the corner.

I got on my bike and rode out of the parking lot back toward home. I own a car but just like a cell phone, using it was asking for trouble. It's like driving home at night after a really scary movie, afraid you might see a zombie step out in front of your car or catch a glimpse of one in your rear-view mirror. That's reality for me except with ghosts. They like to get my attention when I'm driving. Sometimes they'll suddenly appear on the seat beside me to chat my ears off on the way home, and sometimes they'll claw up the hood of my car or pound on my windows. The worst ones are stuck in repeat, re-enacting the last minutes of their lives in front of my eyes. Riding my bike everywhere just made things easier.

I rode my bike down the now-familiar path I first mapped out when I moved to town: stay away from the historic district (for obvious reasons), go down past the new townhomes under construction, by the library and around the corner to a street lined with tiny two-bedroom houses. When looking for places to live, I scoured the entire town for a street that was absolutely ghost-free. I couldn't believe my luck when I stumbled upon the little gem known as Cedar Street. Even the name was generic and unremarkable. It was great.

Every house basically served as temporary rentals for small families just starting out before moving on to something bigger, or for college kids who recently moved out of their parents' house. I was a little worried when I found out there were one or two divorced households, divorce being a recipe for future ghost-like activity should an untimely fate happen, but they all appeared content in their present relationship status and were likely to move on to other, better houses along with everyone else.

The only residents to live on Cedar Street for longer than a year were me and the man who lived in the house right behind mine, and we weren't going anywhere anytime soon.

I turned down my driveway and parked the bike under the carport housing my seldom-used, barely running Honda. My house looked like an exact replica of everyone else's house on the block except for lace curtains in the window and a coat of chipped green paint on the siding. Instead of going up the steps to the front door, I grabbed the plastic bag of groceries from the metal basket hooked to the back of my bike and walked across the alley I shared with the neighbor behind me.

His porch light was on, waiting for me. I bounced up the steps and rapped on the back door three times before unlocking it and letting myself in.

Mortie's house could be described as claustrophobic yet cozy. Oriental rugs covered the hardwood floors. Shelves that stood from floor to ceiling lined every wall, packed to the brim with books. The few flat surfaces available were taken up by antiques and artifacts on display, some protected by glass cases, others just gathering dust. The only furniture to sit on in the living room was a set of plaid wingback chairs facing a small TV perched on a cabinet and surrounded by more stacks of books. A sleek black cat with a tip of white at the end of her tail peeked up from her spot curled up on one of the chairs.

"Hello, Zelda," I cooed, giving her a scratch under the chin. She purred contentedly and curled back up into a ball.

I picked up a forgotten, half-drunk mug of cold tea off a teetering stack of books next to one of the chairs and poured it out in the kitchen sink.

"Evening, Lewis!" A cheerful voice called out to me from the back of the house. No one else called me that. My mother named me Louise after my great-grandmother, but everyone usually just called me Lou, except for Mortie. He settled on Lewis, saying I reminded him of a friend he used to play chess with, back during his college years. I wasn't sure how exactly, but I liked it, and the nickname stuck.

"How was work?" he asked from the extra bedroom he had converted into a workshop.

"Work was fine." I put an emphasis on the first word as I unloaded the groceries onto the kitchen counter and made us both peanut butter sandwiches, being sure to add pickles and potato chips to his.

"Oh dear. Mrs Hammond again?"

I climbed up on the empty stool in his workroom and grunted around a mouthful of gooey peanut butter and bread.

If I thought I was lucky discovering Cedar Street, then finding Mortie living next door was like hitting the jackpot. Besides my mother, he was the only one who knew my secret, which made sense because he had one of his own, too.

He stretched a portion of leather out across the table, destined to replace the cover of an old, damaged book. The already restored innards sat safely on the shelf, up and away from all the little bottles of different glues and sharp tools scattered across his worktable, waiting to be reunited with the spine.

"Who's this one for?" I asked, watching him work. Before Mortie retired, he worked in the restoration department at a museum in Indianapolis. Now, he repaired antiques out of his home to help supplement his social security checks.

He glanced lovingly up at the dissected tome on the shelf. "The Ladies Historical Preservation Society. It's a cookbook," he said fondly. I was pretty sure no one was that fond of cookbooks, but I knew it was the history he felt in it that he loved the most. Normally that was the stuff I veered away from, but it was always nice seeing Mortie happy.

"And what did Mrs Hammond have to say tonight?" he asked, cleaning up little odds and ends and bits of debris left over on his table after a day of work. I watched him put the tops back on open bottles and scoop loose scraps of twine off the cutting mat before answering.

"It wasn't Mrs Hammond. It was Tom," I said.

His hands went still. Usually when Tom made an appearance, there was a damn good reason. Last year, he poked up out of the blue with a warning about Halloween, and it turned out to be one hell of a busy night. Every ghost in Magnolia Grove seemed hellbent on trying to be noticed by the town's living residents that night. And I don't know how they managed it, but it certainly felt as if for a short time, folks got a sense of the spirits that haunted their neighborhoods. Whether it was trick-or-treaters running wild down the sidewalks after catching glimpses of them to late night partygoers swerving at specters stepping right in front of their cars as they drove by the cemetery – it made for a long night of trying to convince some ghostly folks to take it down a notch.

"And what did the little gentleman have to say this time?"

"Something about a veil thinning. He was vague as usual." I left out the part about somebody looking for me, wanting what I had. I didn't want to overburden him, and I knew if I said more, he'd be able to tell that it bothered me. I wasn't ready to admit to myself just how much.

Mortie perched on his own stool and took a crunchy bite of sandwich. He was a short man, a little bit shorter than me even, and had a mostly bald head. The few gray and white hairs that were there stuck out despite an attempt to keep them combed neatly back. He was whisper-thin, something that worried me the older he got, almost like if I wasn't watching him carefully, he might blow away on a windy day. Even though he no longer worked at the museum, he still dressed each day as if he did, wearing a bowtie and a sweater vest over a dress shirt that he rolled up to his elbows as he worked.

The first time I met Mortie, we were both taking our trash cans to the curb for garbage day and exchanged friendly greetings. The second time I came across him, he was in the county cemetery. He'd been kneeling at the base of a dilapidated headstone, covering it with a piece of tracing paper and going over it with chalk, half a dozen ghosts swarming around him, unknown to him at the time. It wasn't what he was doing that drew their curiosity, though. I'd come across loads of people over the years indexing cemeteries, adding the inscriptions of old weathered tombstones to online databases, and like for many others, it was a hobby of Mortie's. No, it wasn't the tracing paper and chalk that intrigued the ghosts; it was Mortie himself.

He finished his sandwich and considered me with a quirk of his head as he dabbed at the corner of his mouth with a napkin. "You're not telling me something," he said to himself, stroking his chin and then nodded, agreeing with his own assessment.

He reached out, and frail-looking fingers with a surprising amount of strength behind them grasped mine. His eyes changed. The irises and pupils disappeared, overtaken by a milky-white film. There was a moment of added warmth between our hands and then it was gone, his eyes already returning to their normal pale hazel color.

"They scared you this time," he said, giving my hand a gentle squeeze before letting it go. "Oh, my dear Louise, you should've said something."

I gulped down the swell of emotion that came unexpectedly from hearing him drop my nickname. "Hey, I'm always scared. This isn't anything new."

Mortie wasn't sure what this particular gift he'd been endowed with was called, but he believed it made him something of an empath. It allowed him to see what a person was feeling just through a touch. He claimed it aided him with his work, giving him a second instinct as he restored artifacts, helping to return them to their original, true selves. It also showed him exactly what I was the moment our paths crossed that afternoon in the cemetery, when I picked up his tracing paper and offered him a hand up off the ground.

"How about a distraction, hm?" he asked, picking up on the fact I wasn't ready to talk more about Tom-Tom. "I have a puzzle for you."

He reached up and took a scrap of thin paper off the shelf, a layer of charcoal covering its surface, making the string of hardly legible letters stand out. He handed it to me as well as his cell phone with a picture of the headstone the paper came from pulled up on the screen.

"What do you make of this one? I came across it when I was out in Cottage Hill Cemetery and haven't quite figured out yet what it says – something that starts with an *I* and ends with an *S*, I believe."

With my help, Mortie pretty much filled up the database with every headstone within a thirty-mile radius of Magnolia Grove whose inscription had been erased by time. He'd since moved on to towns farther out – cemeteries I really didn't venture to. I had more than enough on my hands with the three cemeteries inside the city limits, not to mention the county cemetery.

I didn't need the charcoal to tell him what was written there, but I always liked to give him the idea that it helped. In truth, the picture was enough. Whatever it was that made me, well, me, also came with a few other cursed quirks, including a creepy party trick to be able to look at tombstones of those who had truly passed on and see the details of their lives in my head. Sorta like recalling a memory from my own life. Strangely, it never worked on ghosts. Just graves.

"Imogene Adams. Born May 15, 1851. Died September 12, 1916." I could almost see her face in the headstone. "She loved bluebells. Her husband planted them for her in the garden by their front porch when they first got married. She always loved watching them come into bloom each year."

Mortie's chin gave a little quiver. He was in every sense of the word an empath, gift or no gift, and while I loved that about him, it hurt my heart that he seemed to feel everything for everyone.

"Then she shall have them again the next time I'm out there," he said, fervently.

He quickly took out his laptop to enter the information I gave him into the database.

I hopped off the stool and planted a kiss on the top of his bald head while he typed. "See you tomorrow, Mortie."

Home was exactly like I had left it that afternoon when I first headed out for my shift, before Mrs Hammond happened, before Tom-Tom and the freaky police station wisp. I kicked off my Converse shoes and curled my toes in the freshly vacuumed carpet. The floors were clean as were the dishes left to dry in the dish rack. I prided myself on coming home to a clean house. Nothing was worse than cleaning up an entire grocery store after a full day of customers only to come home to pick up another mess on top of that.

The lamps were on in the living room and bedroom. I always left the lights on while I was gone, the electric bill be damned. The block was ghost-free, but who knew when that might change and a surprise would be waiting for me on the couch when I walked through the door, ready for me to listen to its life story.

While my wardrobe was basically nothing but varying shades of black and gray clothes, my house was a different story. In a life made up of depressing, horrific imagery, I leaned more toward bright colors as much as possible when it came to my surroundings. Outside the house was sage green and inside the walls were pale yellow. The furniture all consisted of mismatched, thrift store finds that were bright and cheery. In almost every corner and windowsill, there was some kind of potted plant. With a life full of dead folks hounding me, it was nice to have silent things nearby to counteract them.

I rifled through the mail I'd dropped on the table by the door before I'd gone to work and looked at my answering machine, which, of course, didn't have any messages on it. I may not have a cell phone, but I did have an older landline phone. No one ever really called me except for Cliff asking if I wanted to cover someone's shift or Mortie wondering if I wanted to share a casserole with him while *Jeopardy!* was on.

I didn't own a TV. That, too, was asking for trouble. My mother had one when I was a little girl and the messages that came to me through the white noise during her daytime shows made me want to scream. Luckily, no one bothered me during my *Jeopardy!* sessions with Mortie. Occasionally, it flickered during the commercials, but that was pretty much it.

I sank down onto my overstuffed couch and picked up a book at the top of a stack on the coffee table. Being without a TV meant a lot of free time for reading. Every two weeks, I usually swung by the library on my way home from work to pick up a new haul of books.

The coffee table was covered with the latest stockpile. There were a few instructional books ranging from how to care for different houseplants to teaching yourself crochet – I had the notion of crocheting a hat for Mortie for Christmas. Mostly, there was a stack of romance novels I was in the process of working my way through.

Thrillers were out of the question. Even cozy mysteries hit a little too close to home. Romance novels proved to be the best respite from the darkness of my everyday life. They always had a happy ending and were refreshingly predictable. I wasn't sure what kind of expectations they were instilling in my subconscious when it came to men, but that really wasn't a problem. There were no romantic leads in my life. Whatever made me what I was also seemed to make me a man-repellent.

Maybe all men had a "crazy lady" detector naturally inherent to them that went off like the Fourth of July whenever I was around.

Either way, there were more than enough men on my coffee table willing to tear off my nightgown and ravish me.

I read for a little over an hour. Going to bed was the worst time of night for me, and it didn't have anything to do with ghosts. For the most part, I was content with my life of solitude, especially in the life I'd made for myself in Magnolia Grove. I had a job that was simple and predictable. I had a ghost-free home on a ghost-free block. Not to mention, the library was less than five minutes away. And whenever I needed someone to talk to, there was always Mortie next door. Still, when I pulled back the quilts on my empty queen bed, it was another reminder of how lonely my life was.

I put a small saucepan full of milk to heat on the stove while I got ready for bed. Warm milk with a teaspoon or two of vanilla syrup did wonders for lulling me quickly to sleep. Whether or not that sleep would be dreamless, was a gamble. At least I wouldn't be lying awake, staring up at the ceiling, thinking about how empty the house felt.

That night, I managed to drift off to sleep as soon as I pulled the covers up to my chin. It was a deep sleep with not a single dream – a rarity.

I should've realized it for the omen it was.

CHAPTER 3

I woke up to rain pounding against the windows. I stayed under the quilt for a few minutes longer, listening to its steady rhythm. A good night's sleep was rare. The few times they did happen, I made sure to soak up every minute of them.

Working the late shift automatically meant I kept a later schedule than everyone else. By the time I'd taken a long bubble bath and done a few chores around the house, it was already past a normal person's lunchtime. Outside, the rain picked up, coming down in heavy drops. On days like this, it was tempting to take the Honda to work but after everything that happened yesterday, it was wiser to stick with the bike.

I pulled on my hooded pink polka dot raincoat, one of the few bright-colored things I ever wore, and headed out to wipe off my bike seat with a hand towel. There was still plenty of time to swing by the cemetery and visit with Mrs H before getting to work. Maybe a quick chat would help me avoid any future untimely summons on her part.

Most people believed ghosts only came out at night. That'd be nice. While ghosts were definitely more prevalent at night, especially with a full moon, they usually didn't keep to any set schedule, at least not where it concerned me.

I rode my bike up to the cemetery's iron gate, leaning it up against the wide trunk of a weeping willow. Thankfully, the cemetery was empty of anyone else alive. I always preferred it that way as it tended to make things easier. On any given day, Magnolia Grove Cemetery didn't really have a lot of mourners to start with. A handful of them sometimes lingered a few days after a funeral, but that was about it. The only real regular besides me was a tall, lanky man dressed in a suit that had seen better days, placing flowers at his wife's grave. I never saw her floating around anywhere, so I assumed their time together had been happy. He always gave me a nod hello whenever our paths crossed. Today it was just me though.

I walked up the row of tombstones Mrs H liked to frequent. The rain lightened to a breezy sort of sprinkle, and the air was crisp. It wouldn't be long before fall was here, and I'd have to rummage in the back of my closet for some sweaters.

"Mrs Hammond?" I called out politely, keeping my tone neighborly, as if I was knocking on her front door asking for a cup of sugar.

No one answered. That wasn't like her. In fact, I tried to remember if there was another time when she hadn't been around the moment I entered the cemetery.

"Mrs Hammond?" I tried again. The breeze kicked up, spitting tiny droplets on my face. I lowered my hood to try to keep out of the rain. Naturally, when I wanted to get this over with, she was nowhere to be found. I stifled a groan. I really, really didn't want to be summoned again. It wasn't the greatest sensation. I decided to try a new tactic.

"Cynthia?" It was the name carved into her tombstone above a pretty bouquet of lilies. Engraved beside it was Mr Hammond's name: Franklin. She hated when I called her Cynthia. Whenever I did, her little nose scrunched up and her usual cheerful demeanor became terse, as if I'd just shouted a string of curse words in the middle of church, right before the minister got up to give a sermon.

She still didn't answer me.

"Tom-Tom?" I ventured, peeking around the stone angel.

Nothing.

I even looked around his own tombstone. It was an old slab made of sandstone that leaned to the side, getting dangerously close to toppling over. Wind and rain had long since removed the words carved into the surface, not even leaving an indent behind to trace.

"Tom?" I tried again.

Silence.

I let out a loud sigh, not caring if Mrs Hammond heard it or not. I guess I would just have to prepare myself for an unwelcome summons in the near future.

It was the second bad omen that I should've paid more attention to.

The workday started as uneventfully as any other day, and I tried to enjoy its repetitiveness, all the while shaking off the nagging feeling Mrs Hammond's odd absence left me with.

I stacked apples one on top of another in a pyramid in the produce section. A few at the top came loose and rolled their way down the sides. I caught them before they could fall off the display tray and awkwardly held out my arms to steady the rest. Somewhat sure the pyramid wouldn't topple to the floor, I let go of my apple embrace, looked back up at the display tray, and right into the eyes of a familiar face. If I thought he was super cute across a dimly lit police station parking lot, then he was drop-dead gorgeous next to a sea of green apples that matched his eyes perfectly. A smile tugged at the corner of his lips, and I nearly swooned right then and there.

"Hey," he said timidly.

"Hey," I replied automatically, my knees threatening to wobble. Was he talking to me? Was there someone else right behind me? Maybe a prettier, less weird girl? I forced myself not to turn around to check.

"Hey," chimed in Diego as he pulled up with a pushcart loaded with boxes of fruit. He grinned mischievously at us.

Officer Super Cute looked like he was about to say something else to me when Cliff's voice blasted over the loudspeakers. "Lou to the back office, please. Lou to the back office."

I opened my mouth to say something to him – God knows what.

Diego, still grinning, piped up. "Better get a move on, Lou."

I hurried off, my cheeks on fire. That could have gone a bit smoother.

Cliff sat in the back office behind the computer with a grumpy look on his face and a cigarette between his lips, begging to be lit. He noticed my blushing cheeks and quickly looked away, undoubtedly not wanting to get dragged into whatever happened that could embarrass me that much.

"I need a favor," he started.

"Sure, what's up?" I didn't take the open seat on the other side of the desk, sure that whatever Cliff had to say, the conversation wouldn't last more than a minute.

"Think you can lock up tonight? My ex-wife suddenly has plans and needs me to take the kids."

This wasn't the first time something like this happened. I'd met Nancy before, and she was no picnic. Let's just say, it was pretty easy to see why Cliff was totally okay with it when she said she wanted a divorce. She probably agreed to go on a last-minute date with someone just to stick it to Cliff, as per usual, trying to make him look like a bad father who wasn't there for his kids when they needed him. I never knew my dad, and had very few expectations on that front. Cliff, however, seemed like a pretty swell dad, all things considered. Just like he was a laid-back boss, he was a laid-back dad.

"Shouldn't be a problem," I told him. It wasn't the first time I had locked up for him. We both had zero aspirations when it came to the store. We both only wanted a paycheck and weren't interested in getting promoted to anything else. In that mutual, unspoken apathy, we worked pretty well together. He said nothing about my random acts of disappearing during my shift, and I was always there for him when Nancy screwed him over.

"Thanks, Lou. I owe ya one."

"No prob." I left the office and took my sweet time walking down the hallway, eyes scanning everywhere. The warmth in my cheeks was gone, thank God. Still, I was pretty nervous about running into Officer Super Cute again and giving a repeat performance of my awkward-ass self. I didn't see him anywhere though and was surprisingly disappointed. I mean, what did I expect to happen? He was probably just making polite conversation. Why would it be anything other than that? I was nothing, no one, just a stock girl that he saw coming out of the cemetery way too often. Maybe he wanted to know what I was up to.

"Your boyfriend checked out at the express lane while you were gone," Diego informed me as he rotated bunches of broccoli.

I didn't bother correcting him. Diego knew very well I didn't have a boyfriend. Time and again, he tried to set me up with one of his neighbors or a friend from school. Diego recently turned nineteen, which made him, and all his friends, nearly five years younger than me. Even if any of his friends wanted to go out with me, which I doubted in the first place, those five years felt like a decade. Maybe it was hearing the stories

of dead people over and over again that aged me on the inside
– who knows. One thing was for sure though, I wasn't all that
interested in dating someone who still had a 'one' in the first
digit of their age.

"Don't you want what Amy and I have?" he often asked.
Of course, I did, but I was also pretty sure that high school
puppy love like theirs tended to fizzle out as fast as it started
and wasn't a lasting relationship goal.

I didn't say that to Diego, though. He and Amy were
inseparable, their lips constantly locked in the parking lot, or
next to the dumpster in the alley behind the store, even in the
breakroom when I was trying to eat lunch.

"Don't you wanna know what he had in his cart?" he said
under his breath, eyes darting around conspicuously. "I scoped
it out for you."

"I'm guessing groceries," I said, trying not to sound at all
interested in what was in his cart. Groceries said a lot about
a person. A lot. I'd been too surprised to see him on the
other side of the apple display to notice anything beyond his
sweatshirt and jeans. The faded maroon Magnolia Grove High
School hoodie went so well with his tousled sandy hair and
worn jeans. God help me if he'd been in his uniform, I would
have likely fainted right then and there.

"Half a gallon of skim milk. Bagels. Reduced-fat cream
cheese. Kale…" Diego scrunched up his nose at that one.

Great. Officer Super Cute was a health nut. I didn't want
to think about how my freezer full of microwave dinners
compared.

"Deodorant. Mouthwash. Oreos…"

Oreos? Maybe not such a health nut after all.

"No baby diapers, frilly-scented soap, or anything like that,"
Diego said, winking knowingly at me.

One load of groceries minus all that did not a single man make. Still, it was interesting. None of it mattered, though, but that didn't stop me from thinking about it over and over again for the rest of my shift.

Hours of over-analyzing later, I came to the conclusion he must have been about to interrogate me concerning my late-night activities in the cemetery. If Cliff hadn't called me away, I probably would have had to come up with some kind of explanation on the spot. I mean, the man was a cop; what else could he want from me?

"'Night, Marge," I said as I locked the back doors and pocketed the keys. I'd moved on from my awkward social encounter with Magnolia Grove's finest and instead focused on whether I should swing by the cemetery one last time to check on Mrs H.

"Good night, kiddo," she said, getting into her minivan.

Diego rushed past us in a hurry to meet up with Amy at the movie theater. "See ya, Lou," he said as he hopped in a car with a few of his friends.

I waved goodbye and headed to where I kept my bike locked up. The flickering streetlight next to the dumpster lit up the empty bike rack. The metal chain I used to secure it dangled from the rack, the padlock broken on the ground.

"Dammit all to hell," I grumbled.

That was swell. I didn't carry a cell phone, not like there was anyone who could come and pick me up anyway. There was always Mortie I could rely on, but he didn't drive all that well at night anymore. Home wasn't too terribly far from work, but it would still take me more than half an hour at least to get there. That ruled out stopping by the cemetery. The odds of an inconvenient summons by Mrs H in the near future kept piling up.

I cursed again under my breath at the loss of my bike and started out on the sidewalk in the general direction toward home. Besides being a pain in the ass to replace, I loved my bike. It was pale green with wide handlebars and a big comfy seat, the kind of bike someone might ride down the streets of France with a bouquet of flowers and a baguette in the basket. At least, that's how it was in the movies anyway. Now I'd have to take the car to work until I could find another bike.

I rounded the sidewalk that led to the new townhomes. Red and blue flashing lights from two patrol cars bounced off the front of the houses at the end of the street.

"Crap."

I walked a little closer hoping it was a public disturbance or maybe a drug bust, but when I saw the front of a car smashed into a tree, I made a U-turn. There was a good chance everyone was fine and had escaped unscathed, but I didn't want to stick around to find out otherwise. Tonight was not the night to be getting acquainted with newly created ghosts who'd just left their earthly shells. I just wanted to get home and go to bed.

My normal route now hindered, I tried to think of another way home that wouldn't take me past any ghostly roadblocks. Park Street contained a creepy pair of twins who wandered outside one winter night in the early 1900s, and woke up the next morning to a whole different sort of existence. They weren't like Tom-Tom, who was a welcome sight in comparison. The twins were mischievous like a pair of poltergeists... almost. Real poltergeists were dangerous. My whole life, I'd only ever come across three of them and was lucky enough to escape with scrapes and bruises. Clara and Ned were just annoying as hell and disturbingly clever, taking to their ghost state too well for their own good.

Crawford Lane was totally out of the question. Josephine drowned almost two centuries ago in the pretty lake the road curved around. Her wails of sorrow over her untimely death echoed out over the surface of the water as she floated around the center of the lake. The first time I heard her wails, I'd been checking out the neighborhood to see if it suited me. She'd managed to lure me out into the water with her cries. I only realized what was happening after finding myself knee-deep in ice-cold water a few feet from shore. It'd been the middle of January. I wasn't sure why she couldn't have waited till August.

That left me with 12th Street and Hank McAllister. Poor Hank got into a fight with his wife one day and went up on the roof to clear out the gutters in hopes of burning off his anger, when a squirrel scared the hell out of him, and he fell off the roof. He loved his wife very much and was sad about things ending in a nasty fight over something he couldn't even remember.

At least Hank wouldn't chat forever. He usually came down from his roof when he saw me and wondered if I might know what their fight was about. I obliged him by taking a couple of guesses, but they were never right and I'd long since run out of all the obvious reasons the two might have fought.

The rain that started the day was gone, but the humidity from it lingered in the night air. Usually, I wore my hair in a straight curtain of black around the top of my shoulders, but the humidity made a few strands turn to wavy curls around my cheeks. I brushed them off my face and looked up at the clouds slowly drifting by in the moonlight. A handful of stars peeked out here and there. In a few nights, there'd be a full moon. Maybe if I was lucky, I could find a cheap bike before then. I didn't want to be driving the Honda when every ghost in town was lurking around.

Hank's house came into view. It was an old, two-story house with a white picket fence covered in vines of morning glories. Oddly, Hank's roof was empty and there didn't seem to be any sign of him on the street. I would have thought more about his peculiar absence if it weren't for the light pouring out of his neighbor's open garage. Inside, pounding his fists into a punching bag hanging from a hook in the ceiling was none other than Officer Super Cute.

Our eyes met from across the driveway.

"Hi," he said, instantly putting a hand on the bag to stop it from swinging.

"Hi," I repeated stupidly.

He jogged the short distance between us and pulled off a boxing mitt. "I wanted to… uh… introduce myself earlier. I'm Scott." He wiped his hand free of sweat against the side of his sweatpants and held it out to me.

I took it and he gave my hand a firm shake. There's something refreshingly genuine about a man with a firm handshake. It's kind of annoying when they hold your hand like it's a limp fish or treat it as if it might break.

"Louise," I said. "I mean… Lou… everyone calls me Lou." I fumbled over my words, the heat rising in my cheeks.

We stood in silence for a moment.

"Would you like a beer?" he asked, pointing to a cooler in the corner of the garage.

"Oh. Um. No thanks, I don't drink." Alcohol and whatever it was that made me… well, me, made for a catastrophic combination. I, therefore, made it a policy to steer clear of it. I waited for the shocked reaction most men my age had when I revealed that nugget about myself. Instead, he simply nodded.

"How about a grape soda then?" he asked, lifting the lid

and rifling through the cooler, which was packed with equal amounts of beer and fruit-flavored sodas.

"Sure, thanks." This was new territory for me. I wasn't exactly sure what to do with myself in this situation. I'd never really been alone with a man for anything other than work-related reasons or hanging out with Mortie, and neither of those situations was at all similar to this.

I took a sip of grape soda and stared at my sneakers trying to think what I should do.

"You and I always seem to see each other at the same time. It's nice to finally be able to talk to you," he said with a genuine smile.

"Yeah, I'm, uh, usually on my way back to work at that time of night, it seems." I guess I owed Mrs Hammond thanks for that one.

I wasn't sure what else to say. I was barely a conversationalist with the people I interacted with on a daily basis, much less a handsome stranger. Already my social skills were getting pushed to the brink.

An awkward silence fell between us.

"I don't suppose I could report a crime?" I said, trying to fill the quiet.

The easy-going smile on his face vanished, replaced by a sudden seriousness. "What's happened? Are you okay?"

The intense shift in his tone almost gave me whiplash, and I realized I probably shouldn't have started a conversation with a cop that way.

"Oh, it's nothing," I quickly assured him. "Someone just stole my bike tonight. It's no big deal."

"I could write up a report–"

"No, no, it's cool." God, I was awful at this. "It's just been inconvenient is all."

"What's it look like? I'll keep an eye out for it when I'm on patrol."

I rattled off a description and quickly took another sip of soda.

"Um… maybe you could give me your number and I can call you if I find it?" he said, and then before I could tell it to him, he shook his head, chuckling. "God, I'm such a chicken. Listen, I'll just ask straight up. Do you want to get dinner with me sometime?"

I blinked stupidly at him. What was happening? Was I dreaming? Did I hear him right? I did. He was waiting for me to respond, looking adorably nervous and uncertain of himself.

"Yes," I answered quickly so I didn't leave him hanging any longer. Absolutely. Yes. Oh God, yes.

"Phew," he laughed. "I wanted to ask you back at the store, but I was afraid that kid might think I was asking him."

I laughed. "Diego would have loved that."

Instead of laughing along with me, he sucked in a breath, his eyes going straight to my lips.

"What? Is there something on my face?" I asked, panicked. Maybe there was something in my teeth. I tried to remember what microwave dinner I ate during my break and hoped it didn't have broccoli in it.

"Nothing, I… I've just never seen you smile before," he said, still looking at my mouth.

He noticed me before? Well, of course, he had. I mean, how many times had our eyes met outside the police station on all my walks back from the cemetery? Quite a bit.

"Really?" I bit my lower lip to keep from getting an even bigger smile and looked away, resisting the urge to cover my cheeks which were now at five-alarm fire levels. I desperately needed to get out of there before I messed things up for myself.

He eagerly handed me his cell phone like any normal person would in this kind of situation, but the second it touched my fingers the bars began to drop like everything else technology-wise. My thumbs rapidly punched in my number.

"I don't have a cell phone," I told him quickly handing it back to him before it could die. "But you can leave a message on my answering machine if I'm not there."

"You got it," he said, looking at my number on his phone and then back at me with the most heart-fluttering smile I'd ever seen.

"I should probably get home." *Before you realize what a mistake you've made, asking me out.*

"Do you need a ride? My patrol car is in the shop getting new brakes, but I have my bike." He motioned toward the shining black motorcycle parked on the other side of the garage.

Of course, this insanely gorgeous man had a motorcycle. My damn knees were going to give out any second just thinking about him on it.

"No, it's cool. I'm not far – just off of Cedar." I nervously tucked my curling hair behind my ears and wondered what else I should say. "Uh… it was nice meeting you, Scott," I said, trying out his name for the first time.

That disarming intensity returned to his green eyes as I said his name.

"It's nice to finally meet you too, Louise."

CHAPTER 4

All the way home my insides felt like they were filled up with helium. Mortie's lights weren't on. It was too late at night anyway and I was pretty sure he'd gone to bed. I wish I'd gotten home earlier; it would have been nice to bounce off him all the things that happened.

I opened up the refrigerator to find a few cartons of leftover Chinese food and a note from Mortie stuck to one of them.

Thought you'd need this.
Hope you're doing okay.
– M

God bless that man. I sank into my couch and ate cold spicy chicken out of the carton, replaying everything all over again.

I was going to go out on a date. With a cop – a cop that looked like the high school star quarterback all grown up. That was a lot to process. There'd been guys in the past who showed interest in me, but they never asked me out and they were never guys like Officer Super Cute... or rather, Scott.

Scott.

I glanced at the stack of romance novels on the coffee table. I was pretty sure none of those men could hold a candle to him.

I changed out of my work clothes and pulled on my nightgown, all the while feeling extra self-conscious. I glimpsed myself in the bathroom mirror above the sink and immediately wished I hadn't. The girl staring back at me was too pale, her hair too dark, her slate-colored eyes too big and nervous-looking. Scott could have asked anyone out. Why me?

I started to run a brush through my hair when I felt the telltale sign of Mrs Hammond's summons pulling me – like I'd been lassoed around the middle and yanked out of the bathroom. I should have landed with my back on the ground in the cemetery, with the breath knocked out of me, staring up at the night sky – but there was no cemetery. There was nothing.

I was caught somewhere between the bathroom and the cemetery, somewhere between the land of the living and a world reserved only for the dead. I tried to move but couldn't. I tried to breathe but couldn't. I tried screaming, but there was no sound. I was stuck in a dark void of nothingness in between worlds.

Something stirred in the muted darkness; an inky black fog that passed over my legs and arms, paralyzing me in an icy cold grip as it snaked its way across my flesh. The shape of a head formed in the fog, emerging out of the black cloud to look me over. Its vaporous face tilted to the side as if curious. It was the most horrific thing I'd ever seen. At least a wisp had eye sockets. These eyes were nothing but bottomless black holes, staring into me as if they could see past my skin and bones, straight into my soul.

The face lowered to an inch above mine, dipping down as if it might place a kiss on my lips – if it had lips. "Mine… mine… mine," a voice whispered in my ears.

No. No. No. I chanted the word over and over in my mind like a mantra.

I saw myself in the barren chasms of its eyes. Alone. Small and insignificant. Life drained away from that insignificant me, sinking in my cheeks, my eyes becoming as empty as a wisp's.

It took everything I had, every crumb of energy and strength, to break free of that invisible tether and shout one single word in the void's face.

"NO!"

I landed with a *WHACK*, face-down in the cemetery between tombstones. Mrs Hammond stood over me, floating in the night air.

"You came for a visit, Lou! How lovely! I was hoping you would stop by again soon," she said in a happy sing-song voice.

I vomited, sobbed, vomited some more, and then sobbed some more.

"Oh my… are you alright, dear?" she asked, hovering closer. She took out her hankie and wrung it nervously in her hands.

I grabbed a fistful of grass in an effort to tether myself to the earth, afraid whatever had taken me might snatch me up again.

I kept my eyes open, scared of the darkness that fell even during a quick blink. My hairbrush was still in my hand. I stared at it. The brush was tangible evidence that I was alive, that I was in the land of the living. I pulled my knees to my chest and clung to the brush as if it were a lifeline.

"Lou?" came Mrs Hammond's panicked voice.

"I – I'm sorry." It was all I could manage to say; the words coming out in a scratchy voice as if I'd been screaming for hours.

I found the backpack I hid under the rose bush and pulled out a hooded sweatshirt and sweatpants. My nightgown was in tatters, covered in a sooty, grimy residue – proof that whatever world I'd just come from was very real indeed. I waited until a pair of car lights disappeared down the end of the street before taking off the ruined nightgown and pulling on the fresh set of clothes.

"Are you alright, Lou?" Mrs Hammond asked again, her voice still rising in panic.

I caught Tom-Tom's eyes peeking out behind the stone angel. Maybe I should have stayed there and tried to get answers from them, but all I could do was shake my head and scramble out of the cemetery. The second my feet touched the sidewalk outside the cemetery gates, I bolted. I'd been too stupid to pack a pair of socks or shoes in the backpack and had to run in my bare feet. They hurt against the old, broken sidewalks, but I couldn't slow down – wouldn't slow down – I had to get away.

I knew the balls of my feet were bleeding. I'd felt each cut as it happened. I didn't stop, though, and embraced the pain. Physical pain meant I was alive. Cars drove by, even a patrol car, but thanks to the sweats, I looked like any other jogger out for a run at night. Thankfully, they didn't slow down enough to notice the absence of shoes.

I ran past my gravel driveway, flinching at the pebbles underneath my feet, but welcoming the pain. *I'm still alive… still alive… still alive*, I repeated in my head. I didn't go to my house. Instead, I ran to the only place I'd ever really felt safe. I bolted up the steps to Mortie's back door and knocked on it, tears streaming down my face. The door opened and I fell inside. Arms came around me, catching me before I could fall to the ground.

"There now, there now," Mortie said in a hushed voice that made me cry harder against his shoulder. I was safe. I was alive. Here was someone who cared about me. I mattered to him. I wasn't alone.

"I – I'm not okay," I managed to say against his shoulder.

He started to usher me inside when the TV set crackled to life. White noise danced across the screen. For a fraction of a second, the screen froze, and a faint voice called out to me through the speakers. *"Mine... mine... mine..."*

I clamped down onto Mortie's arm.

He pushed me back out through the front door, and we hung onto each other as we made our way across the alley between our houses back to mine, me in my cemetery sweats, him in his pinstriped pajamas.

Mortie knew his way around my house almost as well as I did his. He planted me firmly on the couch and went through the house, flipping on all the lights I'd turned off back when I was getting ready for bed, before my world turned upside down.

"Let's get you fixed up, Lewis," he said, taking out the first aid kit I kept in a kitchen cabinet. He doctored up my feet, which were the worst of my injuries. The cut on my foot was right under my big toe and had a solid piece of glass lodged in it. The gash wasn't deep enough to need stitches, but stepping on it hurt like a son of a bitch.

Mortie opened my freezer and came back with a bag of frozen mixed vegetables. The corner of my lip was split from when my face smacked against the cemetery ground. There was also a cut on my cheek sporting an already tender bruise. I alternated between putting the frozen bag against my cheek and lip.

Mortie moved some books out of the way and sat on the coffee table in front of me. He didn't ask any questions. He simply took my hand in his.

I had clearly woken him up when I knocked on his door. His hair, already wild at times, was extra frazzled and his pajamas were wrinkled. His hazel eyes turned milky white. He nodded along as if I were telling him everything that happened. When it seemed he had learned it all, he patted my hand and placed it back in my lap.

"So, who's Scott and where do you think he's taking you for dinner?" he asked instead of mentioning anything about the cemetery.

I half-laughed, half-cried, and pulled him in for a hug.

He stayed with me until I fell asleep. For the hundredth time since I met him, I drifted off to sleep thinking that Mortimer Thornbush, a man who had been a stranger to me four years ago, was better than any father I could ever dream of having.

CHAPTER 5

When I woke up the next morning, every muscle in my body was sore, like I'd been beaten to a pulp and zapped of all energy. I lay in bed staring up at the ceiling. I didn't want to think about last night – didn't want to face those horrors again, but I had to. I learned that lesson when I was a little girl; you couldn't let fear fester inside you. The longer it did, the more power it had over you.

Okay then, what did I know? I knew that something existing between this life and the next wanted me, and it wanted me bad. That was the first fact. The second was that, somehow, in some freaking miraculous way, I'd managed to break free from it. But how? I didn't have the slightest clue. Third, I'd have to make damn sure to visit Mrs H as often as possible. I couldn't risk getting stuck in that place again. The memory of that muted darkness washed over me. It was all too easy remembering the icy touch of whatever that thing was on my skin. I shuddered. That was enough of facing my fears for the moment.

I got out of bed, groaning at the effort, and took a shower, letting the hot water loosen up my aching limbs. It felt good washing off the grime and dirt caked onto my skin. The more I scrubbed it off, the more I felt like me, and with that, came a surprising amount of bravery laced with anger. If that thing came for me again, I wasn't going to be afraid. I was done with that. I knew better than anyone that fear was only going to hold me back.

I felt even more resolved as I wound fresh bandages around the cut on my foot and pulled on a pair of jeans and a T-shirt.

The bruise on my cheek had blossomed into a nasty blue-brown shade, but at least the swelling in my lip was down. I pulled my hair into a ponytail and tried to cover up the cuts on my face with makeup. It didn't help much; I still looked beaten and worn down.

Whatever soot I came home covered in had transferred to my bed sheets during the night. I scooped them up off the bed and threw them in the washer, adding more soap than necessary, hoping it would be enough to wash out the otherworldly residue.

I'm not much of a coffee drinker, but I have been known to guzzle iced tea like there's no tomorrow. I poured myself a large thermos full of it and mixed in a bunch of sugar, desperate for a morning boost. I pulled out an oversized beach bag and loaded it with things I'd need for the day.

Sunlight hit me in the face when I opened the front door. I immediately recoiled, wincing at the bright light, and wondered if this was what it felt like to have a hangover. I almost tripped over a package addressed to Mortie on my front porch step. It wasn't the first time the mailman confused our houses. From the looks of the double-padded envelope, it was another old book in need of repair – and a heavy one at that. I heaved it onto my hip like a baby and carried it across the alley to his house.

A gleaming Lexus sat parked in his driveway. A chorus of feminine voices came from inside the front door as the Ladies Historical Preservation Society crooned over their newly restored cookbook. I propped the package up against the screen door for him to find later and headed out.

My rundown Honda sat neglected under the carport. I walked past the spot where my bike was usually propped up against it and felt a pang of loss at its absence. I threw the beach bag onto the seat next to me and tried to start my rarely-ever driven car. I had to turn the key a few times to get the engine to crank, but eventually it roared back to life.

The drive to Magnolia Grove Cemetery was thankfully uneventful. I had a ghostly passenger treat me like a taxi, but luckily, he wasn't the chatty type. Stuck in repeat, he just sat in the back seat, looking at his watch, and got out before I could slow to a stop at a red light.

I turned into the cemetery's gravel parking lot and parked next to the only other car there. The tall, lanky man who religiously visited his wife's grave passed me on his way out under the cemetery's arched iron gates. He dipped his head in his customary nod hello, but when his eyes met mine, they went wide as he took in the sight of my injured face. He looked as if he wanted to ask about it, but I gave him a smile that hopefully said, "I'm okay, no worries." He nodded and walked back to his car, looking over his shoulder at me once more to be sure.

My skin rippled in goosebumps as I walked through the cemetery. Hours ago, I had run from it like my life depended on it. I fought the urge to do the same thing again now. It helped that the cemetery looked completely different in the bright, sunny afternoon light. Instead of turning tail and running, I marched on, determined as hell to beat back the fear until it was under my control.

"Lou! You came by for a visit, how wonderful!" Mrs Hammond floated around the back row of tombstones, happy to have me voluntarily appear all on my own. Tom was nowhere to be seen, and I decided to take that as a good omen, though I would've liked to hear what he had to say about last night.

I took a bright beach towel out of my bag and spread it out near Mrs Hammond's tombstone. I purposely picked a neon pink and green towel to help drive away the darkness I knew would be plaguing my memories.

I ate a peanut butter and jelly sandwich while flipping through the *Teach Yourself Crochet* book I'd checked out from the library, all the while chatting with Mrs H. She was thrilled to see me learning something she deemed ladylike. She was constantly on me about becoming more domestic in order for me to lure in a man to marry. It was no use introducing her to more feminist ideals. Ghosts aren't really capable of learning. They don't adapt. They simply exist, trapped in the mindset they had before their deaths. Besides, Mrs Hammond usually turned her nose up at me whenever I said I was domesticated enough for my own tastes.

I struggled learning a few stitches out of the book. She hovered over my shoulder to watch me awkwardly hold the crochet hook and yarn, pretending she remembered how to do it and giving me encouraging little claps when I finally figured out how to do a chain and then a single crochet stitch.

After what I thought was a sufficiently long visit, I packed up and broached the subject of last night, hoping that the visit buttered her up enough for it.

"I came by yesterday before work, but you weren't here," I started, keeping my tone casual.

"Oh?" she said innocently… a little *too* innocently. Her hands went to the string of pearls around her neck as she looked anywhere but at me.

"It's funny, Tom-Tom wasn't here either."

"Well… um… he's not usually here, is he?"

"Right." I wasn't going to get anything out of her. It didn't matter. I had plans to swing by again after work to satiate her social needs and butter her up some more in the hope she'd let something slip.

"Did you get into a fight?" Diego asked, staring at my bruised face.

"No. I told you, I fell down," I answered for the third time. He looked at me doubtfully. It was true, I did fall down, right smack face down into the cemetery ground, though all of my coworkers seemed to think I'd borne the brunt of someone's fists.

"Hey, did you happen to see anyone outside last night when you took your break? Someone stole my bike."

"You got beat up and someone stole your bike? Geez, Lou. That's rough," he said, shaking his head.

"Did you see anyone?" I asked again, frustrated at his lack of attention.

"Nah. Sorry."

Cliff passed us by in the paper goods aisle as we stocked toilet paper on the shelves. "Hey, I need one of you to go round up carts in the parking lot."

Amy's pale blond head popped out at the end of the aisle. Her blue eyes looked a little red as she gave Diego a pleading look from behind big, black-framed glasses. Diego sighed, hurt and resignation written all over him. Apparently, there was trouble in puppy love paradise.

"I'll do it," I told him, giving him a reassuring pat on the shoulder.

Outside, night had fallen. The streetlights were on, casting a glow over the somewhat empty Piggly Wiggly parking lot.

Bugs swarmed like clouds under the yellow-orange lights, and there was a heavy, harvest-like scent of fall in the air. I took my time rounding up carts. It was quiet in the parking lot, and the number of customers had dwindled to a trickle.

A patrol car pulled up right as I pushed the last bunch of carts together into the cart return. My stomach fluttered as Scott got out of the car wearing his uniform. *Damn.* He looked way too good in the short-sleeve uniform with a utility belt strapped around his trim waist, a gun holstered to his hip, and a shining Magnolia Grove PD badge pinned to his chest.

He popped the trunk of the patrol car, revealing my pale green bike squeezed in between two road cones.

"You found it!" I said, going right up to it. "Where was it?"

"Someone ditched it on the shore of Crawford Lake. The tires were flat, but they should be good to go now," he said.

"Thank you!" I looked up at him, beaming.

The proud smile on his face disappeared.

"What happened?" His hand came up to my chin, tilting my face side to side as he examined my cuts. A tingle at his touch shot over my skin and right down to my stomach, spreading a low warmth through me. He was close enough that I could smell the laundry detergent on his uniform along with a hint of woods from being outside. I would have happily drowned in that scent.

"Are you okay? Who did this?" he asked, a rising anger taking over the concern in his eyes.

"No one," I said quickly. "I... I fell."

He took on the same doubtful look Diego had.

"Seriously, I did."

"You're sure?" he asked, his hand still on my face.

I nodded, my chin moving against his palm, acutely aware of his touch on me.

"Alright then," he said, still doubtful. He must've realized just how close we were, and the concern on his face turned to sudden bashfulness.

He took a step back toward the trunk. "I... uh... do you need this tonight? I can drive around back and unload it for you."

"No, um, I drove my car to work."

"I can put it in your car then, or, if you want, I can swing by Cedar while I'm on patrol and unload it at your house."

He remembered the street I lived on. My street... awkward, weird me. The attentiveness of this way too-attractive man was baffling.

"Really?" I asked, biting my lip to stop myself from grinning like an idiot. "That wouldn't be too much trouble?"

The smile returned to his lips and a slight dimple formed in his right cheek, threatening to make my knees wobble.

"It's no problem. I'd be happy to."

"Mine's the only green house on the block," I told him, my cheeks starting to warm. God, I was being ridiculously shy. Well, that was going to stop. I'd already decided I was done being a chicken. The theme for the day was all about facing my fears, whether it was ghosts, cemeteries, or even Officer Super Cute, aka Officer S. Campbell, according to the metal nameplate pinned to his chest. Having reminded myself of this, I suddenly felt daring – gutsy even – which was new to me, especially in regard to men.

I stood up on my toes and gave him a lingering kiss on the cheek. "Thank you."

His cheek leaned into my lips.

"Is it wrong that I want someone to steal your bike so that I can find it again?" he said in a quiet, close voice. I laughed and the dimple in his cheek deepened.

"Well then, Louise," he started, eyes gleaming at me. I'd never had a man's eyes gleam at me before. It felt amazing.

"Yes, Scott?" New daring me was having the time of her life.

"When's your next day off?"

"Sunday."

"I'm working a late shift that night but how about an early evening dinner with me?"

"Sounds good."

He got into his patrol car and rolled the window down, grinning at me. "I'll pick you up at six."

I was on cloud nine the rest of the night and all the way to the cemetery. I was even humming on the car ride there. I cheerily saluted my ghostly taxi passenger from earlier in the afternoon as he hopped into my car again. He looked annoyed at my eagerness and checked his watch impatiently.

"Lou!" Mrs Hammond beamed excitedly when I walked back through the cemetery gates. I was just as happy to see her. Hopefully, her being there meant I was in the clear for the night. I placed a bouquet of flowers in the cement vase next to her side of the tombstone.

"You're such a dear. You really shouldn't have," she said, happily floating over them and bending down as if she could smell them.

I had something for Tom-Tom, too, even though he was nowhere to be seen. I placed a cheap plastic truck I picked up at the dollar store across the street from the Piggly Wiggly during my break at the bottom of his weathered tombstone, and laid a hand reverently at the base of the plain slab.

"Thanks for the heads up, kid," I said, and meant it. Without him, I wouldn't have had a clue that something was about to go down.

I finally turned into my driveway for the night. The Honda's headlights poured over my bike under the carport, where it was propped up on the kickstand. A sticky note clung to the basket rim.

Can't wait for Sunday.

Scott's phone number was scrawled along the bottom.

I read it over a few more times, smiling to myself like an idiot. I pocketed it and walked across the alley with one more gift in tow yet to be delivered.

I lifted my hand to knock on the door.

"Over here, Lewis," Mortie's quiet voice came from under the shadow of the oak tree separating my backyard from his.

He sat in one of the plastic patio chairs we used on hotter summer nights to chat and listen to the wind chimes dangling from the branches above us. A cloud of smoke drifted up from the shadows as he took a puff of his pipe. Shit. It had been over a year since he last lit up his pipe. Something was wrong.

"What are you doing out here?" I asked, pulling up the chair next to his.

"Needed a minute outside." He sat in the chair and stared at his house. His bowtie was loose and askew at his neck, his hair slightly ruffled on one side – a clear indication he'd been puzzling over something. Most disturbing of all, though, was the weariness that deepened the creases around his eyes. Zelda paced back and forth at his feet, her fur on end, her ears back. Every now and then, she pressed up against Mortie's legs with a comforting rub.

"I brought you something," I said cheerfully, hoping to pep him up. He was never like this, and it rattled me to see it. I set the tin of Snickerdoodle cookies I picked up from the bakery section open on the table between us.

"My favorite, how thoughtful," he said with a smile – albeit a faint one – that seemed to bring him more to himself.

We sat there in our usual companionable silence, eating cookies and listening to the clink and clang of the metal butterfly wind chime twirling above us.

"How was work?" he asked after a while.

"Good," I said, taking another cookie. "I think Amy and Diego are on the verge of a breakup though." I stuck with work topics instead of prying into what was wrong.

"Well, it was bound to happen sooner or later. I bet it doesn't last long though."

He finished his third cookie, let out a long sigh, and fiddled with his pipe. I steeled myself for whatever was about to come.

"There was a package left on my doorstep this morning." He said it as though he wanted to talk about anything else but that.

"I know, I left it there for you. Someone delivered it to my address, but it had your name on it."

His head snapped up. He said nothing as he took in my words. After a long moment, he nodded and took another slow puff on his pipe.

"That changes a few things," he said finally. "And not for the better, I'm afraid." He tapped the pipe against his palm, agitated.

"I don't get it," I said, more than a little unnerved. "Isn't it just a book?"

"Books are never just books, Lewis. There's power in their written words. There's even power in the paper those words are written on. Sometimes it's nothing but a sliver, a faint residue that clings to it despite how old the book is. Take the cookbook for the Ladies Historical Preservation Society. There's a thimble's worth of power still there. That book has passed through hands, touched lives generation after generation, and the history of those lives still lives on in those pages, begging for someone to know the stories it has to tell.

"Now that book in there," he pointed to the house with his pipe, his fingers shaking as he held it, "that book has way more than just a thimble. In fact, I'd say that book is the most powerful book I've ever come in contact with."

I tried to remember how it felt when I picked it up and put it on his porch. Nothing. I'd felt nothing. How could something be that powerful and I didn't notice anything different about it at all?

"My years at the museum taught me many things. One of them is that objects almost have a heartbeat to them. The blood that pumps through them is either good or evil. I've held weapons hundreds of years old that were responsible for taking thousands of lives. The evil clinging to them was staggering."

Mortie clenched his pipe to his chest as he stared hard at the house. "That book sitting on my worktable right now... that makes all those artifacts look like teddy bears."

CHAPTER 6

I may not have felt anything when I picked up the package that morning and set it on his porch, but I sure as hell felt something when I stepped over the threshold into Mortie's house.

Horror, despair, a hollow emptiness big enough to swallow a person whole… it was all there rolled into one nightmare sensation – a sensation I'd recently become familiar with, one that existed in a world somewhere between this one and the next.

Sitting open on Mortie's worktable was an old book in terrible condition. The black binding had come loose from the spine. The threads keeping the dark pages together were broken and frayed. The whole thing looked like it would fall apart the second someone picked it up, and that was just the outward appearance of the thing. Dread poured out of its pages, radiating out in waves. Mortie stood in the far corner of the room, keeping his distance as much as possible. If I had any sense, I would've done the same, but something pulled me in, luring me towards it with a macabre sort of fascination.

"Where are all the words?" I asked, staring down at empty pages, colored a deep midnight black.

"I don't believe there are any, at least none written in ink," he answered, his voice sounding farther and farther away the closer I got to the table. A low hum drummed in my ears. Despite their frayed edges, the black pages appeared smooth, without even a tear across them. I held out a hand, wanting to feel its velvety texture under my fingers.

"What are you doing, Lewis?" Mortie's alarmed voice sounded like a distant whisper on a breeze.

I ran a hand over the page. It felt softer than I thought it would be. Weirdly warmer too. At my touch, shining silver words lit up across the page as if someone were writing them at that very moment. I tried to decipher what language they were written in, but the ink drained out of the sprawling letters, dribbling down the blank page toward my fingertips as if pulled by a magnet. The silver ink latched onto my skin. A feeling like a thousand tiny needles pricked my palm and the page beneath my fingers disintegrated. A shockwave of blue energy exploded from the book.

"Louise!"

I was on the floor. How I got there, I didn't have a freaking clue, but my butt hurt from the hard fall against the floorboards.

Dazed, I blinked up at Mortie. "What the hell just happened?"

He didn't answer but grabbed me by the upper arms in a fierce grip, pulling me up to my feet. His eyes flashed white as he looked into my face.

"What happened when you touched it?" he asked, apparently not finding the answer in me.

"I – I don't know. There were letters and then, in the next second, it felt like they bit my hand. Then, just as quickly, they were gone, and I was on the floor."

"For half a second your hand disappeared into the book," he said. "And then there was an explosion of blue light and the book... it seemed to throw you off." Mortie sounded pretty shaken up recounting it.

I quickly got ahold of myself. "It's okay, I'm okay," I said to him, and me, hoping the words would reassure us both. He didn't look reassured.

The low hum from the book was still there, growing louder and louder until it howled through the room, sounding like wild winds blowing through the eaves of the house.

"I think we've had just about enough of this," I said and slammed the book shut, silencing it. Still, it wasn't enough. The dread was persistent. I knew Mortie felt it too. Concern knitted his bushy eyebrows together and I was alarmed to see a tremble of worry go through him. I shoved the book's heavy weight back into the padded envelope it came in and marched out the front door, setting it down on the porch as I'd done before, resisting the urge to dropkick it across the yard.

"I'll deal with you later," I said, as if it could hear me.

Back inside, the atmosphere in the house was as different as night and day. The nightmare sensation had completely gone, now it felt just as welcoming and safe as ever. Even Mortie seemed more himself, albeit exhausted. I knew how he felt. All that evil weighed down on me and now that it was gone, it felt like an anvil had been lifted off my back.

Mortie rarely smoked his pipe, and he hardly ever drank, but tonight, he did both. There was a bottle of sherry tucked into the back of his kitchen cabinet. He got it out and poured two glasses. I started to object.

"Just a little, Lewis," he insisted. "To help take the edge off."

Despite the distinct change inside the house and in Mortie, I still felt a darkness lingering in me, twisting around my gut, promising doom. I downed the sherry.

"I got my bike back," I said, trying to add a little bit more happiness to the house.

"You don't say? Cheers to that!" He lifted the glass in salute and poured himself another.

"Scott found it."

A slow smile spread over Mortie's face. "Is that right?"

I couldn't help but smile myself, remembering the moment outside the Piggly Wiggly.

We chatted for a while about my upcoming date, about Diego and Amy, about my work schedule in the week to come, about anything except that damn book looming with dread on the porch. When he tried to stifle a yawn, I said goodnight and hugged him before heading to the door.

"Whatever that thing is, we'll tackle it together," he said, determined. "See you tomorrow, Lewis." It was nice to hear the usual cheerfulness in his voice. Maybe things weren't that bad after all.

I stepped outside onto the porch and went still.

Wisps flooded the yard – way more than I'd ever seen swarming around the hospital or police station. I tried to take a step down, but they drifted closer, gathering tighter to one another, blocking me from passing through. That's when I felt it – the tell-tale pull around my middle. The porch steps disappeared, the wisps disappeared, and suddenly I was somewhere else entirely.

I didn't end up in the in-between world I desperately feared, nor did I end up in the cemetery with Mrs H. Instead, I landed hard on my side, bruising my elbow. The water in the lake off Crawford Street lapped against the shore just a few feet from me. How was this even possible? It was Mrs Hammond who did the yanking, and no way was she out here by the lake.

"What is it?" A woman's voice came from beside me.

The ghost hovered in the air over the shoreline. The old-fashioned nightgown she wore swirled about her legs and her long blond hair floated around her shoulders in a breeze I couldn't feel.

"Josephine?" I'd never been this close to her before. Normally, I saw her from afar, floating over the center of the lake, trying to get me to come in and drown so that she'd have a friend. Now she was on the shore, looking down at the black book that should have been on Mortie's porch steps.

"What is it, Lou?" she asked again. "I can… feel it."

Oh shit. Feel? That was a word ghosts never ever used. You can't feel things when you're dead, can't touch 'em, can't sniff 'em… nothing. And here was Josephine, the woman who drowned in Crawford Lake over a hundred years ago, looking at the black book as if it just kissed her passionately on the mouth.

"It's just a book." I took it protectively in my arms and started marching away from the shore toward the street. Oddly, the dread it emanated at Mortie's didn't seem as strong. Maybe that was because I was outside with it. Perhaps enclosed spaces made it worse.

"But it isn't really, is it?" her voice hovered somewhere close over my shoulder.

I picked up the pace.

There was a whoosh of air as she disappeared. Then came the wailing. Her sobs echoed out from the lake, slowing my steps toward the road. I wanted to cover my ears to block her out, but the book was too damn heavy and required both hands to hold it.

I turned back to the lake. There was something rhythmic to the water rolling up to the shore wave after wave, and the steady slosh of water hitting the smooth rocks. I wanted to hear more of it and took a step toward the lake, then another, and another.

The screech of tires snapped me out of it. A rusted Toyota came to a sudden stop at the curb behind me. The door flung open and a tall redhead wearing a miniskirt and knee-high boots jumped out of the car. She strutted to the edge of the gravel parking lot and put her hands on her hips.

"You must be really stupid," she said to me, with a shake of her head that managed to somehow be disappointed and annoyed at the same time "You left that book outside, unprotected. What were you thinking?" She grabbed hold of my arm and pulled me towards the Toyota.

I gaped at her as she dragged me along. Josephine's wailing got louder and louder in my ears, trying to drown out her words.

"If I'd known you were going to be this stupid," the redhead said. "I would have lugged the damn thing around with me instead of mailing it to Mr Thornbush."

"You know Mortie?" I asked stupidly, still mystified at the sudden presence of this stranger who knew about the book and knew Mortie's name.

"No, I don't know Mortie," she said, mimicking my voice. "Aren't you listening? Whatever. Just get in." She threw open the passenger door and waited impatiently with a hand on her hip.

I hesitated. This person was a complete and total stranger. She could kill me and drop my body off the side of the road, dooming me to haunt passing cars for the rest of eternity.

"Or don't get in. Stay here and get lured into the lake by freaky ghosts who don't know how to stay dead."

"You... you can see her?"

"Sure can't. Glad of that too. Now get in, Louise."

The wailing turned to screams of rage from the lake since I wasn't doing Josephine's bidding. I supposed I could take my chances with the redhead as opposed to drowning in the lake. I got into the car and buckled my seatbelt, setting the book on my lap.

"It's Lou," I corrected her.

"Victoria, but everyone calls me Vick," she said over her shoulder as she reversed out of the parking lot and peeled off down the street.

"You gotta keep that thing inside, hidden somewhere or something." She nodded toward the book. "You leave it outside – let's say on Mortie's steps," she said, rolling her eyes at me in the rearview mirror, "and you're asking for trouble."

"What is it?" I asked, mirroring Josephine's question while staring at it with suspicion.

She sighed but instead of treating me like an idiot, she was genuine for the first time. "I don't know. I just know the person who had it before you said it was crazy important, and you were meant to have it."

I supposed my even wanting the thing was out of the question. If it was meant for me like she said, then why did she send it to Mortie in the first place?

"How did you know where I was? Or who I am?" I asked her.

She didn't answer, groaning impatiently as if I were a child asking a million questions. I thought they were reasonable questions, considering this total stranger knew the exact moment I'd be plucked off Mortie's steps and dropped by the lake... unless she was stalking me or something. She at least knew where I lived, as she had turned her car onto the last street to get to my neighborhood.

"Wait a second. Did you steal my bike?"

She shook her head and laughed. "Jesus, you've gotta be kidding. You have a priceless creepy-ass book on your lap, and you think I'm interested in some stupid bike?"

I started to ask another question, but she cut me off. "I'm going to be straight with you. I can't handle a million questions, alright? You get one more for tonight and that's it, okay?"

"Alright then." I went for the most obvious one. "What are you?"

She sighed again and was quiet for several long minutes during which I thought she might not answer.

"Listen, Lou, there's different kinds of people in this world. There are normal people like Amy and Diego and all those other people working at that rundown grocery store of yours. And then there's people like you. People like Mortie. And people like me. Got it?"

That didn't really answer my question at all, but I nodded anyway. Maybe if I treated her like Tom-Tom, I'd get more out of her. I kept my mouth shut and waited. After a while, my theory panned out.

She bit her lip, seemingly unable to handle the silence. "I don't know all that's going on," she finally went on. "I don't even know what that thing really is," she said, nodding again at the book. "But something's changing, something's going down – something big and potentially horrible, and you're right at the center of it all. Do you understand?"

She was just as vague and unhelpful as Tom-Tom, but the seriousness and general fear behind her words were sobering. I couldn't help but shudder.

She pulled into my driveway. The wisps were gone, and Mortie's light was off in the kitchen.

I opened my mouth to ask her something else, but she held up a hand, cutting me off. "I'll answer more questions the next time we see each other. I promise."

I guess this wasn't the last I was going to see of this woman. Just when exactly would 'next time' be, and what disastrous event was sure to happen beforehand? I opened the door but didn't get out of the car.

"One thing before I go. You said I'm the one that's meant to have this book. If that's true, then why didn't you just mail it to me instead of sending it to Mortie?"

She waited a beat before answering, as if weighing whether or not she should. "Would you have opened it if your name was on the package? Or would you have been afraid of who it might've been from and tossed it in the nearest dumpster?"

I stared hard at her. How in the holy hell could she have known that? No one except Mortie could have even guessed that.

I didn't answer and waited for her to pull out of the driveway, but she stayed parked, biting her bottom lip as the engine kept idling.

"You're wondering what to wear Sunday night," she said, giving me a pointed look. "Go with the red dress – the one with the little blue flowers."

I gaped at her as the Toyota backed up out of my driveway.

She rolled the window down part of the way. "And Lou… have fun. Something tells me you're going to need it."

CHAPTER 7

My stomach flipped around like flapjacks at the roar of a motorcycle coming down my street. I looked at myself in the mirror. There was a little bit of lipstick on my lips and just a touch of blush on my cheeks. None of it mattered though, I still looked pale, and my eyes were still too big – like a frightened owl. Either way, it was the best that was going to happen.

I had gone ahead and went with Vick's advice. Only one piece of clothing in my closet seemed anywhere near good enough for a date, and that was the red sundress with little blue flowers I found at a thrift store. It fit so well I couldn't say no, despite hardly ever wearing dresses. Skirts with black tights? Yes. Dresses and bare legs? No.

I also went with the only pair of nice shoes I owned, which were simple flats that luckily went with the dress, plus one of my nicer jean jackets with sleeves that stopped at my elbows.

Deep in the closet, buried under a bag of winter sweaters, the book pulsed a reminder of its presence.

"That'll be enough out of you," I told it.

The dread I felt at Mortie's had diminished quite a bit since then, but the book's awfulness still lingered. Neither Mortie nor I knew exactly what to do with it. We ended up deciding on my bedroom closet as the safest place to keep it for the time being. Every now and then the book gave off a faint drumbeat of doom from behind the closet door, as if in protest at being hidden away, but I ignored it. After all, I had other things on my mind.

I opened the front door and stepped out onto the porch. It didn't hit me until I was on the bottom step that maybe I should have let him come up and knock. Maybe that's how normal dates were supposed to start.

Scott parked the motorcycle in the driveway behind my Honda and walked up to the house. He was beautiful. I'd forgotten just how much. His faded jeans and dark blue button-up shirt combined with a black motorcycle helmet nearly turned me into a puddle of estrogen right there in my front yard.

He took off his helmet, slowly lowering it as his green eyes drifted over me.

"You look… amazing," he said reverently.

I blushed and smoothed my dress nervously. "Thanks. So do you."

His face lit up with a smile big enough to make that dimple of his resurface. I suddenly wished for black tights to hide my wobbling bare knees.

"You ready then?" He started toward the bike and then looked back at me. "Oh shit. I should've told you I was coming on it."

"It's fine," I quickly told him. Luckily, the dress fanned out enough that I was sure I could tuck it around me in a way that wouldn't have it flying up in my face.

"You sure?"

I nodded eagerly, inwardly cursing myself for listening to Vick when I picked out the dress from my closet.

He helped me put on the extra helmet and then straddled the motorcycle, leaving room for me to get on the seat behind him. I hesitated, doing mental gymnastics to make sure my legs remembered how to climb on things so that I wouldn't awkwardly fumble my way onto the bike. It wasn't the most graceful attempt, but I managed well enough.

"Might need to move a bit closer," he said, looking toward the empty space I'd left between us.

I scooted up on the seat and bit my lip as the inner part of my thighs graced his hips. At least he was in front of me and couldn't see the fire rising in my cheeks.

"I've never really been on a motorcycle before," I admitted.

"I'll go slow," he said over his shoulder. "Just put your arms around me and hang on tight."

Oh Lord. I nervously put my arms around his waist, feeling his muscles firm under my fists. The butterflies started up a barn dance in my stomach. Oh, my sweet Lord.

He started the engine, roaring it back to life. I tightened my grip on him out of instinct. His hand came down over mine, giving it a squeeze. And then we were off, and I quickly forgot just how scared I was.

The air flew over my arms and bare legs. I wanted to take off the helmet to feel the wind on my face and hair, but it wasn't safe. I also didn't want a mouthful of bugs by the time we got to wherever we were going.

The city limits of Magnolia Grove disappeared in the side mirrors and the rolling Southern Indiana countryside unfurled before us.

My arms loosened their death grip on him.

"Faster?" he asked.

I nodded against his shoulder, and we sped off down the empty highway, the sun setting on the horizon.

When we finally did roll to a stop, my legs were Jello, but I didn't care.

"That was amazing!" I said as he helped me take off the helmet, my cheeks hurting from smiling so hard.

His grin was just as big. "I had a feeling you'd like it." He leaned in close – close enough that for one heart-racing second, I thought he might kiss me. Instead, he brushed a hair off my cheek and took a shy step back.

Dozens of food trucks filled the parking lot, and the smell of tacos, fried food, and ice cream mingled in the air. The entire scene had a festive vibe with lights strung up all over the place and a band playing music somewhere. Beyond the food trucks, houseboats decorated with brightly colored Christmas lights, despite it being late summer, were tethered to the docks, bobbing up and down on the rolling river waves.

Scott ordered us street tacos, and we walked away from the swarm of people to a lonely dock in the distance.

"I've never been here before. Where are we exactly?" I asked, taking it all in. For the moment, we were in a ghost-free environment, which was rather surprising considering the body of water and the amount of people hanging around the food trucks.

"Kind of feels like a party in the middle of nowhere, doesn't it? We're not all that far from Bloomington," he said. "It's always busy here on Sundays, but during the weekdays it's quiet."

He sat down at the end of the dock and took off his shoes and socks, rolling his jeans up to his shins. He held out a hand for me as I slid off my own shoes and sat down next to him.

I was worried it would get awkward when the inevitable silence fell between us, but it was more like a companionable quiet, accented by the sound of the river lapping against the dock in a steady rhythm.

He looked out at the rolling river, watching as the waves went by. "Sometimes on my days off, I like to come up here and just listen to the water," he said.

This little nugget of information held a promise of hidden depths. Beyond his handsome exterior was a man who sought out peace and calm along the shore of a rolling river. What other gems were waiting to be discovered in him?

"I have a place like that," I told him and instantly wished I hadn't. Things were going so well. If I elaborated, then my ruse of being normal would evaporate into thin air, leaving nothing behind but my creepy self, which would likely send him running for the hills.

"Where's that?" he asked.

"It's not really all that special," I said, dismissively.

He nodded but looked disappointed. I stared down at the taco wrapper crumpled in my lap. "Actually, it's a cemetery…" I didn't dare look up. "Right before twilight. No one goes to cemeteries in the evening – I'm not sure why – but it's quiet then. You can hear the wind rustling in the grass. Even the birds in the trees are quiet."

He didn't say anything, and I was sure then that I'd scared him off.

His hand found mine. Long fingers intertwined with my small ones. "Sounds peaceful."

I looked up into his face. There was no disgust, no judgment. Instead, there was something else entirely. Wanting. My cheeks burned and I quickly averted my gaze, sure that I had misinterpreted what I saw.

We sat there together, hand in hand, a little while longer and then took a walk down the shoreline to get some ice cream. I was worried he'd want to ask normal date questions – stuff about my past, where I came from, what my family was like, but he didn't. Instead, he told me about some of the crazy police calls he'd been on and listened as I talked about Mortie and work, both of us laughing over some of my funnier customer stories.

It was the most normal time I'd ever had outside of the Piggly Wiggly, and I loved every second of it. For an entire evening, I felt like Cinderella, if her wish had been to feel like a normal, average girl going out with a boy. It was perfect. Naturally, it was destined for disaster; those were the rules in my universe.

By the time we pulled back into my driveway at the end of the night, my legs weren't as shaky as I got off the motorcycle. I handed him the helmet and straightened a few flyaway hairs.

"I... uh, had a great time," I said, unsure of how to end things.

"Me too. Do you think – I mean, would you like..." He ran a nervous hand through his hair. "I'm going to have to get better at this," he said to himself with a bashful smile. "Listen, can I see you again soon?"

I shook my head in disbelief and his face fell. "No, no, no, I didn't mean it like that," I quickly corrected myself. "Yes, of course, I'd love to see you again. It's just... I'm surprised, is all. I mean, why me? I'm just a grocery store stock girl."

He stepped closer. "With big gray eyes and pouty lips that I could stare at for hours. The first time I saw you smile at me, it nearly knocked me off my feet."

What he said was impossible. He could have anyone, and yet here he was, standing in my yard right in front of me with a look of wanting in his eyes I'd never seen before in a man, pointed in my general direction. Suddenly, I couldn't think any more about how crazy it was. I could only think about how his hand was on my waist, pulling me in close as his lips pressed against mine. The kiss was sweet and warm and nearly melted my brain.

"See you next time, Louise." He straddled the motorcycle and revved it back to life.

I held up a hand in a small wave and watched as he rolled out of the driveway and took off down the road. My fingers flew to my lips, desperately wanting to burn into memory how his lips felt against mine, the taste of his mouth, the pressure of his hand on my hip.

An hour later, I was still in a dreamy state as I stepped out of the bathtub after a long bubbly soak and pulled on a nightgown. Scott and Louise. It didn't seem all that far-fetched when I thought about it now. Maybe I could see a little bit of what he saw in me in the bathroom mirror if I looked hard enough. I wiped away the condensation from the mirror and touched my lips. Pouty? I never thought about it before but maybe they were a little pouty.

There was no tell-tale pulling this time, just one forceful yank around my midsection. The bathroom disappeared and I fell with my back hard against the ground in the cemetery, the full moon shining directly above me in a cloudless sky. Crap. How could I have forgotten? By having a date with a gorgeous man who seemed totally into me, that's how.

"This really isn't the best time for a visit, dear," came Mrs Hammond's panicked voice. She'd never said anything like that before. I sat upright so fast my head started to spin.

An icy mist pooled on the back of my hand. The glow of a small boy's ghostly fingers wrapped around mine. "You have to get out of here, Lou. He's coming."

Tom-Tom knelt on the ground next to me, fear in his innocent eyes. Mrs Hammond floated behind him, constantly looking over her shoulder and twisting her hankie fiercely. The cemetery around them was packed. Ghosts I'd never seen before huddled between the tombstones. All of them focused on me.

"Go... Run... Leave." They all said it and if they couldn't say it, they mouthed it.

I'd never not heeded a single ghost's advice before, much less that of a hundred ghosts, and I wasn't about to start now. I scrambled to my feet. The second I stood up, they disappeared. The cemetery went dark as if a light had gone out taking every last ghost with it. I bolted for the backpack hidden under the rose bush.

I'd been smart when I packed it and this time it had everything, even shoes. I pulled on black leggings and a long-sleeved black T-shirt and slipped my feet into a pair of running shoes. I shoved the nightgown into the empty bag and stowed it back under the rose bush.

"Who's there?" an authoritative voice called out.

Shit, shit, shit. I recognized that voice. I dropped down out of sight and army-crawled from one tombstone to another, my stomach sinking, my heart thumping wildly. His flashlight beam danced over each grave I left behind, catching up to my movements. I ducked behind the old oak tree, pressing my back flat against the trunk hoping to God it covered me. It didn't.

"Get out from behind there." Scott's voice was forceful.

Oh shit, oh shit, oh shit.

There was nowhere to run, no other place to hide. Cemetery strolls at twilight were one thing – dressed all in black darting around suspiciously in the middle of the night from one creepy grave to the next... that was something else entirely. That landed me right in freak territory with no good way to explain it. I sucked in a breath, preparing myself for the end of all my hopes and romantic dreams of a life filled with Scott, and stepped out from behind the tree.

CHAPTER 8

Everything happened at once.

I stepped out from behind the tree at the same time the cemetery's iron gate squeaked open. The flashlight beam went dark. I darted back behind the tree and peeked out. Scott was gone... totally gone... like 'vanished into thin air' gone. I scanned the cemetery, but there wasn't any sign of him.

Three dark silhouettes moved through the cemetery entrance, floating over the dirt path. At least, it looked as if they were floating. It was hard to tell. The streetlights that normally shined orange light down on the graves were suspiciously dark. There was still moonlight though. Soft beams of it streamed through the drifting clouds, adding to the newcomers' otherworldly vibes.

All three figures were covered in black cloaks with hoods so deep it seemed there were only shadows where faces should have been. The tattered hems of their cloaks brushed across the grass making it seem as if they moved with the wind.

They looked terrifying, but I was used to terrifying things and remained steadfast in my hiding place behind the oak, watching their progress through the cemetery.

It wasn't only ghosts that I'd come across in my life. It would be nice if that were the case. There were other things – creatures I rarely came across to be sure – but they very much existed, and believe me, they were the stuff of nightmares. I'd seen a banshee, a few wraiths, and something I highly suspected might be a demon. Who knew what else was out there, just waiting to scare the bejeezus out of me? Were these shadow-like beings from that same nightmarish blend? The jury was out.

A week ago, there'd been a new addition to Magnolia Grove Cemetery, a Mrs Edna Renwick. Mrs Renwick had gone on to her eternal slumber easy-peasy, probably on account of living a full life all the way into her late nineties. The dirt heaped on top of her casket was no longer loose, but the roses her grandson placed at the base of her tombstone were still fresh. The three mysterious shadows floated in a curious beeline straight for her plot.

There weren't many new plots left in the old cemetery. The newly deceased residents of Magnolia Grove tended to be buried at New Bethlehem Cemetery on the other side of town. Mrs Renwick must've picked out her plot a long time ago, choosing to be buried next to her brother and parents. Unfortunately, the family's plots were located close to the big oak where I hid. I crouched down and kept to the wider portion of the trunk.

Where the hell was Scott? What was the point of having a cop out here if he wasn't shining his flashlight on them, demanding to know what they were doing in the cemetery in the middle of the night? Why would a police officer be patrolling a cemetery anyway? It's not like any of these dead people were on the verge of committing a crime. And how come he just up and disappeared right when a cop would've been needed most?

A beam of moonlight hit the landscaping shed and, for a moment, I glimpsed a shimmer, a sort of metallic gleam, beside the shack storing the groundskeeper's lawn mower and weed whacker. Clouds passed over the moon, swallowing up the dwindling light, and then it was gone.

One of the cloaked figures knelt, placing a very human hand on Mrs Renwick's headstone. Not a nightmare creature then, but a living flesh-and-blood person. He reached within the folds of his cloak and pulled out a velvet box, the kind you get when you buy a ring or necklace at a jewelry store. He opened it, revealing what looked like a raw-shaped piece of quartz bigger than my thumb. A braid of twine encased it like a net with two long straps tied around it in a knot.

"Let us begin," came a man's voice from within the depths of the hood.

Two others positioned themselves around Mrs Renwick's grave – one beside it, another standing at the foot of the mound of dirt. The man kneeling at Mrs Renwick's headstone delicately lifted the gemstone from its velvet bed.

"First, an offering. The blood of life must be shed," he instructed.

The shadowed figure beside the grave took out a pocketknife and drew the blade across his palm. He clenched his fist until drops of blood fell one after another onto the pile of dirt. The man at the foot of the grave took fistfuls of dirt and poured them over the drops of blood, burying them like a body.

"With this blood, may you find new life once more and rise out of the sleep you've been forever damned to," the man with the quartz said in a reverent tone.

What ridiculous sort of nonsense was this? Poor Mrs Renwick. Her resting place was being defiled by a bunch of nutjobs.

Having spent a lot of time in cemeteries – and I mean a lot – I'd definitely run across my fair share of weird things; teenage girls pretending to hold seances (which usually just entailed them lugging around a bunch of candles in backpacks, waiting to see which one of them could stay in the cemetery the longest before they all got scared and ran home). Then there were couples engaged in amorous, um, acts. I wasn't sure who would want to do it in a graveyard with a bunch of ghosts watching, but to each their own, I suppose. And then there were the grave robbers – people shamelessly stealing flowers and wreaths meant as memorials to loved ones. But this – grown men dressing up in ragged cloaks, pretending to raise the dead? This was a first.

"And now for the summoning," the man at the headstone said, holding the gem out expectantly toward the one with the cut palm. Obediently he smeared his bloodied palm over the stone's jagged surface. He then held the dripping quartz by the twine straps and dangled it over Mrs Renwick's grave. "We call out to the one who sleeps, the one with the power to raise the dead, and beg him to restore what has been taken."

The three of them dipped their cloaked heads and began to chant in unison, the words sounding like mumbled gibberish from where I stood.

Once again, where was Scott? This was the perfect time for a cop to bust this bunch of wackos.

All of it was completely ridiculous… at least it would have been, if not for the gemstone's changing appearance as it swayed back and forth above the grave. It started with a drop of black, like ink, swirling inside the quartz, spreading until it filled every crevice of the stone, turning it deep black, like obsidian.

The air in the cemetery changed. For a moment, it felt like the world had a tangible, finite edge to it, and the only thing separating us from the abyss beyond was a thin shred of air as fragile as tissue paper.

A cold chill crept over the bark beneath my fingers. My stomach flipped as if I were about to be yanked away again. I gripped the tree trunk, anchoring myself.

The dirt on Mrs Renwick's grave shifted.

The earth trembled.

And then the impossible happened.

I blinked and blinked again, not believing what I was seeing. A casket emerged from the ground, hovering in the air. The man with the cut hand collapsed beside the mound. The casket fell with him, landing hard on the ground next to the gaping hole in the earth.

"Help him to his feet," the man at the headstone ordered the other cloaked figure who scurried to do as he was told.

The gemstone vibrated, now emitting a blue glow. The radius of the glow pulsed wider and wider until it encompassed the entire back corner of the cemetery. The chill beneath my fingers turned to bits of frost that crept up my arms and into my throat, prickling it with little ice crystals that made my breath come out in a puff of steam.

With a flick of the hand from the man at the headstone, the casket lid flung open, and there, in her best Sunday dress, was Mrs Edna Renwick.

Something I didn't expect happened next.

I was angry. Furious. This was *my* cemetery. Mrs Renwick was in my care, whether or not she haunted the rows of gravestones or slept peacefully beneath the ground. How dare they defile her and her final resting place?

The chill retreated, and the bits of frost melted away into droplets of water on my skin. Trembling with rage, I gritted my teeth and gripped the bark, willing myself to remain put. Pissed as I was, I still had enough sense not to go up against three guys in creepy cloaks who were much bigger than me.

The man at the headstone approached the open coffin and reached in, gently caressing the old woman's embalmed cheek. "Beautiful," he breathed.

Living Mrs Renwick would've been appalled. She was the same breed of woman as Mrs Hammond, both taking great care to present themselves as downright proper ladies. Back in their day, their worlds had been full of bridge parties and church potlucks. I'd heard more than my fair share of such mind-numbingly boring stories from said events from Mrs H. I wouldn't be surprised if she and Mrs Renwick had even crossed paths at a potluck or two at some point, even though they moved in different circles and belonged to different churches. But while Mrs H was timid and quasi-submissive in a passive-aggressive sort of way, Mrs Renwick could be described as prudish and rigid, especially in her expectation that everyone should display good manners and stay within their own personal boundaries. An intimate touch from such a man as this would've earned him a solid slap across the face and a stern talking down at the very least.

He held up the gemstone over Mrs Renwick's corpse.

"Rise," he whispered.

The glow emanating from the stone retreated in on itself. The black inside drained away, returning the stone to its clear state.

Mrs Renwick's eyes fluttered open.

Impossible.

I'd seen all manner of crazy shit in my life but this... this was absolutely impossible.

Her long, graceful fingers gripped the sides of the coffin. She pulled herself up into a sitting position, looked curiously at the man in front of her, and then, right smack dab at me. In life, Mrs Renwick's eyes had been hazel. I'd seen them in the picture placed in the library's lobby over her obituary on the bulletin board when she passed away. Now they were pitch black, the same black that had been in the quartz.

"Lou," her voice came to me, and I jumped, expecting to see the mouth on the corpse move but it didn't. The voice had come from behind me, from Mrs Renwick's apparition.

She didn't look at all like the corpse in the coffin. This Mrs Renwick was young and lovely, with her hair piled into a loose bun and soft tendrils framing her oval face. Her aura wasn't the warm white of Mrs H's but more like the bright white of a daylight light bulb – definitely not an aura I'd ever seen before. This was no normal ghost. In fact, this ghost wasn't even supposed to be here at all. I knew that as sure as I knew that she was Edna Renwick despite the age difference.

"Lou, it's almost time," she said in a quiet voice, looking over my shoulder toward the landscaping shed. "When you hear the crash, you have to run. They must not find you here."

A sliver of light danced behind Mrs Renwick's aura, a thin ribbon streaming vertically in the air, drifting and twirling as if caught up in a gentle breeze. Before, there had been a deep chill where I stood against the tree trunk, but now as I faced the ribbon, warmth poured over me. Looking at it felt like walking on a beach on a sunny day or lying on the grass just as a sunbeam peeked out from behind the clouds to blanket your skin. It was wonderful... and terrifying. Facing it was like facing my own death. I knew that if I stepped into that ribbon, I'd never come back from it.

No longer bearable to look upon, I turned my back to it. There was relief in looking away, almost as if I'd taken a step back from the edge of a cliff. The warmth of it continued to pour over my back, reminding me that it, and Mrs Renwick's aura, were still there.

The ritual went on around Mrs Renwick's cemetery plot, except now the cemetery was darker, without the glow from the quartz. The clouds covering the moon now filled every inch of sky, hanging lower and lower like they might drop a rain shower over us at any minute.

"Wake from your rest, dear Edna, and follow my voice to the land of the living," he commanded, sounding like one of the silly teenagers who pretended to do seances in the cemetery. He held the gemstone up in front of her face. It gravitated toward her, attracted to her corpse like a magnet. "Tell us where to find it... where is the key to restoring life?"

Mrs Renwick's corpse tilted her head curiously at the man holding the necklace made of twine, considering what he said. Her arm lifted, and those graceful fingers of hers that had played the organ every Sunday in church pointed right at me.

I gasped and all three cloaked heads looked at my oak tree. I froze like a deer in the headlights. A thunderous crash came from the maintenance shed.

"Run, Lou!" Mrs Renwick shouted.

I took off, bolting up over the fence. I was nowhere near the athletic type, but I had just enough adrenaline pumping through my system to get me up and over. I landed hard on the other side, scraping my knees on the pavement.

"Find out who that was!" the jewel-holding man shouted after me.

I ran like an animal fleeing a wildfire, not really thinking about where I was going, just desperate to escape where I'd been. My heart pounded in rapid fire against my ribs. What the hell just happened? Who were those guys? How was that kind of power even possible? And then, on top of all that, where in the hell had Scott gone? People didn't just vanish into thin air. I mean, technically, I did from time to time but that wasn't my fault, that was Mrs H. At least he hadn't seen me. I was pretty sure about that. If there was a silver lining in all this mess, it was that.

I wasn't paying attention to where I was going, focusing only on whether or not I was being followed. I didn't notice the accumulating wisps until they were all around me.

They blocked the roadway ahead, flooding the entire area, floating in a massive swarm growing denser wisp after wisp. These wisps weren't acting like the ones outside the police station or hospital. Just like outside Mortie's with that damn book, their eyeless sockets focused solely on me. I doubled back, making a run for a nearby side-street.

The floating specters hovered, crowding in closer and closer to one another. They poured into the street behind me in droves, corralling me to the point where only two paths were left: one curving back to the cemetery, the other leading left toward a gravel road. I took the left.

A house loomed at the end of the street, partially hidden by old walnut trees, some of which were rotting and sagging dangerously close to the power lines overhead. I knew the house, having seen it once before. I'd come across it while mapping out routes to and from work when I moved into town. Back then, I took one look at the sign out front, *Osgood Funeral Home*, and made an abrupt U-turn for home.

Now that U-turn was blocked by wisps. The wisps circled around me, filling my ears with cries that echoed in my head, reverberating deep inside me. They closed in, nudging me closer to the funeral home's extra-wide garage, which was big enough for hearses to unload their deceased passengers. I desperately wanted to run back to the cemetery, creepy cloaked nutjobs raising the dead be damned, but I couldn't. I couldn't run, couldn't move, couldn't even stand. Their cries were too much. I crumbled to the gravel road, shaking my head, trying to rid myself of their horror-filled sobs in my ears.

The funeral home's double doors flung open. Brilliant light exploded from within, almost as bright as the ribbon I'd seen behind Mrs Renwick's aura. A darkened silhouette stood bathed in that light.

"Back! Get back you cursed things!" someone shouted.

A man ran down the front steps.

The wisps within the radius of light shrieked, shrinking back long enough for him to hook his arm around my waist and half-drag me up the steps into the safety of the funeral home.

CHAPTER 9

He pressed his back up against the closed doors as if the added force was needed to keep them out.

I'd seen him before, several times, in fact. Tall and lanky, he usually wore a rumpled suit frayed at the hem as he carried a bouquet of flowers to his wife's grave in Magnolia Grove Cemetery. All those times I passed by him, I never realized he was the funeral home director.

I sank into the nearest velvet-covered pew in the main chapel and watched, stunned, as he opened the curtains, putting a lit candle on each windowsill.

"I've never seen this many before," he said with a shake of his head as he lit the last candle.

"You... you can see them?"

"Why, of course, I can." He looked at me, baffled, as if it were a ridiculous question, as if I asked him if he knew the sky was blue.

I cried. I couldn't help it. All these years I thought I was alone in this curse. When I was a teenager, I'd wondered if I was going insane, if I'd imagined these shadows of the dead, conjuring them out of thin air like some creepy version of imaginary friends. For years I'd thought something was wrong with me, that maybe I had deep psychological problems. Eventually, I'd accepted that the ghosts I saw were very much real and this was just who I was, though doubt always lingered there at the edge of reason. Now, here was someone like me, someone who could see all the dark and scary things I saw. The relief was overwhelming.

"There, there," he said, taking a seat next to me on the pew and awkwardly patting my hand. "It's alright."

"How – how long?" I asked between sniffles and a hiccup.

He handed me a tissue from his pocket. "All my life."

The toll it had taken on him was clear. He might've been a handsome man if it weren't for the sunken, gaunt cheeks and the dark circles under his gray eyes. I wasn't sure how old he was, but the thin streaks of gray in his black hair seemed premature. There was defeat in his pale face and a resolved tone of acceptance in his voice. I knew both those things all too well.

"And yet you work here. How is that even possible?"

He mostly ignored my question, answering it in merely half a shrug. "I was just about to make some tea. Let me bring you a cup," he said and left me alone in the chapel.

I'd been inside a funeral home before. Once. Back when my great-grandmother died. She was the only relative my mother and I knew, and it was the very first time six-year-old me ever saw a ghost. It wasn't Great-Gran Louise's either, but the aura of the man in the closed casket in the back room. He asked me politely enough if I'd seen his dog that ran off; all the while his face flickered back and forth between how he looked before and after his death, which was, unfortunately, from a grisly car accident. Ever since then, I'd sworn off funeral homes for good.

Now granted, this particular funeral home didn't appear all that bad. It was clear he lived here. There was a stairwell hidden away in a corner of the room, blocked off by a velvet rope with a small sign taped to it that read: "personal residence."

At the front of the chapel was an empty pedestal just waiting for a casket to hold. I shuddered and averted my eyes. Strange, I'd seen all manner of horrifying ghosts in my life, but it was this simple, plainly decorated chapel that gave me the shivers.

He returned, the swinging door moving in a hush against the carpet. I glimpsed the kitchen beyond it, one with an open layout large enough to suit a mourning family gathered for a wake or a luncheon.

He carried two steaming teacups and took a seat in the pew across from me.

"Chamomile with milk and honey," he said, offering me a cup.

"Thank you." I took a sip and cradled it in my hands. I stared down at the sweet murky liquid as a long silence fell between us.

"My name is Ivan Osgood," he said, breaking the silence.

"Everyone calls me Lou."

Another awkward silence fell. I took a long sip of tea. The sweet herbal mix was soothing and despite all the awkwardness, I was starting to feel a little better.

"There's no ghosts in here," I said, my voice coming out almost muted in the hushed chapel.

"No." He looked around with a peaceful smile. "Never in here."

"Why is that?" I thought the question was an obvious, natural one but from the uncomfortable look on Ivan's face, apparently, it wasn't.

"I think, perhaps, because they themselves do not want to mourn," he said. "It would be like facing the ultimate reality, an unavoidable truth that would force them to pass from this world to the next regardless of whatever was keeping them here."

I'd never thought of it that way. "You're suggesting they want to be here?"

His discomfort vanished and a passion filled his eyes, like someone in a book club discussing their favorite novel.

"Have you ever had a memory so awkward and uncomfortable that it creeps up on you in the middle of the night, unsuspecting? Something you might've said wrong in the past, perhaps an embarrassing faux pas? You wish you could let that memory go but you can't and maybe if you looked at it hard enough – if you took it apart piece by piece – you might find that you don't *want* to let it go. The memory hurts a little, twists at your gut but at least it proves you can feel; that you're alive even though you know the memory will only come to haunt you again another night. Perhaps the reason they stay in this world is a little like that."

I stared at him dumbfounded. I never thought of it that way before, but damned if it didn't ring a little true, at least for some of the ghosts I'd encountered.

Having unfurled himself to me with that little nugget of otherworldly insight, his awkwardness ebbed.

"Forgive me, Lou. I've known about our… mutual affliction for quite some time now. I should've introduced myself before. She told me I could trust you, and I should've believed her, given all that she knows about the future. But I was afraid – afraid of what I might learn about myself through you. For that, I am terribly sorry. It was foolish to be afraid, I can see that now."

He rattled all that off, most of it not making a lick of sense. I latched onto the one bit that did.

"Vick?" I breathed.

He nodded. "Yes, Miss Ingram, or rather, Victoria."

A puzzle piece fell into place. I looked him over in a new light. "It was you that made her send me that book." But how in the hell did the two even know each other? More importantly, though, how could this lanky, quiet man ever be in possession of something that horrifying and nightmarish?

He hung his head in shame. "A burden I had no right to place on your shoulders. Believe me, though, when I tell you I saw no other choice."

I tried to grapple with everything he threw at me. He'd known I could see ghosts this whole time. How? I certainly didn't know *he* could all those times our paths crossed in the cemetery. And the book – why did he think he had no choice but to give it to me?

"Were you..." He hesitated, not meeting my eyes. "Were you able to read it?"

"I mean, I saw words and stuff, but I didn't understand them. I don't think it's written in English." I wavered for a moment before saying the rest. Should I tell him what it did to me? What the hell, might as well take it all the way considering he started this. "It also knocked me back on my ass when I touched a page."

He sputtered his tea. "You were able to touch a page?"

I set aside the tea and folded my hands in my lap giving him my best 'I mean business' face. "What exactly is in that book? And why send it to me?"

He didn't immediately answer and got up to peek out the windows. "It seems our friends have gone."

I gritted my teeth. I really hated not getting answers. Why did everyone I meet insist on evading my questions?

He went from window to window blowing out the candles. "It's the warmth in the light that keeps the shades away," he said, holding onto the last burning candle.

"Shades? I've always called them wisps."

His lips turned up in a hint of a smile. "A less threatening name to be sure."

I wanted to ask him more about all the different ghosts he'd seen. I was desperate to, but I pursed my lips tight, saying nothing, determined to get an answer to my first question even if it meant enduring a whole host of awkward silences between us.

He sat back down, cradling the burning candle in his lap.

"The book has a name, at least I know that much about it." He paused. His fingers fidgeted with the base of the candle holder. "The Book of Souls," he whispered. "Many years ago, it was given to me much in the same way I gave it to you. I don't know where it came from or who had it before me. Alice, my wife, believed it must've belonged to someone like me." His eyes met mine. "Someone like us."

Someone like us. Just a short time ago I thought I was the only one in the world who could see and talk to the dead. And now, Mr. Osgood was suggesting it wasn't just him and me but others who might've come before us.

"In the beginning, I thought I might try to read from it." His brows furrowed in pain at the memory. "But even trying to open it took a toll on me. From then on, I kept it locked in the basement, tolerating its dread all these years. Alice said that even dark things can serve a purpose," he said quietly, his eyes drifting over the chapel. "I always wanted to believe she was right, though I don't think she could feel what I did."

"Why give it to me?"

"Something is changing, Lou. Have you felt it?"

I stared hard at him. How many times had I heard that now?

"Tom-Tom said something similar to me in the cemetery a few nights ago. What do you mean by it?"

"Tom-Tom?" he asked, confused.

"You know, the little boy in a sailor outfit that haunts Magnolia Grove Cemetery. I mean, he doesn't come out all that often, but surely you've seen him."

"Yes, yes, I've seen him. Are you saying he actually spoke to you?"

"Of course."

He stared at me in awe and then sank back against the pew.

"And the woman in pearls, does she speak to you too?"

"Mrs Hammond? All too often." I chuckled.

"Astonishing! And the shades? Er– the wisps, as you call them, what do they say?"

"Nothing really." That wasn't entirely true. Tom wasn't the only one to warn me that night, but I kept that to myself. After all, the wisp technically hadn't said anything, it was more like her voice had been inside my head.

"It appears we're not as alike as I thought," he said. "I've never heard a ghost speak. Frankly, I didn't even know that was possible."

"There's a lot of impossible things happening lately." I told him what I'd seen tonight in Magnolia Grove Cemetery.

Intrigued, he leaned forward as I told him about the men in cloaks and their color-changing crystal. He sucked in a breath as I described the casket rising out of the ground, his eyes widening when I got to the part where Mrs Renwick sat up in her casket.

He sat quietly considering all that I said. Wax slowly rolled down the candle's long stem to drop in the holder sitting on his lap. His long silences were frustrating. When I talked to Mortie about this kind of stuff he always gave me quick, insightful advice. I set aside my teacup and clasped my hands together to try to be patient and to stop me from shaking him till he spoke.

"I don't know how much help I can be to you, Lou, except to tell you what I, myself, have observed as of late. Alice used to think that there was a veil between this world and the next, like a solid curtain. She was a very perceptive woman," he said with a sad sort of smile. "She even saw right through me the first time we met, discovering my secret.

"In this line of work," he went on. "I've felt that curtain brush up against me on several occasions. Sometimes it's more substantial than a curtain, almost a brick wall, but it's always been there. In the last few weeks, I've done three funerals, poor Mrs Renwick included. The Veil no longer feels like a curtain but more like tissue paper, thin enough I'm afraid it might tear. The book changed too, humming as if coming to life, and the dread it carried intensified. The book and the Veil are linked, I'm sure of it. The answers to whatever is happening are sure to be in its pages. It won't give those answers to me, but maybe it will to you."

Goosebumps rippled over my skin. I knew the dreaded hum he spoke of. Moreover, I was pretty sure I knew the Veil he talked about. I'd been inside it, trapped there momentarily somewhere between my home and the cemetery. Worse than that though, I knew something lurked inside it. A terrible thought came to mind, one I was almost too scared to put into words.

"What if that's what happened tonight? What if those men in the cemetery ripped a bit of the Veil open to conjure Mrs Renwick?"

Ivan blew out the candle, sending smoke dancing high into the air. "If that's true, then the power these people have unlocked could only be the beginning."

CHAPTER 10

My little green house sat waiting for me as if nothing had changed, as if I were just coming home from a shift at work. A long night filled with dead things, and conversations about dead things, had taken its toll on me.

I walked up the front steps, feeling like I shed a second skin belonging to the outside world as I stepped over the threshold. Inside, all the lights were on, and warmth flooded over me, chasing away a chill I didn't realize had settled deep inside my bones.

I walked past the bathroom, remembering all my happy fluttery post-date feelings just before I'd been torn right out of my naivety and dropped in the cemetery to have reality slap me across the face. The world as I knew it had turned upside down. The power to bring the dead back to life was a reality. I'd seen the proof right before my eyes.

Despite all the night's revelations, there was one nagging thought that kept refusing to be ignored. Scott. All my time in cemeteries and I'd never come across a cop patrolling them. It seemed odd that on a night where nutjobs showed up, so did he, but then again, he certainly didn't do anything to bust them. Isn't that what cops did? Maybe I was overthinking it too much. Maybe he *was* just out on patrol. And if he was, what if he *did* see me? A flutter of panic came with the thought. If he had, I was pretty sure that was the first and last date we'd have. It wouldn't be a surprise. Catching me hiding behind gravestones in the dead of night for no sane reason probably would have killed it. And if I was being honest, whatever was between us was doomed before it ever began really. No one normal could be in a life with me. I was a creepy, weird, cursed girl. If that wasn't a relationship killer, I wasn't sure what was.

A pulse of dread emanated from the bedroom closet where I'd buried the book. According to Ivan Osgood, the answers to what happened tonight could potentially be waiting inside, if only I could figure out how to read from it. Well, I wasn't interested in finding answers, at least not tonight. I ignored the closet with its drumbeat of doom and threw myself on the bed, not even bothering to undress.

I woke with a start a few hours later. I sat upright, rubbing my eyes, and blinked drowsily. Maybe I was delirious with sleep or maybe it was the lingering effects of the nightmare that woke me, but whatever it was it had the hair on the back of my neck standing on end, insisting I wasn't alone.

It was still night. A ray of moonlight streamed through the window and glinted off something beside the dresser. I stared hard at the shadows where I'd seen the shimmer until my eyelids were too heavy. Feeling ridiculous and exhausted, I gave up, rolled over, and went back to sleep.

Hours later, I woke up again, stiff and groggy. Sunlight poured in through the bedroom windows.

What time was it? And what day, for that matter? Did I have a shift to cover that night? I tried to focus on each question, searching for its answer, but in the end, all I could think about was how thirsty I was. I tucked my feet into a pair of worn-out bunny slippers, their pink fur long since faded to gray, and shuffled to the kitchen to pour myself a cup of water. I gulped it down and went through the usual morning motions of filling up the teapot, setting it on the stove to boil, and popping some bread into the toaster.

My sluggish mind barely registered the black object on the table. It wasn't until I rubbed the sleep from my eyes that I saw it.

Sitting there in a beam of light on my lace-covered kitchen table was the book – definitely not where I'd left it in the closet. Even more puzzling, was the absence of dread that usually accompanied it. Maybe I was just too tired to feel it.

Everything that happened last night came rushing back. Scott. A very dead Mrs Renwick sitting upright in her casket. Ivan Osgood. The funeral home and all the wisps around it.

The teapot whistled and the toast popped up from the toaster. I fixed my breakfast all while keeping a resentful eye on the book, wondering if it would disappear and reappear somewhere else, as it apparently liked to do. I sat down at the table with my cup of tea and munched on toast and jam, staring at its black binding.

After the last bite of breakfast, I reached for the cover and flipped it open. "Fine then," I said, giving in. "Let's see what you have to say for yourself."

My hand hovered hesitantly over the open book. My muddled morning mind waged a battle over whether touching the page would be a good idea or a really, really stupid one. Stupid won out.

I pressed my open palm against the page. The paper gave a soft tremble beneath my touch. Silver ink letters flooded the page just as before, the language still unrecognizable. I stared at the letters, waiting for them to vanish like they did before, but they didn't.

And that was it.

Nothing else happened. No knocking me on my ass, no filling me with dread. Nada.

I took a shower and got ready for work, feeling more like myself as I pulled on a pair of wine-colored tights and a jean skirt.

Every now and then I stuck my head in the kitchen just to be sure the book hadn't disappeared. And every time I checked, it was there sitting on the table pulsing a sort of: 'Hi, yeah, I'm still here.'

I shoved it into the backpack usually reserved for hauling library books and slid my lunch for work next to it before setting out across the yard toward Mortie's. I hesitated before stepping off the porch. It wasn't just the lack of dread that was different. The yard was completely empty of the wisps that flooded it the last time I had the book out in the open. I walked, unsettled, the rest of the way to Mortie's, looking over my shoulder more than once just in case I was mistaken.

"Lewis!" He called out cheerfully from the workroom after my customary three knocks on the front door. Zelda leaped down from her warm bed in the window to snake around my ankles until I gave her a scratch under the chin.

Instead of working on something, Mortie was tidying up his workspace. Zelda followed me into the workroom and jumped up on an empty stool. She watched him bustle back and forth between the table and shelves for a moment, then lost interest and began licking her paws clean.

"Word of warning," he said. "The ladies from the historical society are going to show up any minute with another project for me. You're welcome to stay. I know how much you love chit-chat and scones," he teased.

"Sounds lovely," I groaned, earning a chuckle out of him.

On the way over, I'd decided not to overburden him with everything that happened just yet and to sound as upbeat and chipper as I could. I didn't want to worry Mortie any more than I was about to.

"Hey, how was the date?" he asked eagerly.

"The date was great." It wasn't a lie, the date went perfectly, but the rest of the night... not so much.

"I wondered if you might take a look at something for me," I quickly went on, before he could ask more and find out I was holding back. I heaved the backpack onto the nearby stool and started to unzip it, then stopped.

"You don't feel anything?" I asked, surprised.

He thought about it for a moment before shaking his head. "No, why?"

Weird. The last time the book was in his house, dread practically dripped from the walls. Now... nada once again. Even Zelda seemed unphased, curling up to go to sleep on the other stool.

I slid the book out and set it on the worktable, taking care not to bump any of the other projects nearby. "You've met before."

Mortie's smile faded in grim recognition. He pushed up his glasses and looked uneasily at the book. "Yes. I believe we have."

He took a steadying breath, reached out a reluctant hand, and placed it flat on the cover.

Again, nothing happened.

"Interesting," he said. He picked it up, turning it around to closer examine the back cover.

"Apparently, it has a name." I decided to give him that much information, hoping he wouldn't ask how I knew. "The Book of Souls."

"That sounds ominous, albeit fitting." He opened the cover and touched the first page. His fingers flew over the letters scrawled across the page, a shimmer of silver following along with his touch. "How very interesting."

A car door sounded outside followed by the high voices and laughs from a chorus of women.

Mortie closed the book carefully. "May I look at it while you're at work?"

"I was hoping you would, on the off chance we might find out more about it now that it's no longer oozing with terror."

I zipped up the now lighter-weight backpack and shouldered it.

He opened his file cabinet and tucked the book inside and out of sight from the incoming gaggle of ladies. "Maybe when you come back, you can tell me what really happened last night to make you so upset, hmm?" he said over his shoulder.

My silence hadn't worked on him after all. I should've known better.

"I'm sorry. I will," I said, giving him a kiss on the cheek. "I promise."

The ladies from the historical society made their way up the porch and rang the doorbell.

"I'll head out the back if that's okay." Chit-chat with scones was almost worse than corpses coming back to life.

"Just one more thing, Lewis," he said, ignoring the door. He patted the closed file cabinet. "Books like this don't just up and change their nature. I'm not sure why it feels different this time, but I have a hunch. Books have owners. I don't know who owned it before, but it's making itself pretty clear it's picked you now, and I'm not entirely sure that's a good thing."

* * *

I rode my bike down to Magnolia Grove Cemetery. My legs were stiff from running around all over town last night and I had to pedal a little harder than normal to loosen up my muscles.

Police tape cordoned off the entry and exit to the cemetery. The parking lot was full, with three hearses all from different funeral homes, backhoes, squad cars, and even a news van. I slowed my bike to a stop and got off, walking it along the sidewalk next to the perimeter fence.

Holy shit. Apparently, the creepy cloaked trio hadn't stopped with Mrs Renwick after I took off last night. Mound after mound of graves had been opened and caskets were everywhere, lying askew next to piles of dirt.

Backhoes broke ground re-digging cemetery plots while workers from funeral homes all across the county loaded broken caskets into the back of hearses. A police officer interviewed the groundskeeper next to the maintenance shed, who kept shrugging and lifting up his baseball hat to scratch his head.

I craned my neck searching for Mr Osgood but couldn't find him. There was a hearse with his logo on it though, and some men in overalls loading up a body that was nowhere near the coffin it came out of. At the center of the cemetery, a camera crew had set up. A pretty brunette reporter in a blazer held a microphone up to an annoyed officer.

Mrs Hammond was nowhere to be seen. I wasn't sure if that was due to the influx of people in the cemetery or some other reason.

Among it all, tucked away in the background, wearing shades and looking hotter than Hades in his uniform, was Scott.

His eyes had been on me before I'd noticed him, but for how long? My cheeks burned as he made a beeline across the cemetery straight toward me. I pinched the hem of my jean skirt against my thigh to keep from fidgeting as he came around the fence to where I stood on the sidewalk.

What was he going to say? Maybe he did see me last night after all. Would he confront me about it, question me about what I was doing in the cemetery in the middle of the night? Maybe he was going to arrest me. I didn't break any laws last night, did I? Of course, I didn't, but then why did I feel so guilty?

I opened my mouth to say something – God only knew what – when he pulled me into his arms and kissed me.

This wasn't like the kiss we shared last night after our date. That one had been soft and sweet with a hint of shyness. The perfect first kiss. This was different. Possessive, passionate, territorial. Could a kiss be territorial? This one certainly felt that way. It was as if, with just a kiss, he had planted a flag on my face, declaring me off-limits to everyone else in the cemetery. It was startling to get such a kiss, and from him, no less. More startling, though, was my reaction to it.

I melted into him, taking him into me, and returned the kiss, deepening it into something harder, something heated, something intense enough that it took us both by surprise the moment our lips parted.

His breath caught and he stared down at me, his thumb on my lower lip where his mouth had been. I'd been so wrapped up in the moment that I didn't even think till now that maybe I hadn't kissed him very well or that I'd done something weird. I couldn't tell from his reaction one way or the other because whatever was in his eyes was a mystery behind those dark sunglasses.

And then another transformation occurred. An easy-going smile that didn't quite meet the lower rim of his sunglasses changed him from the shy, sincere Scott I was just starting to get to know, to a confident, laid-back, maybe even a little cocky Scott, a version of him I was not at all familiar with.

"Work was crazy last night," he said lightly, as if we didn't just have both our brains explode with the most intimate kiss either of us ever had. I blinked stupidly up at him, trying to catch up to the sudden change in him.

Yes. Last night. I'd forgotten. I'd also forgotten we were very much not alone, and that the cemetery was packed with cops, funeral home workers, and EMTs, some of whom were looking curiously our way. The blush on my cheeks burned all the way up to five-alarm fire levels.

"A bunch of kooks broke into the cemetery and really trashed the place," he said, nodding at the mayhem behind him. His words and their meaning were enough to pull me back into the here and now. Did that mean he hadn't seen me last night after all? It sure sounded that way. If he had, I doubted very much I'd be in his arms right now, sharing mind-blowing kisses and whatnot.

I let out a relieved breath and eased a bit in his arms, listening more closely to what he was saying. "It sure is good to see you though," he said. "I meant to call this morning, but it's been absolutely crazy here."

His voice dropped to a quieter tone, and for a split second, I glimpsed the Scott I was used to – genuine, earnest Scott. "I really did have a great time last night."

"I, uh, had a great time too," I managed to say, trying to recover from another round of whiplash.

"Campbell! I'm not paying you to make out with your girlfriend," the police captain barked across the cemetery. "Get over here and bring a fingerprint kit with you."

"Yes, sir!" Scott shouted back.

All eyes were on us then, if they weren't already.

"I better go before he really starts to lose it," he said, completely unphased by the attention he garnered. "Talk to you later?"

I nervously smoothed the front of my jean skirt and nodded. "Um, sure."

He pulled me in for a hug and a passing officer grinned at us.

"Campbell!" the captain shouted.

Scott brushed a hand over my elbow in parting and jogged off to his patrol car to dig out a black case before returning to the shed.

What in the holy hell just happened?

For starters, that cop said "girlfriend." Was that what I was? I'd never been someone's girlfriend before. Did one date count as girlfriend status? I didn't think so but then again, that kiss seemed more intense than just a girlfriend/boyfriend kiss. That was some next-level kissing. And then there was Scott's demeanor, the shifting disposition. What was that all about? Not to mention, he hadn't even been embarrassed to be seen with me like that, to hug and kiss me in front of everyone – weird, creepy, awkward me. In a way, the whole moment felt way odder than corpses coming back to life. That, at least, made sense in my world, but a boyfriend who casually kissed me in front of an entire police department? Now that was crazy.

While Scott disappeared into the shed, the pretty reporter who'd been recording stand-up segments in front of tombstones managed to corner another officer.

"How many suspects are you guys searching for? A vandalism job like this, that would have to be half a dozen at least, wouldn't you say?" The reporter pushed the microphone closer to the officer.

"I'm sorry, ma'am, the statement I gave you is all Magnolia Grove Police is prepared to say at this time."

"Digging up bodies and moving them around the cemetery seems like something that would take quite a bit of time. How is it that Magnolia Grove's finest didn't stumble upon these perpetrators in the act while they were out on patrol? Are shift duties lagging in the department? Did an officer neglect passing by the cemetery on his watch?"

He didn't take the bait. "Ma'am, your news van is blocking a hearse. Please move it out of the way." He walked off and the reporter dropped the microphone to her side, scanning the cemetery for someone else to interview.

Behind her, a pair of paramedics loaded a stretcher with a covered body into the back of an ambulance. The paramedic latching the door closed looked across the cemetery at the reporter. He was big and burly with a tattoo of a bird's skull peeking out from the collar at his neck. His glance lasted less than a second, but it was definitely intense – more like a targeted, focused attention that zeroed in on her and no one else. It happened so fast that afterward, as he jumped into the passenger side of the ambulance, I wasn't entirely sure what I saw. Maybe I misinterpreted it. Maybe she just said something that caught his interest. What did I know about it anyway?

The reporter was in the process of winding up her microphone cable when the police captain walked by.

"Captain Roberts!" she called out, hurrying to catch up to him as he marched out of the cemetery. "Can I ask you a few questions off the record?"

"You're kidding, right? I've got a cemetery that's been gutted, funeral homes scrambling to match corpses to caskets, and I'm up to my eyeballs in dental records. I gave you your soundbite."

"But–"

"Sorry, Sharon. That's as much information as you're gonna get right now," he said over his shoulder.

The reporter gave a gesture to the cameraman to stop rolling. "Pack it up, Toby."

Our eyes met through the cast iron fence that walled off the cemetery.

"Spooky stuff huh?" she said to me with a wolfish smile.

"What happened?" I asked, feigning ignorance.

If she was annoyed by the question, she didn't act like it. She seemed eager just to have an audience. "Last night a bunch of kids broke into the cemetery while the cops were out doing who knows what and decided to dig up a bunch of bodies. The cops are being tight-lipped but what else could it be? The alternative is that a bunch of corpses just up and climbed out of their coffins. Real-life Halloween shit if you ask me."

She leaned in closer toward the fence. "What they're not saying publicly is that the same thing happened at New Bethlehem Cemetery. Total upheaval – could be grave robbing, could be satanic rituals, who knows. Now they're checking out all the cemeteries in the county. God only knows what else they'll find."

She took my silence for shock. "You really haven't heard any of this? Don't you watch the news?"

"I don't have a TV."

She balked at the statement, looking at me as if I'd grown a second head. "What are you? Amish?"

She scrunched up her face in a disapproving frown and started towards the news van. "Let's go, Toby. I want to get back to the station and have this edited before the five o'clock news."

The cameraman rolled up cords and shoved them into a big bag. "Don't mind her, she's just uptight since she didn't get a good soundbite," he said by way of explanation. "She also exaggerates. New Bethlehem Cemetery was nothing like this. Only three graves were disturbed there, and I really doubt they'll find anything anywhere else."

"Toby!" the reporter shouted. She waited impatiently with a hand on her hip, twirling the microphone in the air while he hurried to catch up.

CHAPTER 11

Now that I'd seen the ruckus at the cemetery, there was one more place I needed to go, but I'd have to pedal fast to get there and still make it to work on time.

The funeral home looked different in the light of day. Not as grim perhaps as last night. There was a flower box filled with marigolds in the window that I hadn't noticed before, and the bushes surrounding the house were neatly trimmed with bright green leaves offsetting the home's dark gray paint. Still, the house repelled me, and I had to fight the urge to turn my bike around and pedal as fast and as far away as I could.

I needed to see Ivan, though. Besides Mortie, he was the only one I could talk to – the only one who knew my secret, knew it even better than Mortie ever could, because Ivan shared that burden, too. I might not get the patience, listening and understanding Mortie offered, but Ivan was a chance to share with an equal, someone who knew just what it was like to come face to face with a ghost.

A hearse was parked in the driveway, its wide back door open. A driver slid out a gurney loaded with an occupied body bag. I leaned my bike up against a nearby walnut tree and waited as he pushed the gurney through the funeral home's side doors. The driver got back in the hearse and pulled out onto the street, more than likely headed back to the cemetery to load up another body.

The left side door to the funeral home stayed open a crack. I walked up the driveway and peeked my head in.

The gurney with its deceased passenger stood at the center of the room. Two empty caskets in the back corners of the room were also propped up on adjustable stands, similar to the gurney. Ivan stood over the body with a clipboard, flipping through papers.

Just like the funeral home, Ivan Osgood looked different in the light of day. He seemed rested; the dark circles were gone from his eyes and his black hair, with thin gray streaks, was neatly combed back. There was no longer a nervous energy about him, though maybe that had something to do with there being no wisps swarming around his house this time. Instead, he appeared engrossed in what he was doing.

"Lou!" he said, his eyes lighting up at the sight of me standing in the doorway.

I was worried that by coming here I might have been overstepping a boundary and intruding. After all, this place wasn't just his home, it was his workspace. Sure, we shared the same curse, but that didn't mean he'd welcome a pop-in visit. My worry turned out to be unwarranted, though, as he pulled me inside the room, eagerly talking to me.

"Have you heard the news? It wasn't just Mrs Renwick. I've been working all morning matching bodies to coffins."

Speaking of bodies, I wearily eyed the bag on the gurney. Mr Michael Freeman. I didn't need a chart to tell me that thanks to my good ol' cursed party trick. Curiously, I wondered if Ivan did. It looked like he did. Perhaps this was yet another difference between us.

Interestingly enough, just like with Mrs Renwick, I knew I wouldn't find Mr Freeman floating around anywhere haunting or stewing over unfinished business. Strange. Just how many of these disturbed graves even belonged to actual ghosts?

I skirted around the gurney and kept to the wall. While the inside of the funeral home reminded me a bit of being in a church, this room felt more cold and sterile, like a laboratory. Ivan stopped flipping through his papers and tilted his head curiously at me.

"Are you uncomfortable with the dead?" he asked, surprised.

"No, of course not. It's just…" I paused, trying to find the right words. "It's not often I see them in this current state, if you know what I mean."

"Ah." He nodded and went back to the body bag, unzipping it to reveal a very dead, and slightly decayed, Mr Freeman. I reminded myself that Mr Freeman wasn't here in this cold room of stainless steel, and that he was at peace, that his life had been filled with family barbecues and working in his shed to make beautiful carved wood sculptures.

I got really angry again. Mr Freeman's body wasn't supposed to be here. His family had said goodbye to him and now they would be forced to relive their worst day. The cemetery where he rested was hallowed ground, ground that had been violated.

Ivan seemed unaware of just what an infringement Mr Freeman's being here meant and looked down at the body with detached curiosity.

"Imagine, Lou, reanimation. It's almost impossible to conceive, and yet here is the evidence of it. If someone is capable of this, then what else might be achieved?"

He should've been angry. Why wasn't he angry? He needed to be as upset about this as I was.

I checked myself. Ivan could see ghosts, but he couldn't talk to them, and apparently, he couldn't see them the way I did – the lives they led, the people they'd been. Maybe if he could, he wouldn't be as apathetic and analytical as he sounded. Not just that though, Ivan was different. He lived here in this place where sad endings played out before him over and over again. That kind of thing had to change a person, maybe force them to become more emotionally distant in order to do their work. I tried to forgive the tone of wonder in his voice.

"Are you saying they're attempting to do something more than just reanimate the dead?" I asked.

He looked at me, taken aback. "Why, isn't it obvious?" He gazed down at Mr Freeman as if considering it. "Eternal life."

"That's impossible."

"A lot of impossible things appear to be happening as of late," he said pointedly. "Speaking of which, have you read more from the book? Did you uncover any clues yet as to what might be happening?"

"I'm working on it," I said, hoping at this moment Mortie was deciphering something we could use. I looked at the clock on the wall. I really had to get to work but I still had one more question.

"A reporter said that what happened last night in Magnolia Grove Cemetery happened in New Bethlehem, too. Did any of those bodies come here?"

He didn't answer me at first, and I wondered if he heard me. He jotted something down on his clipboard, seemingly preoccupied.

"New Bethlehem?" he repeated, and then flipped through the rest of his papers, looking for the answer. "None. At least not yet anyway. Did the reporter say how many?"

"Three, I think. I'm going to check it out after work and see what's going on."

He looked up from his clipboard, alarmed. That seemed to get his attention. "Do you really think that's wise, Lou?"

"Wise?" How else was I going to get answers?

"I mean, surely it's not safe. You were able to get away last night, but what if you're not that lucky next time? Perhaps you should stay out of any cemetery until we know more about what's happening."

Stay out of a cemetery? As if I had a choice in the matter with Mrs Hammond in the mix. I didn't say any of that, though, and nodded because he stood there waiting for me to agree. "Yeah, you're probably right."

CHAPTER 12

"They were digging dead bodies up all over the place and then moving them around, who knows why. I mean, that's some real creepy shit. I saw on the news that..."

I vaguely listened to Diego as we finished breaking down boxes in the backroom. Everyone at work was talking about what happened last night – at least the local five o'clock news version of what happened, which apparently decided on either vandalizing teenage ne'er-do-wells as culprits or Satanists. The real answer definitely leaned closer to the Satanist side of things.

Throughout my entire shift, I'd been consumed with overthinking everything that happened last night and what the reporter said about New Bethlehem Cemetery. What happened in Magnolia Grove Cemetery happened there too. How was that possible? And why? Did that mean there were more than just three of those cloaked dudes wandering around raising dead bodies? Would there be a lot of police at New Bethlehem Cemetery like there was at Magnolia Grove? Would I be able to sneak in there and check it out unnoticed? And how long did I have until Scott connected the dots that super creepy stuff happened around the creepy-ass girl he was dating? I quickly pushed that last thought away as it as it would probably lead to a whole slew of other Scott-related questions and went back to thinking about police surveillance at the cemeteries.

"And then tonight, out of nowhere, she says I'm not paying enough attention to her. How was I supposed to know her blue sweater was new? She said that Drew noticed. What the hell does that mean?"

Diego looked at me expectantly waiting for an answer to his question.

"Huh? What did you say?" I wasn't sure how we made the leap from cemeteries to Amy, but it wouldn't be the first time all roads of conversation with Diego led back to her.

"Come on, Lou, you're the only other woman I know. I would try Marge but last time she told me I'd just grow up to be an old man with a beer belly who'd end up disappointing Amy." He folded up a broken-down box and tossed it on the growing pile in the dumpster. "I'm starting to think Mr. Romano must be a real asshole."

"He is. I met him once when he was standing in line at the meat counter. You should've seen Marge. She's never been that pissed. I'm pretty sure that was the last time he shopped here. Now, what's this about Amy?" I asked, determined to listen this time as I got stuff out of my locker.

"I think she wants to break up with me. At least, I'm afraid she does."

"I'm sure everything is fine. You're probably overthinking it." Like I was.

That clearly wasn't the answer Diego was looking for. He rolled his eyes, probably wishing he'd stuck with Marge. She knew more about relationships than I did anyway. Hell, I didn't even know what was going on with the one man I'd ever dated.

"Good hustle tonight, guys." Cliff sailed into the back room in his usual rush to be done for the night, flipping off the store lights, a cigarette bouncing between his lips as he spoke. "I think we finished in record time."

He opened the back door, and the lighter froze halfway to his lips.

"Holy Mother of God," he breathed. The unlit cigarette fell to the ground.

Diego let out a quiet whistle under his breath. He quickly averted his eyes and muttered a brisk, "'Night, Lou," before running off toward a furious-looking Amy waiting for him near the loading dock in her father's borrowed Buick. That blue sweater was about to be the least of Diego's problems.

At the center of all the ruckus was Vick. She leaned up against her rusted Toyota, wearing a tiny tube top along with a tight mini skirt that showed off one long leg gracefully crossed in front of the other. She stood waiting for me with her hands on her curvy hips and a wicked grin on her lips at Cliff and Diego's reactions. A bike rack had been installed on the trunk of her Toyota with my bike already loaded onto it.

"That is the most beautiful woman I've ever seen in my life," Cliff said reverently. Vick caught a trace of his whispered words. She fluffed up her hair and smiled wider, looking like a wolf about to go in for the kill.

I shouldered my backpack and tried not to fidget with my own appearance. Next to Vick, I felt every bit the short, plain grocery store stock girl I definitely was.

"Vick, this is Cliff, my, uh… boss." Technically, he was just the night shift supervisor but whatever. He puffed up his chest at the inflated title and I bit the inside of my cheek to keep from grinning. "Cliff, this is Victoria."

She tossed her long red hair off her shoulder and held out a hand, her fingernails painted a bright pink to match her lipstick.

Cliff stared at the offered hand as if it were made of solid gold. I nudged him in the side with my elbow. He quickly took her hand, holding it gingerly in his.

"Ma'am," he said in awe. The wicked smile on her face faltered the second his hand touched hers.

"Nice meeting you," she said in a tone that didn't quite mean it. She turned to me, though her eyes, filled with suspicion, lingered on Cliff. "You ready to go, Lou?"

"Sure." I wasn't sure what she was doing here or what she was up to, but maybe I could convince her to scope out New Bethlehem with me.

"I'm really – I mean, it's really… uh nice meeting you… Victoria." Cliff stumbled over his words but managed to say her name with a heavy dose of admiration.

I rolled my eyes and got into the passenger side of the Toyota.

"What is with that guy?" she asked when we pulled out of the parking lot.

"Cliff?" I glimpsed him in the side mirror, still staring longingly after Vick's car. "Nothing. He's harmless."

"No, not that. *What* is he? I can't get a read on him."

Boring, normal, comb-over Cliff? Surely she was mistaken. Cliff was about as mysterious as a box of cereal.

"He's just the supervisor."

"If you say so," she said doubtfully.

I pushed aside this potentially baffling new nugget about Cliff and focused on the unexpected appearance of Vick outside work after my shift.

"Why the lift?" I asked.

"To try to convince you not to do something stupid." She glanced at me sideways with a knowing look. "And to be there with you when you decide to do it anyway." She said it like she plucked my idea to ask her to come with me to the cemetery right out of my head.

I rolled my eyes, irked at her continuing this whole fortune-telling grift even though she had yet to be wrong. "What makes you think I'm about to do anything except go home?"

"Please," she scoffed.

"Fine. Let's say you're right," I said keeping my tone skeptical. "Why do I need you around for that?"

"Cuz, kid, who do you think is gonna get you past the cops?"

The Toyota turned left onto Forest Street and passed the Baptist church. Vick looked at the clock above the car radio. "Now we have about fifteen minutes for you to scope out whatever it is you're looking for before those officers on patrol come back from eating their Whoppers at Burger King. Got it?"

She quickly changed the subject before I could respond. "So, how'd your little date go? Did you swoon all over him?"'

I remembered it all again for the hundredth time and let out a contented sigh. "It was perfect. Minus having to wear a dress on a motorcycle." I narrowed my eyes at her. "Thanks for that by the way."

"Oops." She grinned wickedly. "I bet it drove him wild though."

I wasn't used to talking about boys...or men...whatever, with another woman, especially one like Vick who seemed like she probably knew them inside and out and had come to the conclusion that they weren't worth the effort. I might have been on the fence about her being any sort of fortune-teller, but she was probably an expert in this arena. "I don't know," I admitted, honestly. "Scott is gentle and quiet, and we haven't–"

"Oh 'Scott' is it? For some reason, I thought he'd have a more exciting name than just plain ol' Scott.

"Do yourself a favor, kid. Get your kisses in. Have your fun. And then move on." She pulled into the dirt alley behind New Bethlehem Cemetery and parked under the shadow of a tree. "None of 'em are worth the heartache."

The cemetery was dark and empty, pretty much like every other cemetery in the dead of night, though there were tire marks in the dirt in front of Vick's car where I was willing to bet a patrol car had just pulled out.

"Are you absolutely sure about this? You don't think they're going to come back early or anything?"

"You're kidding, right?" She looked down at me, personally affronted at my hint of doubt. "We have fifteen minutes, but I'm not a freaking stopwatch so try not to push it, okay?"

We both got out of the car and started for the cemetery. It had an open layout with no perimeter fence, leaving plenty of room for future expansion. The alley where Vick parked was on the opposite side of the entrance and we ended up having to walk across a quarter acre of empty land, destined for future plots, just to get to the first row of graves along the back.

"I don't go traipsing around creepy-ass cemeteries for just anyone, you know." Vick tiptoed around the grass, her high heels sinking into bits of ground made soft from a few days' worth of passing rain showers.

"As far as cemeteries go, this one's pretty tame," I told her. "Just be glad it's not the county cemetery out in the middle of nowhere with its spooky pine trees and howling winds." That place even creeped me out and that was something. Her pretty brows shot upward in fright, and I grinned, happy to have the upper hand for a change.

Lightyears different from the county cemetery, New Bethlehem was also different from Mrs Hammond's stomping grounds in Magnolia Grove Cemetery. That graveyard was the permanent residence for some of the town's oldest citizens – even a few of the first settlers were buried there. New Bethlehem, on the other hand, was, well… new. There were entire sections of empty plots just waiting to be filled by the town's currently living residents. As a result, not many ghosts hung out in New Bethlehem, if any.

"What are you looking for, anyway?" Vick jumped back, startled by a battery-operated glowing cross someone had decorated the base of a tombstone with.

"Ghosts." At least that was the short answer.

"Great," she said sarcastically.

In reality, I didn't know exactly what I expected to find. I counted two graves that had been disturbed, but by all accounts, their inhabitants were already back in their coffins, nestled deep underground.

"Ivan talked about a veil," I went on.

"Had a quaint little talk with our other creepy friend, did you?" She shined a flashlight on a tombstone with a face etched on it and gasped before realizing it was just an angel's face next to an engraved poem. I bit the inside of my cheek to keep from laughing.

"How did you find him, anyway?" I asked, kneeling down to read some of the names on the headstones.

"Osgood? Same way I found your creepy self," she said, pointing to her head. "The only other freak in this town I was unaware of is that boss of yours."

"Cliff is… well, he's just Cliff."

She wiggled her fingers at me. "The hands don't lie, kid." She changed the subject. "What do you think of our Ivan Osgood then?" she asked.

"He's very…"

"Withdrawn? Quiet? Awkward? Entirely too pensive?" she finished for me.

"I was thinking lonely."

"Yes," she said softly. "I was thinking that too."

I wove in and around the tombstones and thought about Vick's description of Ivan. Withdrawn… quiet… awkward. She might as well have been talking about me. Were he and I that much the same?

I pulled a few overgrown weeds from the base of a headstone the landscaper missed and thought about the loneliness that clearly plagued Ivan. I had Mortie, but who did he have except for a world filled with echoes of the dead?

"Last night in Magnolia Grove Cemetery I think I saw what looked like a rip in the Veil."

"You mean when…" She held her arms up like a zombie.

How in the hell did she know about that? "Yeah, something like that."

"Jesus," she whispered in fear.

"I don't suppose you thought that might warrant a warning or some kind of heads up," I said annoyed. "Or are you limited to inappropriate fashion suggestions for dates?" What was the point of having an actual psychic around if she didn't tell you the important shit?

"Hey, don't look at me. Creepy dead bodies… that's your turf. I just happened to hear about it on the news." She hurried to catch up to me as I stepped around a third freshly dug grave.

In the few times I visited New Bethlehem, I'd never seen a ghost before. There'd been a few on the streets nearby stuck in repeat, but no one really lurked inside the cemetery – until now. Familiar blue eyes peeked out behind an older tombstone at the edge of the cemetery, far away from where he was supposed to be.

"Tom-Tom?" I said in disbelief.

"Oh. My. God," Vick breathed. "You're seeing one of them right now, aren't you?"

"One that shouldn't be here."

She looked around frantically, not at all near the direction of Tom. "I should never have come with you."

"No one put a gun to your head," I said over my shoulder and walked toward his ghostly apparition.

"Tom?" I called out to him.

He shook his head and sank back behind the tombstone out of sight.

"Something's wrong," I said to myself and went still. The air changed. There it was again, the same sensation as the night before, like a layer of tissue paper brushing up against my skin.

"Shit, shit, shit," Vick whispered, looking around in a panic.

A gust of cold air hit me in the face.

"Get down!" I shouted and yanked Vick to the ground.

Screams erupted over our heads, the air whooshing above us like large birds flapping their wings right beside our ears, except these were definitely *not* birds. There were two of them, flying low, their screeching echoing throughout the cemetery. One more than I'd ever dealt with at a time. Their rotting bodies were covered in vaporous rags, the faces looking down on us nothing but decaying skin clinging to skulls. Their screams were loud enough to pierce my ears and make my eardrums ache.

"Vick!" I shouted to be heard over the screaming.

Her hands were clamped down over her ears making it hard to hear me.

I pulled her hands away. "It's okay, they can't hurt you." That was partially a lie. I didn't really know for sure having never actually tested that theory before.

"I – I thought only you could see ghosts." Her voice trembled as she stared up at them in horror.

"They're not ghosts. They're banshees. Vick!" I shook her to get her attention. "Vick! Do you have a mirror in your purse?"

"Y–yes," she said and with a shaky hand rummaged in her oversized pink purse.

I snatched the pocket-sized powder mirror from her hand and flipped it open. I took a deep, fortifying breath and stood up. Their ragged forms flew closer, brushing by me, taunting me. From a distance, their screeches would've sounded like a howling wind but up close they felt like needles stabbing their way into my ears to reverberate inside my head.

When I didn't cower, they came closer, one of them hovering right in front of me. Underneath her matted bits of hair, she looked like a shrunken head, her decayed skin stretched and leathery. Her sunken eyes were still there, the pupils black and the whites of her eyes long since turned to yellow.

I shoved the mirror at her, her wretched face reflecting back at her in a bath of moonlight. The screech on her rotted lips withered and died out as if it'd been robbed of the breath needed to fuel it. The rags turned to ash and vanished altogether as they drifted to the ground.

The other banshee circled above Vick, darting low to scream in her ears. Vick kept her arms over her head as she cowered on the ground.

"Hey, you!" I shouted to the banshee. Her rotted face turned on me. While the first one had been curious by my unphased demeanor, this banshee seemed extra pissed I'd put an end to her little friend and took off in an angry beeline straight for me.

I shut my eyes at the coming impact and held the mirror out like a shield. Her shriek wilted and died in a blast of warm air that rushed over me.

An eerie silence fell on the cemetery. The thin, invisible tissue-like layer that I was sure was Ivan's Veil, hardened, becoming more like a brick wall, returning the night air back to a gentle breeze brushing against my bare arms. Tom's head peeked out behind a distant tombstone and nodded at me. I gave him a little salute before he disappeared into a shimmer of blue vapor.

Vick slowly unfolded her arms, her eyes darting around anxiously.

"Who knew makeup mirrors could fend off banshees, eh?" I said and tossed her the pocket mirror.

She caught it in a fumbling grip and shoved it back into her purse. "I am *never* going to another cemetery with you *ever* again."

CHAPTER 13

"And here I thought this whole time you just sat around in cemeteries shooting the shit with Casper. What the hell are you even doing? You could be killed! Does Mortie let you do that shit? If there's such things as banshees, what the hell else is out there that you're stupidly running into?"

Vick hadn't stopped berating me since we got back in the car. I'd long since given up trying to get her to chill out and let her drone on, tuning her out for the most part. We'd barely missed the returning shift of patrol officers, which was another thing I got blamed for.

"Seriously, I am never going back. I can't believe I thought it was a good idea to–" We turned onto my street and her ranting came to an abrupt stop.

"Son of a bitch," she seethed under her breath.

"What is it? What's wrong?" I asked but didn't have to wait long for an answer.

A patrol car was parked in my driveway and sitting on the porch steps waiting for me was Scott. He wasn't in uniform – just a sweatshirt, jeans, and baseball cap. He raised his head as the beam from the headlights poured over him.

"I'm glad you had fun on your little date, but let me give you a piece of advice," she said with a vehemence I didn't expect. "All men are shit. Just you remember that."

Vick got out of the car, slamming the door behind her. She leaned up against the car like she'd done at the Piggly Wiggly except there wasn't any playfulness in her eyes this time, only open hostility.

"Scott, um, hi," I said shyly. Hours ago, I'd been in his arms, our lips locked in a passionate kiss and now... now I could barely lift my eyes to meet his. When I finally dared to, they were met with the same disarming intensity that had a tendency to warm every inch of me.

"I was wondering if maybe we could talk," he said.

My heart sank at his words, like the Titanic hitting an iceberg called Reality. Even I, as naive and new to the dating scene as I was, knew that nothing good could come from those words. I nodded solemnly.

"Ahem." Vick cleared her throat. "I don't believe we've met."

She launched off the side of the car and sashayed her way between us in a lengthy slow stride like a cat about to pounce. He looked at her as if noticing her for the first time and I waited with a clench in my stomach for the same bug-eyed reaction the guys had shown at the store. It didn't happen. When he looked at her, there was only unease laced with suspicion.

"I'm Victoria," she said, holding out a hand.

It was a trap, but only she and I knew the power in that waiting touch. He looked down at the offered hand with mounting suspicion but after a second's hesitation took it anyway. After all, handshakes were harmless, right?

"Scott Campbell," he said.

Her lips pursed as she shook his hand and then she was nodding along as if agreeing with whatever it was she saw in him. He was the first to pull his hand away.

"Nice to meet you, *Officer* Campbell," she said with a sarcastic lilt in that single word.

He went still. His jaw clenched tight and where there was a hint of suspicion in his eyes before, now they were filled with it, reassessing her in a whole new light.

A tense, heavy silence fell over my driveway as the two stared each other down, neither one showing signs of backing off. I didn't know what the hell was going on, but I felt like I'd just walked in on a conversation I knew nothing about. What was with Vick? And how could one little word cause such a drastic shift in Scott?

"Do you mind giving us a minute?" I asked Vick and tossed her the keys to the house.

"Sure thing." She snatched them out of the air. "See ya around, *officer*." She swished her hips as she passed by him and went up the front porch steps.

His eyes followed her, scanning her with a cold analytical cop's glare. I thought about what it would be like to be on the receiving end of that glare and fought the inner urge to cower.

"You, uh, wanted to talk?" I said when the door shut behind her.

The cop glare flickered off, disappearing altogether the second he turned his attention back to me. He dipped his head and focused on prodding the loose gravel in the driveway with the toe of his running shoe. Again, the sudden change in him was jarring. It was a stark contrast between hardened cop and, well, I wasn't sure exactly what he was now, except I guessed maybe nervous. But why anyone would be nervous around me, I had no idea.

"I wanted to apologize," he said. "I'm afraid I came on a little too strong this afternoon. It wasn't really… uh… me. I mean, I'm not actually like that. I–"

So, I hadn't misread that moment in the cemetery after all. I probably should've asked him why the change but there was something else I wanted to know, something my insecure self was desperate to hear the answer to. I bit my lip and dared to ask about the elephant in the driveway.

"Does that mean you wish you hadn't kissed me like that then?"

Flustered, he lifted his hat and ran a hand through his hair. "No. I mean yes, I just–"

I leaned in and kissed him, repeating the question in a different way. I'd never done something so bold. It startled even me, but I couldn't *not* do it, because more than wanting to kiss him – which I wanted to do so very badly – I had to know; he might not have been himself before, for whatever reason, but was that kiss we shared real?

Instead of backing away, he answered my unspoken question by deepening the kiss. His hand came up to cup the back of my head, returning the kiss to that same mind-blowing magnitude as before.

"I guess I hadn't imagined that after all," he breathed against my lips; his words mirroring my own thoughts.

Those green eyes gazed down at me and it felt like I was basking in a beam of sunlight. I tried to imagine that cop glare zeroed in on me like it had on Vick, but it was impossible.

He moved us toward the cement steps and together we sat down, side-by-side. His hand shyly found mine. Long fingers intertwined with my small ones and suddenly it felt like we were picking up right back where we left off down by the riverside, with our feet hanging off the docks.

His thumb swept back and forth against the base of my palm. "For a minute there, I really thought I might have ruined things," he said, sounding relieved.

I bravely rested my head against his shoulder and breathed deep the scent of his sweatshirt. "I was worried I might've too."

He quirked his head to the side to look down at me. "Why would you have ruined anything?"

Shit.

Oh, only because I thought you saw my creepy ass in the cemetery in the middle of the night at the same time dead bodies were coming back to life.

"It's just that, um…" I reached for half the truth. "Well, I'm all weird and awkward and creepy." The half-truth was more like ninety-percent true. I was afraid that now I'd put it into words, he might realize that was exactly right and want nothing to do with me.

Instead, he laughed, his shoulder moving up and down against my ear. "You're none of those things."

He seemed so sure with how he said it, that part of me wanted to believe it might actually be true.

He lifted my chin with his fingers and gave me another kiss. And there it was again – that feeling of the sun shining down on me.

It started simple and sweet, like that very first kiss when he dropped me off after our date. Except now that I'd had deeper, more passionate kisses from him, I found myself longing for another one. I pressed my lower lip under his, letting him feel the fullness of it. The fingers on my waist dug deeper and that feeling of sunshine turned more to cloud nine and I forgot everything – ghosts, banshees, cults raising the dead… everything except for his lips against mine.

With my head up there in the clouds, I didn't realize the exact moment our kiss ended until his slow, steadying breath came soft on my lips.

"I should probably go," he said, glancing at the kitchen window as the lacy curtains fell back into place. "I have a feeling if I stay here any longer, your friend in there is going to come out here and rip me to shreds."

"Don't mind Vick. Her bark is worse than her bite."

He stared suspiciously at the window. "Somehow I doubt that."

He walked to the patrol car and opened the door.

"And just for the record, Louise," he said, turning back to me. "You're sweet, kind, knockout gorgeous, and when you kiss me like that, I almost forget who I am."

I watched him drive off, smiling stupidly to myself as I walked up the front steps.

I stepped inside and my smile evaporated.

The kitchen was transformed. Every flat surface, every inch of counter space was filled with lit candles and sitting at my dining room table with her arms out and palms facing upward sat Vick. The only thing missing was a crystal ball.

"Ready for some answers, kid?"

CHAPTER 14

"Nope, nope, nope."

I went around the room blowing out candles. For the first time since meeting Vick, I really started to doubt the extent of her powers. If she was as gifted as she claimed to be then she would've known there was no way in hell this was going to fly with me. At all.

"I'm not your mother, Lou, and this isn't like that," she said.

I didn't listen and snuffed out the last candle. I chose to pretend she wasn't set up like a fortune teller in my kitchen and opened the refrigerator to scour over what little leftovers I had.

"Something to eat?" I asked over my shoulder.

She didn't respond and went around the room lighting the candles again.

"Ever since you touched that book, I can't see straight when it comes to you. It was the same with Ivan, except this time I'm hellbent on getting answers. And I'm sorry but that means the candles are a must." She flipped off the kitchen lights, leaving only the candles and the dim bulb above the stove for light.

I found a container of partially eaten rocky road ice cream in the freezer and handed Vick a new pint of mint chocolate chip that she ignored.

"Tonight, I watched two ghosts run rampant in a cemetery," she said. "I actually *saw* them. What if this rip in the Veil gets worse? What if someone gets hurt? We need answers."

There was genuine worry in her eyes this time instead of her usual overconfident skepticism. And, dammit, she had a point. What if someone did get hurt? What if my little parlor trick with the pocket mirror back in New Bethlehem Cemetery hadn't worked and Vick got hurt tonight?

"They were banshees, not ghosts," I corrected her.

She rolled her eyes and gestured to the chair next to her. I sank into it with a huff. She held out an upturned hand.

"You're joking, right?" I said, looking doubtful at her offered hand.

"Listen, the future is a crazy huge thing to take a gander at. I don't need physical contact with someone to see it but when I touch them, I can narrow all that down to a focused sliver. And I got news for you: it's going to take more than a sliver to get the answers you're looking for."

I relented and took her hand.

It was surreal to be on this side of the table. A long time ago, at a different table, in a different part of the country, it had been me sitting where she was, except with a fake crystal ball in front of me and a curtain of beads covering the doorway behind me, waiting for my mother to bring in the next easy mark.

It'd been easy back then for my mother to turn my cursed gifts into a profit-making venture. It didn't matter that her only child – her little girl – could see and speak with the dead. I imagined for any normal parent it would've been horrifying just witnessing what their offspring had to endure day in and day out. Not for my mother. She was only consumed with how much cash her circus freak kid could bring in. It didn't matter that it drained me emotionally to deal with the sorrow my child-like mind didn't know how to handle, only that I gave a good show when customers brought in cemetery photos or were unknowingly trailing ghosts behind them when they came for readings.

Oddly enough, and rather curiously, I don't think she ever cared, or fully believed, that I could actually see and speak to ghosts. Though I suppose to grifters like her, everyone is either a liar or a mark, and the truth kind of becomes irrelevant.

Vick's voice took on a faraway breathy tone. "Ask and I shall answer."

Now it was my turn to roll my eyes. "Fine," I said, playing along. "What did you see when you shook hands with Scott?"

She groaned and turned her hand back over, drumming her pink fingernails impatiently on the tabletop. "Not those kinds of questions, Lou."

"Why not? You said to ask."

"I believe I answered that one already. I told you *all* men were shit, didn't I?" She took a spoon and dug into the mint chocolate chip ice cream.

"Scott isn't." I raised my chin defiantly.

"You sure about that?" she said around a big bite of ice cream. "'Cuz I got news for you, kid. Ain't no way in hell that guy is a cop. Your handsome little boyfriend is a liar who likes to play dress up. Now, does that change your mind?"

Scott wasn't a cop? I tried to think about all the times I'd seen him in uniform, in his patrol car.

"I told you, Lou, *all* men are shit."

It didn't make any sense. He had the uniform, the cruiser, not to mention a standard-issue Glock on his hip to prove it. Heck, even the police chief ordered him around in the cemetery. But then again, there was something off about him and I wasn't sure if it was his changeable demeanor or something else.

Vick watched me over the rim of the ice cream pint as every thought passed over my face, daring me to contradict her.

I opened my mouth to question her, but she interrupted me. "I'm not gonna say anything else about it. Some things you have to learn the hard way."

"And you're the one who gets to decide that?"

She shrugged away my question, dismissing me, and pushed aside the ice cream. She spread out her arms again, palms facing up. "Now ask me something good this time."

"Fine." I took her hand again, intending full well to circle back to her claims about Scott after this little endeavor and press her further. I started with an easy one. "The bodies taken from their graves in New Bethlehem Cemetery, were they disturbed by the same people I saw in Magnolia Grove?"

"Now that's a start." Her eyes fluttered closed, and her head tilted to the side as she peered inwardly in search of the answer. The kitchen was silent as she sat there, the crease between her brows getting deeper with each passing second.

"I… I don't know… it's hazy," her voice took on a far-off tone. "But you missed something tonight. In New Bethlehem Cemetery. You didn't see it, and you should've."

"What?"

"Give me a second, I'm trying to find out." The crease between her brows deepened into an angry scowl. Her eyes flashed open. She slammed her fist onto the table making me jump. "Goddammit! This is worse than I thought. I can hardly see a damn thing."

She rolled her shoulders and cracked her knuckles like she was about to go into a fight and then shoved her open hand back at me.

"Ask me something else."

"The men in the cemetery last night, the creepy cloaked guys, who are they?"

Her lashes fluttered against her cheeks. The tension between her brows softened as she found the answer she was looking for.

"They call themselves the Brethren of the Eternal Blood." She opened her eyes and scoffed. Vick seemed happier to finally have an answer, one that was presumably easier to find. "Nothing but a bunch of morons really, searching for eternal life or some such bullshit." Eternal life. Ivan mentioned the same concept at the funeral home. I mean, it didn't seem like that big of a leap to think that might be what they were after. There could only be a handful of reasons to try to raise the dead. Still, it was odd to me. Mostly because I, of all people, knew there was no such thing as eternal life. There was death and the finality of it was pretty damn certain.

"Ask me another one."

"Alright," I relented. "They may be ridiculous, but they were packing some serious power. Where did they get it?"

She squeezed her eyes shut. The crease in her brow got deeper with every passing moment of silence.

"Hold on. I can almost see it." She bit her lip in concentration.

I waited patiently as the seconds ticked by on the orange, kitty clock hanging on the wall by the oven and still, she said nothing.

"You know, Vick, this is turning more and more into my mother's kitchen table."

She let out a faint gasp and slumped forward, her hand going slack around mine.

"Vick?" Was this part of the shtick? It didn't seem like it. I nudged her arm. She didn't move. "Vick!" I jumped up and ran to the other side of the table.

She sprung up faster than I could blink. Her hand gripped my throat and threw me down on the tabletop. Black swirling fog filled her eyes.

"I see you. Little, insignificant, Lou." Her voice wasn't entirely her own, paired with another – a raspy, deep voice I'd heard before. Twice now, in fact. First, inside that in-between world and then paired with another man's voice coming out of the depths of a hooded cloak. Her face lowered an inch above me. "Do you think you'll be able to hide from me much longer? Soon I'll be free, and you'll be *mine*."

I scratched wildly at the fingers clamped around my neck, but they didn't budge. Vick's face twisted into an evil grin as I struggled, hatred contorting her beautiful features. She had the power to crush my throat. Why didn't she?

"Mine," she whispered in my ear, her cheek nestling against my face. "Mine." Her thumb rubbed with pressure against my throat.

Something shot through me, cold and angry, sending a sharp pulse from my heart straight to my fingertips. I grabbed Vick by the shoulders and let that building energy go.

Blinding blue light exploded in the kitchen. There was a scream. A loud thud. Anything beyond that didn't register with me. There was only the flash in my eyes and the breath that got knocked out of me.

The front door burst open. I tried to think, tried to feel. The blue light faded away, retreating into the dim light above the kitchen sink. Small realizations came back to me one after the other. Vick was no longer on top of me but crumpled on the floor up against the wall, Mortie kneeling beside her. Blood dripped from Vick's nose and the corner of her mouth. Mortie's head snapped up as I rolled off the tabletop, his eyes flashing white as they looked me up and down.

I was always used to seeing love and kindness in his face when he looked toward me. Now there was only fear, and it hurt to see. Vick groaned and his attention reverted to her.

"Easy there, Firecracker," Mortie said as she trembled in his arms. Her eyes were back to their normal blue color but when they fell on me, they were still filled with terror.

"I'm sorry, Vick," I said in a quiet voice, not sure what happened, only that it felt like my fault. She clung to Mortie for dear life as he held a tissue up to her nostrils to stop the bleeding.

Vick raised a shaking finger at me. "She's – she's…"

Mortie covered her hand with both of his. "I know, I know. It's okay," he murmured.

I wasn't sure what she was about to say but I felt horrible. I took a step toward her, and she flinched against Mortie.

"Give her a moment, Lewis," Mortie said sternly, holding a hand up to block me.

"I – I didn't mean to."

Vick continued to cling to Mortie and after a moment she glanced down at their linked hands and another horror fell into place for her.

"I can't see." She touched his hands, his face. "I can't see!"

It wasn't normal sight she was talking about.

"You're okay, Firecracker," Mortie murmured in a soothing voice. "It'll come back. Give it some time."

She cried then, sobbing into his chest. They stood as one, holding onto each other as they walked to the front door, her terrified blue eyes following me all the way.

"I'll be right back," Mortie said and then they were gone, the front door falling shut behind them.

I stood alone in my kitchen. What in the holy hell just happened? It was me that had been attacked, wasn't it? My neck still felt sore from her grip. Then why did I feel guilty? I don't know how long I stood in the kitchen waiting, thinking, trying to wrap my mind around what happened only to come up with nothing.

The front door opened and Mortie reappeared. Gone was the fear in his eyes. Here was the old Mortie I knew, holding his arms out waiting for me. I ran into them and cried, not exactly sure why.

"It's okay. She's okay. I called a cab and she's on her way home."

"I – I don't know what happened," I said through a snotty round of sniffles.

He stroked my hair. "I'm not sure either but it lit your house up like a lightning bolt bright enough to shine through my living room window. Want to try telling me what happened?"

"One minute Vick was sitting here, reading my future and then…" I gulped down the feeling of her hands on my throat. "And then it wasn't her. It was someone else. It was that…that thing. I think it's trapped inside the Veil."

Mortie listened intently, nodding along at words that sounded impossible even to my ears.

"I thought it was going to kill me and then I… I…" I stared down at my hands. Vick's face flashed in my mind, terror in her eyes as she pointed at me. 'She's… she's…' What? What was I that could be capable of such horror?

My hands trembled. Panic rose up my neck, closing around my windpipe. "Oh God. What am I?"

Mortie's hands came around mine, clasping them in a steady grip. "You're Lou," he answered simply.

"But I –"

He shook his head, adamant. "Nothing else matters. Not really. No matter how much power is brimming inside there," he pointed to my chest. "You have control over who you are and you'll aways be Lou. I promise."

I ran the back of my hand over my running nose and quieted, letting myself bask in his calm presence. I wasn't sure if I believed him, but I didn't want to think about it anymore.

He patted my wet cheek. "Maybe it's wise if you girls decide to pass on any fortune telling sessions from now on, eh? You're both just a little too powerful for that to be a good idea. Besides, there's too much bad history for you to be doing such things as that anyway, hmm? It's sure to bring too many bad memories to the surface."

He deposited me on the couch and began rooting around the kitchen, filling a small pan with milk and starting it to heat on the stove. He poured us both a mug full of steamed milk and sweetened it with a touch of caramel syrup.

"Why don't you catch me up," he said, sitting on the coffee table in front of me.

Everything that had happened in the last 24 hours poured out of me. Mortie listened as I rambled on. His eyes never flashed white, though his eyebrows shot upward when I got to the part with Mrs Renwick rising out of her coffin, and then he grew thoughtful as I described the wisps around the funeral home.

"I can't say I know Ivan Osgood," he said. "I've seen the house before, but I've never been inside. When it came time to bury Peter, I went with a funeral home in Indianapolis since that's where his parents were buried."

Mortie hardly ever spoke of Peter. Even in that one sentence, his voice choked up a little at the use of his name. As a result, I didn't know all that much about him. I knew he died of lung cancer more than a decade ago and that Mortie kept a picture of him in a pocket watch tucked inside his sweater vest pocket.

I knew they shared a good life from the pieces I put together and the few stories he told me, confirmed by the fact I'd never run across his apparition.

"Strange to think that all this time that book was in his basement. It makes me wonder what kind of man Mr Osgood is to have been able to abide its presence as long as he did."

"Well, I wish he found someone else to give it to. I have enough problems as it is," I said, rinsing out our empty mugs in the sink.

"Ah, but then you wouldn't know what's in it and why it's probably what those boys in that cult your friend was talking about are looking for." He sat back grinning.

"You've found out something about it then?" I spun around, surprised.

"More than that." He leaned forward. "I can read it."

The book sat open on my kitchen table looking no different than it had before. Still dark, still creepy. The only difference was in Mortie. He was excited, more than when he came back from a cemetery with a new charcoal tracing of a tombstone. After retrieving the book from his house, he now placed a hand on its cover. I wasn't sure if it was a trick of the overhead light, but I could've sworn it trembled in response to his touch.

"You can read what's in that?" There were words, no doubt. I'd seen them. But they weren't written in any language I'd ever seen.

"Perhaps 'read' was a bit of an exaggeration. It's more like an understanding," he said, gingerly opening the cover.

"What's in it then?"

"Spells."

"Spells," I repeated, unsure if I'd heard him right. "As in magic spells?"

Call me crazy but magic seemed a rather ridiculous notion. I mean, I know it doesn't sound like much of a reach to think that there would be magic in the world. After all, *I* existed. Mortie existed. And Vick was out there doing her thing too. But I more or less thought all those quirks about us were sort of mutations, mutations with rules and boundaries that tethered us to the real world. Magic sounded limitless, like making something out of nothing.

"Actually, it's only the one spell, so far." His fingers flipped through the pages with a sense of familiarity until he landed on the one he wanted. "The other pages have spells too, I'm sure of it. The book just hasn't…" his voice trailed off as he searched for the right word. "Shown them to me yet. If I didn't know better, I'd say the book is purposely hiding the rest from me, at least for the moment."

That was a disturbing notion. But then again, this thing definitely had a mind of its own.

"What does this one spell do then?"

He touched the page, and the silver letters lit up everywhere his fingers met the paper. His eyes, looking straight ahead instead of down at the book, turned white in response.

"Raises the dead."

Well, holy shit. I sank into the kitchen chair, staring at the open page with its mysterious letters practically purring against Mortie's fingers. "That can't be a coincidence."

"Agreed," he said.

Mortie hesitantly lifted his hand off the page. "There's something else you need to know about it, Lou."

He closed the book and nudged it away, putting a bit of distance between him and it.

"When I look into it," he said, staring at his open palm. "It looks back into me."

I didn't like the sound of that. "How do you know?"

"What I do, my gift, it operates kind of like a window. When I use it, I can glimpse the emotion that's on the other side of that window. But when I use my gift on the book, it's almost like... there's something looking back at me."

I sucked in a breath. "What are you saying?"

"I don't know," he said, pushing up his glasses with his index finger as he considered the book in the middle of the table. "I'm not sure. I've never experienced anything like it."

I sagged against the back of the kitchen chair. I was used to all sorts of crazy chaotic things happening, but most of the time they were situations I was pretty sure I could manage. But this? Tonight with Vick, cults, a magic book with a mind of its own... it all reeked of creatures I had the least experience with.

The living.

"I think I'm in over my head this time, Mortie."

"You're not," his voice softened. He reached across the table to cover my hand with his and gave it a squeeze. "Whatever is going on, you can do this. You were meant to do this."

"If that's true then what do I do from here?"

"I'm not sure, Lewis, but if our fiery new friend said you missed something tonight at the Baptist cemetery, I'd say that might be the place to start."

CHAPTER 15

I woke up the next morning with a sore neck, evidence that Vick choking me had been very much real and not just in the nightmares I kept waking up from all night. Over and over again, I dreamed about her fingers wrapping around my throat and the black swirling in her eyes. The nightmares ended with a burst of blue energy that woke me up with a start every time.

Mortie went home last night, taking the book with him, leaving me with a promise that he'd do more research and let me know if any other spells decided to show themselves.

With the Magnolia Grove Cemetery likely still full of people working to get it fixed up again, visiting with Mrs H was off my schedule, unless she had other plans. I felt in a rut, a useless rut with no clear course of action ahead for me to take. All I could do today was work my shift at the Piggly Wiggly and swing by New Bethlehem Cemetery afterwards, hoping the cops weren't there and I could find out what it was Vick said I missed.

I grimaced when I saw myself in the bathroom mirror above the sink. The bruises on my neck were too dark to hide with makeup and it was still too warm outside for a turtleneck. I pulled my hair up into a ponytail and tied a light scarf around my neck, hiding the marks. It was a retro look, but it worked. Mrs H would probably approve. At least Diego and Cliff wouldn't see the bruises and pepper me with a bunch of questions.

"Lou to the back office," Cliff's voice crackled over the loudspeaker. "Lou to the back office."

His cheeks were blushing crimson when I walked into the office. Right smack dab in the middle of the bald spot on his forehead was the imprint of a kiss in vibrant red lipstick.

"What's up?" I asked, trying not to stare at it.

"A message for you." He handed me a sticky note.

Sorry about last night. It was my fault. Seriously, Lou, it was. Stop worrying about it, okay?

An address was scrawled underneath.

Keep this for when the shit really hits the fan.
-V

"Everything okay?" Cliff asked. He never really ventured into anyone's personal affairs, and he shifted uncomfortably in his swivel chair at just asking that much.

"Yeah, it's fine." I crumpled up the note, shoving it into my pocket. "She didn't want to give me this herself?"

"She said she had something she couldn't be late for."

I quickly glanced at the stain on his forehead and remembered what Vick said about him – that he was different. Like us. Could that actually be true? I tried to imagine him predicting the future like Vick or being an empath like Mortie. None of that fit in regard to Cliff. He was just… Cliff – boring and normal like I wished I could be. Vick hadn't been wrong yet, but this? This seemed like a bit of a stretch.

Cliff smoothed the hair over his head, smearing the lipstick in the process. "Victoria is… well, she's something else, isn't she?"

"That's putting it mildly," I said, getting up to go.

"Hey, Lou?"

I expected him to ask for a favor, maybe to close up for him again or to have me put in a good word for him with Vick. Instead, he tried to take on a serious tone that came off more as awkward and uncomfortable. Cliff was never one for serious conversations.

"You're a good kid," he said, even though he was barely seven years older than me. "If you're in trouble or anything... if you need help or whatever, just let me know, okay? I'm here if you need it."

I stared at him, taken off guard.

"Uh, sure. Thanks, Cliff."

"Hey, no problem. You'd be there for me. Hell, you always are." A softer blush spread on his cheeks as he gave me a genuine smile. We shared a mutual nod, and I awkwardly scooted off back to work to finish closing up.

The second Cliff locked the back door, I was on my bike tearing off down the road toward New Bethlehem. My mental itch had turned into a full-blown rash. Also, I was miffed. Vick should've given me the note herself, maybe then I'd know just what the hell I was riding into. What good was having a psychic around if she couldn't tell me what was waiting for me at New Bethlehem Cemetery?

I immediately chastised myself. Vick's gift wasn't meant to be used willy-nilly for my gain. I, of all people, knew better than that. Besides, Vick had a life beyond randomly showing up to tell me snippets of the future. The next time our paths crossed I'd make it a point to learn more about my fellow "freak" as she put it.

It was a humid night with the fog hanging low to the ground. The mist made the few hairs that came loose from my ponytail curl at my neck.

It turned out I didn't need Vick after all. There were no cops around, no patrol cars waiting. Nothing. I propped my bike up against a nearby streetlight and walked right through the front gate.

There was no Tom-Tom. No banshees. Someone had planted flowers on the recently disturbed graves but other than that there was no one, just the fog clinging to the cemetery grass, creating a muted sort of quiet. I sat on the marble bench at the center of the cemetery and looked around, wondering for the umpteenth time what I might have missed only to come up short yet again.

Outside the cemetery, the streetlight on the corner flickered and went dark. I would've dismissed it as a blown out light bulb or an electrical short in the wiring if it weren't for the second streetlight flickering and going dark in the same way. And the next one on top of that. The hairs on my arms stood on end. Whatever instinct I had when it came to ghosts tickled to life and I knew I wasn't alone anymore. I hesitantly walked toward the front entrance where the streetlight outages were getting closer and closer.

The fog along the sidewalk turned to a dense blanket hugging the ground. I dipped my hand in it expecting to pull away with beads of moisture on my fingertips. Instead, the swirling cloud was weirdly dry and cold, sending a chill up my arm.

Empty footfalls formed in the fog, moving one step and then another, coming straight for me. Out of that dense fog, the shape of a hand emerged, reaching out to the last streetlight that was still on – the one that I propped my bike up against. Fog fingers wrapped around the light pole and then it, too, flickered and died out, dousing the entire cemetery in darkness.

A thin ribbon of light danced vertically in the air, the same kind of ribbon I'd seen behind Mrs Renwick's aura at Magnolia Grove Cemetery. A face emerged from the shadows around the darkened streetlight. A ghost, and by the looks of her, not one from Mrs Hammond's era. She wore a simple wool skirt that went down to her knees and a cardigan buttoned at the top. Her shoulder-length hair was parted down the middle and pinned halfway up at the sides, sort of like how I'd seen my grandmother's hair in pictures from the 70s. Eyes behind big circle-rimmed glasses stared back at me. Her aura was the same unique daylight light bulb temperature glow as Mrs Renwick's.

"Lou, you came back," she said sweetly.

I knew pretty much every ghost in Magnolia Grove. Most made it their mission to seek me out to tell me their life story – as much as they remembered of it anyway. All except this one. I'd never come across her before. She wasn't a malevolent ghost, that much was clear. In fact, the peaceful, happy way she looked at me was like she was looking at a friend she hadn't seen in a long while. I'm not sure why, but that freaked me out more than banshees.

"I – I was told I missed something," I ventured, repeating Vick's words from my kitchen table.

"Yes. I was afraid you wouldn't come back and–" She stopped suddenly, her eyes scanning the cemetery around us. "Something's wrong. There's someone else here."

I looked around. A car rolled to a stop at the intersection at the corner but then kept on, eventually disappearing down the highway.

"They're looking for you," she whispered, her eyes darting around in a panic.

Again, I didn't see anyone except her. Could it be she was stuck in repeat like so many other ghosts I encountered?

"They found you," she gasped and vanished, leaving me alone at the front gate to wonder what the hell just happened.

"Are you looking for something?" A voice came from over my shoulder.

I spun around with a start and then relaxed. It was someone I recognized. It was the cameraman from the cemetery, I think his name was Toby, and from the looks of it he was still working. He had a camera bag with the station logo on it and a work badge hanging from a lanyard around his neck.

His eyes followed mine to the camera bag hanging off his shoulder. "I'm just shooting some B-roll for tomorrow's newscast. Do you need any help? You look like you're looking for something."

"No, I – uh…" What exactly would a normal person be doing in a cemetery after dark anyway? "I was here visiting my grandmother's grave yesterday and I think I lost an earring."

God, I was a terrible liar. It sounded pathetic even to my ears and speaking of ears, if he looked close enough at mine, he'd see they weren't even pierced.

But apparently it was convincing enough, because he seemed to believe me. "Oh geez, that sucks. Let me help you," he offered, setting down his camera bag.

"No, it's okay. I've been out here awhile," I lied again. "I'm just going to give up for the night."

"What's it look like? I'll keep an eye out."

Since my last lie wasn't nearly as convincing as the first, I didn't bother trying to come up with another. "Don't worry about it." I gave him my best smile and waved goodnight.

I felt his eyes on me as I started to walk away.

"Wait a second," he called after me. "Is this it?"

I shouldn't have turned around. I should've made a run for it. But I didn't. Maybe it was the urge to defend my lie and make it more believable. Maybe it was subconscious pressure to keep up social norms, the notion that I should at least be polite. Either way, it was a mistake.

He held out the black jeweled necklace in his hand, the same one I'd seen raise Mrs Renwick from the dead. He caught the flicker of recognition in my eyes and a slow smile spread across his face.

"You know, when I saw you yesterday, I thought you might be the one that I was looking for but then your boyfriend came up and planted one on you and I was sure I'd been mistaken. Seems I was right. And now here you are."

I spun around to bolt but came face to face with a gun and an up-close look at a strikingly familiar bird skull tattoo. I remembered the paramedic from the cemetery, the one who stared down the reporter with skin-crawling intensity. Except now it was me he was staring down. In close proximity, I could see that the tattoo wasn't just a skull but an entire dead bird that was reborn in another tattoo near his clavicle. He cracked the muscles in his massive neck and yet another tattoo appeared, this one of the bird taking off in flight up the side of his neck.

"You were there the other night in Magnolia Grove Cemetery," Toby said, knowingly. "*You're* the key we've been looking for."

I went for one last desperate lie. "I – I don't know what you're talking about."

It didn't work.

"You've seen what we're capable of, the power bestowed upon us. All that power is nothing," he said, looking at me with an odd sort of reverence in his eyes, "compared to you."

I didn't like the way either of them looked at me. I mean, beyond the my-life's-in-imminent-danger aspect to the situation that was already there. No, the glimmer in Toby's eyes was like a kid who found a brand-new toy he couldn't wait to play with.

"You're wrong. Please, just let me go home," I pleaded but he ignored me.

"With you, we can finish the work we've started."

And then he did something else absurd. He bowed, kneeling right there on the ground in front of me. "Forgive me for not seeing your true power earlier."

His gun-wielding friend didn't seem as inclined to worship me and kept his weapon trained right at my face.

My stomach turned with the tale-tell signs of Mrs Hammond's summons, giving me a glimmer of hope that I might still have a way out of this.

Toby got up off the ground and draped the necklace over my head and around my neck. "Can you feel it calling out to you? Begging for you to use it?"

The weight of the jewel against my chest smothered Mrs Hammond's pull, anchoring me right where I stood, snuffing out any hope I had for escape.

Three more men stepped out of the shadows wearing the same ragged cloaks I'd seen before. This time, up close, I could make out faces and eyes within the depths of their hoods watching me. All five men shepherded me deeper into the cemetery and farther away from the front entrance.

"The p-police will be here any minute." I tried to sound confident and failed.

"Well, that would be unfortunate." Toby smiled. "Luckily, many of us are already stationed within their ranks. Law enforcement, emergency crews, paramedics like Freddy here," he nodded toward the bird tattoo guy, "are the most eager to join with us. They've seen up close the end of life and yearn for something more."

I latched onto the first words he'd said. Law enforcement. Maybe this was what Vick meant about Scott not being a cop. Could he be with the Brethren? I tried to imagine him among them, playing at being a necromancer in some silly little ritual, but I couldn't. It didn't make sense. Besides, Toby said Scott kissing me in the cemetery had made him discount me as anyone of importance. To him, it seemed Scott was just a guy kissing me and not anyone significant, so him being one of them couldn't be right.

Toby stepped close to me, too close. I inched back, as much as I could, now that all five of them surrounded me. He reached out to hold the black jewel dangling against my chest and I flinched, repulsed, as the back of his fingers grazed my skin.

"But death is not the end we are led to believe," he said, stroking its surface. "Our time in this world is not limited. We've just not yet been bestowed the gift that reaches beyond the realm of the dead to restore lost life." He looked at me, and that feeling of being a shiny new toy returned. "Until now."

What he said was a lie – a lie I had no doubt he believed by the earnest, hopeful look in his eyes, but it was a lie all the same.

"No one can live forever," I said. It was the closest I'd come to admitting I knew anything about what he was saying.

"You don't believe that." He lowered his face close to mine. "You *can't* believe that, not after the miracles you saw that night."

"What you did is a lie," I snapped back at him. The same anger I felt that night quickly bubbled to the surface. "A perversion."

"That's because we are limited to the power of the jewel. But now that we have you, we can finally finish what we've started. You must call upon the necklace and summon its powers."

"I wouldn't even know where to start. Whoever – whatever – you think I am, I promise I'm not that person." It was the damn truth, and it must've sounded pretty convincing, even to Toby, because a moment of hesitation flashed in his eyes.

He shook it off, still adamant. "No more lies. Call upon it," he ordered.

"I told you, I don't even know what that thing is, much less how to use it." I lifted the necklace up over my head and held it back out to him. My fingers brushed up against the jewel and it was like a spark, an ignition being switched on. Brilliant blue energy lit the jewel, way brighter than when they used it on Mrs Renwick.

Shit.

Toby's eyes lit up like a kid on Christmas morning.

I threw the necklace as hard as I could and made a run for it.

Pain exploded in my head and my feet were no longer planted on the ground. The earth met my cheek in a jarring collision as I came face to face with Freddy's black boots.

A ringing in my ears muffled all other sounds as I tried, and kept failing, to focus my vision on the blades of grass in front of me. Time slowed down into painful, throbbing pulses instead of seconds as my disoriented, jolted mind tried to process the shock of what happened. I'd never before been the victim of such raw violence. With shaking fingers, I touched my cheek where the pistol had slammed against it. The skin was broken along my cheekbone and already starting to swell. I pulled my fingers away to find bits of blood coating them.

"What have you done?!" Toby cried out somewhere above me. There was a hard slap against skin followed by a grunt from Freddy who muttered an apology.

Hard plastic cinched around my wrist and suddenly I was being dragged across the ground. Frantically, I kicked my heels into the dirt and grass, at the same time twisting and turning to try to break free. The dragging stopped and I blinked away flickering bouts of blurred vision only to find myself zip-tied by the wrist to the thick stem of a cement vase securely concreted to the base of a tombstone.

Retrieve the jewel!" Toby ordered with a shout.

A misty drizzle began to fall in the cemetery.

Toby pulled a cloak out of his camera bag. "Forgive Freddy, Blessed One," Toby said, draping it around my shoulders. "He does not have the faith that I do."

He pulled the hood up over my head, shielding me from the rain before joining the others in the search for the jewel.

Desperately I yanked against the plastic restraint. I tried pushing and slamming into the stone vase to break it, but it didn't budge. I stupidly even tried to use one of the stems from the dead lilies planted in the vase, shoving it between my skin and the zip-tie to try to wiggle my wrist free, but it only broke in pieces and scratched up my already chafed skin.

I slumped defeated against the headstone.

Horrible thoughts raced one after the other in my still throbbing head. Was I going to die here? Were the Brethren going to kill me after forcing me to do whatever they intended with that stupid cursed jewel? And would the ghost of me be damned to haunt New Bethlehem forever?

A cold chill fluttered against my fingers.

"I'm here, Lou," came the quiet voice of my new ghost friend as she knelt in front of me, taking my hand. "You're not alone."

I squeezed my eyes shut. Tears escaped, the salt in them stinging the open cut on my cheek. When I opened my eyes again, she was gone, and in her place stood Toby looking down at me, the jewel dangling in his hand.

Sinking dread quickly replaced the defeat threatening to overwhelm me.

"It will take more than that to stop us," he scolded me in a determined voice. "We've come too far and searched too long for you."

"I – I told you," I winced at the sharp pain in my cheek as I spoke around the tangy taste of blood on my tongue. "I'm no one."

He knelt beside me. "That's not true and we both know it. Look at how the jewel hums when it nears you."

He was right. The damned thing wasn't just glowing brighter the closer he held it to me; it was vibrating, too.

"The jewel was given to us by the spirit that awaits on the other side – the guardian of the doorway to what lies beyond. Through him, we've been shown a path of true restoration is possible."

God, these people were insane. Once again, I desperately wished for Mrs Hammond's summons, that she could somehow miraculously yank me away from all this. I wanted nothing more than to brush the wet blades of her cemetery's freshly cut grass off my tights while she droned on about bridge parties and potlucks.

"All the guardian requires to open the doorway–" Toby's eyes zeroed in on the cut on my cheek, "– is a payment of blood." He grazed his index finger against the blood on my cheek and smeared it over the hardened edges of the jewel.

The ground trembled.

Every coffin buried in New Bethlehem trembled. I felt it and so did Toby.

"All that with just one drop," he said to himself, mystified. He turned to me with a look of awe. "You truly *are* the Blessed One."

He reached into the pocket of his cargo pants and pulled out a pocketknife, flipping it open. "Forgive me, but if you won't give your gift freely, then perhaps He has meant for us to take it from you."

I heard a thud as something sharp landed in Toby's arm. He staggered back, the pocketknife falling out of his shaking fingers as he stared in shock at the dagger lodged deep in his forearm.

Two things happened almost at once. A partially invisible distortion, like heat rising from a grill, rushed across the cemetery and an eruption of gunfire from Freddy and the others chased after it. I grabbed Toby's fallen pocketknife and scrambled behind the tombstone for cover. With a spray of bullets flying all around, I shoved the small blade underneath the zip-tie and dug it into the plastic until it broke apart, snapping open to reveal an indent left behind on my wrist, I turned back around and peeked out as much as I dared from behind the headstone.

Suddenly, where there had been a blurred distortion, now stood a man in a motorcycle helmet, dressed head to toe in black. Strapped to his thigh and around his chest were sheaths holding half a dozen throwing knives. Knives that went flying in the air with a flick of his wrist to land in the chests of two of the cloaked men.

The figure in black dodged more gunfire with a roll between tombstones. He landed, kneeling, and drew another knife from the sheath at his chest, flinging it straight at Freddy. He died with his finger on the trigger, unleashing a spray of bullets, a few striking the tombstone in front of me, sending bits of cement flying from it like shrapnel.

There were more whizzing bullets, grunts, gasps, thuds...

And then it was over.

The cemetery was silent except for the crickets who resumed their chirping.

I peeked out from behind the tombstone, clutching Toby's pocketknife.

The dark figure stood over the three bodies. Toby was gone, I had no idea where, but he'd left something behind. The jewel. No longer glowing or vibrating, it lay there abandoned on the cemetery gravel path. The figure in black took the hilt of a knife and slammed it down on the jewel, breaking it into a dozen shards.

He kicked them aside and walked through the carnage, yanking out one of his knives from a body to wipe it clean on his leg, and then came straight for me.

"You think you can hide from me?" he growled.

My heart fell to my stomach at the sound of the cold, detached voice behind the helmet. I cowered deeper into the shadows of the hooded cloak. He pulled off the helmet, confirming my worst fears, and threw it to the ground.

He knocked the pocketknife out of my hand, grabbed me by the front of the cloak and pulled me to my feet. The tip of his knife pointed at my chest. "For years I've hunted you. Just how many of you do I have to kill before I get to the right one?" He yanked the hood off my head and the Brethren's cloak fell to the ground.

Scott sucked in a breath as he took a step back.

The knife lowered to his side.

"Louise." He whispered my name to himself, almost doubting what he saw right before him.

We stared at each other, the silence in the cemetery growing to deafening levels. There were about a thousand questions in that silence, but all I could focus on was the sense of betrayal in those beautiful green eyes of his that mirrored the betrayal twisting around my gut.

A cold mist brushed against the back of my neck. "It's not over," my new ghost friend whispered.

The shards vibrated in the grass. A black fog rose out of the broken pieces and snaked across the ground. A low laugh came from one of the bodies, bubbling up out of Freddy's unmoving mouth.

Scott moved to my side, his knife coming up again, this time in a protective stance.

"Mine…" the voice purred.

A very dead Freddy sat up. Inky black eyes stared me down. They were eyes I'd seen before, once in Vick's eyes and again at Magnolia Grove Cemetery in an equally dead Mrs Renwick. And just like she'd done, Freddy raised his hand and pointed right at me.

"Mine… mine…" the voice coming out of his mouth seethed. Panicked, I scrambled backwards, tripped over a flat stone slab, and tumbled down against the ground.

Scott grabbed the corpse by the head and in a crunching jerk, twisted its neck, silencing it.

I blinked stupidly at him as he stood over the body. All of it was almost too much to take in – the ghost still floating among the ruined tombstones, the carnage that lay sprawled out at her feet, and Scott.

Vick was right all along. He was not just a cop, or even a cop at all. He was… well I didn't know what he was, and I didn't have time to think about it.

The other bodies began to move. It started with a shoulder here… a hand there… and then they were up off the ground, coming for us both.

"Mine… mine…" they all chanted.

"Get down!" Scott ordered.

I took cover once more behind the tombstone and watched

stunned as he moved from body to body. His movements were quick, violent, efficient as he broke one neck after another, being sure each body couldn't reanimate. He was clearly an expert at this... whatever this was.

"Mine! Mine!" the voice raged out of their mouths in protest, echoing across the cemetery, as he fought one after the other.

I was so caught up in this new version of Scott, I didn't realize just what I had taken cover by until it was too late.

A hand from one of the dead Brethren, fallen and obscured by the shadows of a nearby grave, moved up my leg as if it were just figuring out how to bend its joints for the first time. His fingernails dug deep into my thigh, breaking the skin hard enough I cried out.

Toby's pocketknife lay on the ground nearby where Scott had knocked it out of my hand. I'd never used a weapon of any kind in my life, but I picked it up without thinking and plunged it into the dead man's neck like it was a reflex.

It didn't affect him. His hands continued to burrow deeper into my thigh.

My new ghost friend appeared in the air above me. Her aura changed from white to blood-red with the horrifying outline of a skeleton underneath. Her shriek filled the cemetery as she rushed forward into the body of the dead man. Red light exploded out of his eyes and mouth and nose, burning out every inch of the inky black inside him, returning his eyes to an empty blue-eyed stare. Her aura poured out of him and once again appeared pure white as if she hadn't just turned into a nightmare creature from another realm.

And then Scott was there, pulling the body off me, throwing it out of reach.

He knelt beside me. His hands moved over me methodically, checking for injuries. I wasn't used to being this close to action movie, killer Scott. Somehow, I managed not to flinch at his touch. I felt so many things all at once – betrayal, gratitude, even anger. From the Brethren overtaking the cemetery to their violent annihilation at the hands of this latest version of Scott, it was entirely too much to take in and wrap my brain around. All I could do was stare as he moved with laser focused intent, somehow fully in command of the absolutely insane situation we were in. And of course, on top of all that, he was still beautiful as ever with his hair mussed up from the helmet and a gleam of sweat on his brow.

I sucked in a harsh breath as his fingers brushed across my thigh. It felt like a dozen barbed thorns made of ice digging deep into my leg.

He shoved the tip of one of his knives into my pant leg, ripping the stretchy fabric all the way up past my thigh. He tore away the rest of the fabric till it looked like I was wearing a pair of short shorts on one side and leggings on the other.

"Shit," he whispered under his breath.

A nasty gash ran the length of my thigh oozing something dark, and it wasn't blood. Thick inky liquid pearled around the gnarled wound before rolling down my skin in black streaks. I moved to wipe it away, but Scott grabbed my hand and firmly held it back.

"Don't touch it," he ordered.

He untied the scarf around my neck, paused for a beat at the sight of the bruises on my neck, then quickly used the scarf as a tourniquet above the gash, being careful not to get his own fingers anywhere close to the wound.

"We don't have much time," he said to himself.

"What do you mean? What's wrong with my leg?"

He didn't answer and scooped me up in his arms.

"Wait, Lou!" My new ghost friend called after me. "Look! You missed it before," she said, motioning to the tombstone I'd sought shelter behind during the gunfire.

The headstone wasn't old like Tom-Tom's, but it wasn't new either, maybe fifty years old. It was a double headstone, the kind that belonged to a husband and wife buried side by side. The dirt piled on top of the left side of the tombstone was fresh, marking it as one of the graves recently disturbed. There should've been two names on the stone, one on the left and one on the right, but whatever letters were once etched into the granite had been violently scraped off, purposely vandalized. It shouldn't have mattered; I'd been able to read tombstones in worse condition. Except for this one.

This one gave me nothing.

Scott sprinted me out of the cemetery, the no-name tombstone getting smaller in the distance. The world started to blur, turning fuzzy at the edges of my sight. Only then did I realize why I couldn't read it. Under the heaping pile of dirt there might've been a newly buried casket but there damn sure wasn't a body inside.

CHAPTER 16

I'd never been inside a patrol car before. There were buttons and screens everywhere and they all swirled together in a dizzying dance as the cruiser tore off away from the cemetery, police lights flashing, sirens blaring. I leaned back against the passenger side headrest and tried to focus. My brain still pounded in my skull from getting pistol-whipped, but it was nothing compared to the icy splinters inching deeper and deeper into my thigh, spreading their chill up and down my leg. The shivers started, and no matter how hard I tried I couldn't stop them.

"We're almost there. Hang on, Louise," Scott said behind the wheel, his voice entirely too serious.

"C-cold," I managed to say between chattering teeth.

"I know, babe. Just a little longer."

He couldn't see the ghostly passenger as he got into the back seat, my repeat ride-along friend who always treated me like a taxi.

"Does it hurt?" I asked the ghost. "Dying?"

His vaporous hand reached through the metal mesh separating the back seat from the front and covered mine. There was a small bit of warmth there, the stinging kind that comes with frostbite. It spread over me and for a moment it seemed like the cold splinters had slowed their deep drilling.

"You're not going to die," Scott answered. Was there more hope in his tone than surety?

Not going to die. I thought about those words, and they felt suddenly ridiculous to me. Of course I was going to die. It was the 'when' that was still up for grabs. Was my time now? Was my next stop the cold metal slab in Ivan's funeral home? I suppose the bigger question was what came after. Would I be lucky and pass on like all the people whose headstones told me their life stories? Or would I be damned to never find rest like the ghost next to me, watching me intently as if he could hear the thoughts work their way into my mind one after the other.

I stopped thinking about it and turned all my focus to the world outside the window. Houses blurred by. Where was the medical district? Why weren't we going to the hospital? Would a doctor know how to fix the cut turning my leg black? The sirens and lights cut off. My ghostly passenger friend disappeared and next thing I knew we were parked outside Scott's house.

Hands grasped onto me, lifting me up out of the police cruiser and carrying me over the threshold.

He sat me on the kitchen counter like a kid with a scraped knee that needed a Band-Aid, though it was a bit more serious than that. I tried to keep my head up but the lights in his kitchen blurred and I felt myself slumping forward, slipping into the swirling tile floor.

"Stay with me," he said, his hand firmly gripping my shoulder to keep me upright as he opened the cabinet beside my head. He pulled out a first-aid kit, though what was inside looked nothing like any first-aid kit I'd seen before. There were metal cylinders and white tubes. I picked one up; my fingers fumbled as I popped the cork and looked curiously inside. The only distinguishing quality was a scent like a mixture of herbs I couldn't place that wafted up out of the tube. Nothing was labelled, the only differentiating quality to them were colored bands of tape. He took the tube from me, put it back in place, and slid out a pouch made of saran wrap, unfolding it to revealing a silvery glittering substance.

"What's that?" I asked, resting my head back against the cabinet.

"The good stuff."

By the look of it, I thought it would have more of a powdery feel to it but when he dabbed it over the length of the cut, it smeared like toothpaste, a toothpaste that started to fizz then burn. His hand came down over my mouth muffling my scream. I writhed against him on the countertop, my leg burning like it was on fire.

"Shhh… shhh, it's okay." Scott tried to comfort me as the imaginary fire burned deeper and deeper into my skin, searing all the way to the bone. "I know it hurts, babe, just a little bit longer."

The fire faded to warmth and then, at last, numbness. I sagged against him. He removed his hand from my mouth to brush away my tears with his thumb.

"What was that?" I asked weakly.

He took a wet dishcloth and wiped away the fizzy residue. "They call it Devil's Tears. An infection like that one can latch on to pretty much everything and spread like crazy. Devil's Tears is the only substance that can burn it out completely."

His answer only raised more questions. He'd seen infections gotten from undead people before? Did that mean Devil's Tears was some kind of special medicine? And who were "they?"

His fingertips gently brushed over my skin where the gash had been. Gnarled flesh had formed over it, creating a scar that looked months old but was still inflamed. How was that even possible?

"I'm sorry, but you're going to have one hell of a scar."

There were a hundred other things I wanted to know. If he wasn't a cop– and it seemed Vick was right, how could he be after what I'd seen – then what was he? What were all the different vials in the first aid kit and what did they do? What was he doing in the cemetery? Did he follow me there? But then if he did, why had he been so surprised to see me?

I should've asked any of those questions. Instead, there was only one that came to mind.

"What happens now?" I asked exhausted and weary.

His hand still lingered on my thigh, and it hurt that it did. Not physically, but emotionally. How I would've enjoyed that single touch before now. It would've been my whole world for as long as that touch lasted. But that was back when he was just Scott, and I was just Louise. Now that hand was a reminder of what would never be. His eyes were on his hand on my thigh too and I wondered how much he was thinking the same thing.

I shifted my leg, unable to bear his touch and the echo of what could've been any longer. He pulled his hand away as if I'd broken a spell and took a step back from me, putting a small bit of space between us. It might as well have been a football field's length by the look that came into his eyes when they finally met mine.

"Devil's Tears take a minute or two to work, but already they should be taking the pain away. Maybe even make you sleepy." The detachment that came into his voice felt like a blow to the gut. The sound of it made me want to cry or scream in rage, I wasn't sure which.

"I'm not sleepy," I insisted, defiant, even as my head started to feel woozy, and my eyelids got heavier with each blink.

I grunted in protest as arms came around me to lift me up off the counter, but I begrudgingly gave into his hold as a weakness settled into my limbs. Damn, whatever was happening, it was happening fast. A shiver took over me and I could barely keep my head up as he carried me through the house to a bedroom in the back.

He sat me on the bed and a sweatshirt came up over my head. I swayed sitting upright and he braced me with a hand on my shoulder as I managed to push my arms through the sleeves. His touch lingered on me once more and the sleepiness made it hard to push away the sorrow I felt at what was surely forever gone between us. I was so tired I wasn't sure if I was dreaming or not, the fingers that brushed lightly against the side of my neck, flitting as light as a butterfly over my bruises.

"Who keeps hurting you, Louise?" His voice floated somewhere above me.

"Vick this time, but she had black eyes. Wasn't really her," I mumbled incoherently, my lips heavy as they worked the words. "It's... complicated."

I melted down into the pillows. He pulled a blanket up around me. A hand touched my hair, brushing it off my cheek.

"Everything's complicated now, isn't it?" he said, his words sad.

I meant to nod in agreement but only nestled deeper into the pillow. I fell asleep thinking about his hand against my cheek and trying to remember why it made me so upset.

A persistent, painful throbbing in my thigh pulled me out of a deep sleep. I blinked heavily, trying to focus on the curtainless window in front of me. Purple-orange light from the setting sun gave the room a dark pink glow. The room was empty, sparse, worse than a hotel room. There was a nightstand with nothing on it but a lamp and nothing at all on the walls. It took me several long seconds of blinking stupidly around to remember that I was in Scott's house. It wasn't at all what I imagined.

Now that I was fully awake, some very real and unfortunate truths hit me. My hair was probably a complete wreck having, slept for the better part of a day, and I hadn't had a shower since before I went to work, which seemed like forever ago.

I got up and tip-toed to the nearby bathroom. Once again there was zero decor, just a towel and wash rag neatly folded waiting on the counter.

I glimpsed myself in the mirror above the sink as I washed my hands and winced. I was a mess. Dirt smudges and bits of blood caked my face. My cheek wasn't swollen anymore but there was a nasty cut surrounded by a deep blue bruise. At least the bruises on my neck had started to fade, turning to an ugly yellow and brown. The residue from whatever Scott applied to my leg was flakey and smelled terrible. I didn't have much of a choice but to use what Scott had set out for me and take a quick shower.

The warm water helped the throbbing in my leg a little, but as soon as I got out and toweled off the pain turned to a full-on pounding that went deep into my thigh. The scar was no longer red, just a long, gnarled string of flesh midway up my thigh. I didn't have any clean clothes and had to pull back on everything I had except for the leggings, which were pretty much destroyed with one entire leg cut off.

I would've killed for one of my backpacks stowed away in the cemetery. I wadded up the leggings and threw them in the trash can. It left me with a super short jean skirt and bare legs, but it was better than nothing. The only thing that wasn't covered in dirt and grime was Scott's Magnolia Grove High

School sweatshirt. It smelled like him – that fresh soap smell mixed with woods which immediately made me think of the night he found my bike. I ignored a sudden pang of sorrow at the memory and pulled the sweatshirt back on, shoving my arms through the long sleeves.

I checked myself once more in the mirror, ran my fingers through my wet wavy hair and decided it was the best it was gonna get.

If I thought the bathroom and bedroom were empty, the rest of the house was even more barren. There were no signs of anyone actually living there. The hallway emptied out to the kitchen where the only furniture was a square table and two chairs. There was no tablecloth, no houseplants, no knick-knacks or family photos anywhere, just Scott, a fast-food bag on the table, and a manilla folder tucked under his arm.

He leaned up against the counter still dressed in black, his arms crossed in front of his chest.

"How are you feeling?" he asked.

"Confused… and stiff," I said, lowering myself into the only chair at the table. "How long have I been asleep?"

"It's Saturday evening, a little after seven."

I sucked in a breath. I was over an hour late for work. I started to stand up, but Scott held out a hand to stop me.

"It's been taken care of. They think you're home sick." He picked up the fast-food bag and placed it in front of me. "Apparently you don't take many sick days. I had a hard time convincing someone named Cliff that you were okay and not on death's doorstep."

No doubt. I don't think I'd ever taken a sick day the entire time I worked there.

"Eat," he said, nudging the bag toward me. "It'll make you feel better."

I took a bite of a double cheeseburger and fries and tried not to wolf everything down at once in an attempt to maintain some amount of dignity. It was hard, because I was famished. Meanwhile, Scott kept silent, watching me. I felt his gaze fall on the scar peeking out from the hem of my skirt and shifted around in my seat between bites of burger to try to push the short skirt lower to cover it.

When he finally did speak his voice came out stern, with that same cold, detached tone I was growing to hate.

"Louise Helena Cordova," he said.

The cheeseburger turned to a rock in my gut.

"Or is it Carson?" He dropped the folder on the table in front of me and flipped it open.

There I was in black and white, crossing a street in Kentucky three years ago. It was the first place I'd run to. Back then my hair had been dyed red and kept cropped short at the ears, way shorter than my current, naturally black, shoulder-length hair. Past me's big, scared eyes looked around the town square, paranoid. Paranoid and scared were my perpetual states of being back then.

I reached out with a trembling hand and turned the page to find a copy of my driver's license from when I was seventeen. My real name was printed in bold letters at the top, Louise Helena Cordova, not the fake last name of Carson that I used to get hired at the Piggly Wiggly.

I turned the next page, and my hand froze. In front of me was a missing person's report from a year and a half ago. On it, my mother's pleading words for me to be found, that she desperately wanted me to come home and that she loved me, which of course, was a lie.

"Does my mother know where I am?" I wasn't sure if I said it out loud or not, but I must've because he answered.

"I wouldn't know," he said dismissively as if that wasn't the most important thing in my world. "What I do want to know is, what does a cult of necromancers want with you?"

I stared at the papers in front of me as if they were on fire. "How did you get all this?"

"I have a whole police department's database at my disposal that I didn't ever think I'd need to use on you but that's an interesting question you ask." He leaned down and stared at me face to face, but this wasn't the Scott I'd shared kisses with. This was the Scott who looked suspiciously at Vick and who was analyzing me in a cold hostile glare that twisted my stomach.

"I told you a cult of people hell-bent on raising the dead is after you and this," he thumped the missing person's report, "this is what you're worried about?"

I stared at the page. Cult or no cult, the real danger was right there, or at least it used to be. I had no intention of letting that danger back into my life.

"Your favorite place to go is a cemetery in the middle of the night when the breeze goes through the grass," he repeated my words from our date in a tone that made me want to cry. "I actually believed you. You're a damn good liar, I'll give you that. And all those nights in the cemetery, just who were you talking to? Was it the Brethren? How long have you been with them? Who is their leader?" His rapid-fire questions came one right after the other, his sharp words demanding an answer. None of those questions mattered to me, there was only the contents of the file. Here was my past refusing to be forgotten, continuing to ruin everything I ever wanted.

And it was definitely ruined. The Scott in front of me would never again be the Scott who took me to the riverside, the Scott who shyly put my hand in his, or looked at me with wanting.

"Liar?" I echoed his word for me with my own frigid tone. "I suppose it could be worse. At least I'm not a murderer," I fired back. Now true, his killing the Brethren in the cemetery had saved me but I was furious.

A flicker in his steely, indifferent eyes was the only indication I might have landed a blow.

What had I been thinking, going out with him? I should've known better. In what world did I actually think that would work out? This life never allowed me any of those things. That was all for normal girls. Maybe I should've been grateful that any of those moments with him happened in the first place. Instead, I only felt angry, and cursed, as if I was damned to wander alone for eternity like any of the ghosts stuck in this world.

I grabbed the missing person report, crumpling it in my fist. "Thanks for dinner," I said and marched out the door.

"Wait! Get back here," he called after me. "Louise!"

There was no yank, no tell-tale pull. It was more like stepping one foot off Scott's front porch and diving face first into the Veil. I spun around in place. There was Scott looking shocked that I'd disappeared right in front of him. I reached out to him, and it felt like my finger was pressing up against the inside of a bubble.

CHAPTER 17

I turned around and there he was, standing on his bottom porch step, shocked at my sudden disappearance and scanning the area for me. His lips formed my name, shouting for me but I heard nothing through the clear, distorted wall separating us. I reached out a hand, placing it flat against the surface. It felt like being inside a bubble, a very thick bubble.

This bubble world was exactly like the one I'd left except desaturated and dark. The fading light from twilight didn't shine inside the bubble and everything – the street, the houses, the curbs – were all covered with dust or ash, big fat flakes of it that coated everything.

I'd been somewhere like this before. Once, not that long ago, when I'd been ripped out of this world and caught between it and Mrs Hammond's summons. Except, as far as I could tell, there was no inky black monster waiting to suck the life out of me, at least none that I could see on the empty streets.

A small hand grasped mine.

There, standing next to me and coming up to my waist, was Tom-Tom. Not apparition Tom-Tom but in the flesh Tom-Tom, his very real hand dwarfed by mine. Like the world around him, Tom-Tom was desaturated, his usual blue eyes appearing light gray.

"Where am I?" My voice didn't echo. The words came out close as if we walked through a heavy fog or dense snowfall.

In true Tom-Tom-like fashion, he didn't answer.

"Come on," he said, tugging on my hand until I started to walk with him. "She's waiting for you."

The street we were on stayed a street but the world around me changed, buzzing by in a dizzying blur even though we walked at a normal pace.

Every now and then a random object littered the street, bright in color, standing out in the desaturated world. It wasn't the usual stuff you'd find lying in a gutter. A pair of gold glasses, the lenses intact. Rolled up socks with red stripes on the legs, clean and fresh like they were right out of a dryer. Car keys with a purple springy loop on them to wrap around your wrist. Sometimes there were bigger items, like a blue and black hockey stick and a pair of yellow skis. I'd never thought about it before, but could ghosts take objects out of the living world and dump them in here? And just how easy was it for them to do that?

I stopped walking. "Tom-Tom, did you steal my bike and bring it here?"

"It wasn't me!" he said, in the affronted, adamant way of a toddler unfairly accused of something. "It was the twins. They like to take things."

I didn't have to ask who he meant. Ned and Clara, the two little poltergeist wannabes who haunted their block of Park Street. I scanned the monochrome world around me, searching for Clara's bouncing ringlets or Ned's slicked hair with a cowlick sticking up at the front that never laid down right. They weren't anywhere to be found. In fact, there was no one, just me and Tom-Tom alone in this world void of everything.

"They weren't being bad this time," he said in their defense. "They even took it back!"

Well, that didn't explain how it ended up at Crawford Lake with Josephine. Though I maybe shouldn't have been surprised the mischievous pair didn't return it back to where they'd taken it from behind the Piggly Wiggly.

"She told them to take it," he went on. "Said it would set you on a path that would keep you safe."

That brought up a whole slew of new questions. Especially considering that taking my bike that night made me cross paths with one particular person. Scott. And after what I'd just been through, it was up in the air how "safe" I really was with him.

"Who told them that?"

He walked on, ignoring my question. Apparently, apparition Tom-Tom and in-the-flesh Tom-Tom had the same penchant for evading straightforward questions.

He tugged on my hand, urging me along. "Come on, she's almost here."

The world blurring past us came to a jarring stop.

We weren't on the paved street anymore but on grass facing the back of a dark gray house with the shutters closed in the windows. An empty clothesline stood in the backyard, a neglected vine of morning glories not in bloom traveled up the steel post. I'd never been in the backyard of this house, but I still recognized it right off. Osgood Funeral Home.

A brilliant ribbon of light danced next to the clothesline. I'd seen it twice before now but inside the Veil, this world void of color and light, it was brighter than ever and damn near blinding. My ghost friend from New Bethlehem stood in front of us.

Here, in this world between worlds, Tom-Tom felt tangible and real, still not alive of course, but his hand in mine felt just like that – a hand. This spirit in front of us was not at all like that. She was still an aura, the difference was in how bright that aura was. Similar to the ribbon, here inside the Veil, she appeared many degrees brighter than she had in the land of the living.

"Thank you, Tommy." She touched his chin, and he beamed proudly up at her. For half a second, he looked like the boy he must've been in life. With sunlight dancing off his blonde hair, his cheeks pink from playing outside in the cold. Then it was gone, and he was walking away down the street, leaving us alone.

She stared, forlorn, at the back of the funeral home. "We don't have much time, Lou," she said.

The screen door at the back of the house opened and out stepped Ivan. With dark circles under his eyes, he seemed more tired than the night we first met. He stood in the yard near a patch of daylilies, their blooms were supposed to be red and yellow but appeared only gray and darker gray here in the Veil. For a moment I thought he'd seen us, staring right where we stood, but he didn't; and turned his gaze up at the night stars, his shoulders slumping in defeat.

My ghostly friend floated across the yard toward him. Longingly, she reached out to him, the Veil stretching and bending at her fingertips as if only a thin layer of plastic wrap separated them. He closed his eyes and leaned into her touch, almost like he could feel her there.

"You're Alice," I breathed. "Ivan's Alice."

The woman who'd understood him, who knew his curse… our curse. Seeing the two of them together, this close and still definitively separated was enough to tear a person's heart out.

"He searches for me, but I'm not here to be found." On the surface, it sounded ridiculous, but I knew exactly what she meant, at least by that latter part. She wasn't here, as in, she wasn't an actual ghost. Like Mrs Renwick, Alice was a spirit and one that had most assuredly passed on.

She withdrew her hand and floated back away from him. Ivan rubbed his forehead in frustration and began pacing back and forth in the yard.

"They don't yet know what you really are, Lou, but they'll figure it out and when they do..." She looked angry, her aura flickering red as it had done in New Bethlehem, snapping and popping at the edges like electricity.

The light from the ribbon poured over her like a sunbeam and her anger ebbed. "They'll protect you, Lou. Help you. All of them... if you let them," she went on. "You don't have to be alone anymore. It's okay to need them. People like Mortimer, Victoria, and so many others... they'll anchor you there in the land of the living and remind you in the dark why being alive is such a gift."

Alice hovered over to the daylilies and reached out to touch one of the petals. For a moment the bright light coming from her fingertips illuminated the flower, and I could see the rich red and bright yellow of the petal surrounded by vibrant green leaves. She withdrew her touch, and the varying shades of gray returned.

"Life is temporary. Fleeting. That's what makes it so precious." She looked toward Ivan, a sad frown on her lips. "He's forgotten that in his search for me."

An explosion detonated in a black cloud in the sky high above us, rocking the inside of the bubble-like world. The desaturated sky darkened as if evening was giving way to night. It wasn't long before another explosion landed, this time in a different part of the sky. A giant plume of black slammed up against the Veil's invisible walls, pooling in on itself as if it were trying to get in.

Alice's aura flashed that dangerous fiery shade of red. "He's coming back..."

The sky turned iridescent in the spots where the black bombs struck the clear surface. The texture of the Veil's barrier changed, no longer bending like a bubble but becoming hard like an enormous glass ball that fractured and splintered in places as if someone were beating their fist against it.

"Take her home now, Tommy," Alice instructed.

Tom-Tom reappeared at my side and obediently hooked his hand in mine.

"Find me, Lou," she pleaded and floated forlorn back to Ivan one last time. "Maybe then he will have peace."

The ribbon shrank in on itself and she was gone. The bubble hardened where it fractured, the splinters cracking at the crevices, sending bits of the Veil crumbling down on the street like ash.

Tom-Tom tugged on my hand, and we were gone, Ivan and the funeral home disappearing in a blur behind us as we ran down the street.

CHAPTER 18

Coming out of the Veil was like getting smacked in the face with color, all of them, and in every shade. It was late at night, judging by how empty the streets were, but even in the dark, there was color everywhere. I didn't realize just how much my eyes had missed it. I drank in the bright red of a nearby fire hydrant underneath a streetlight, the deep green leaves of a bush beside it, and a birdhouse in someone's yard painted a rich blue. There was also warmth. The night was cold, sure, but it was filled with the warmth of life, something that didn't exist inside the Veil. I breathed the fresh night air, letting it fill my lungs, grateful to be rid of the stale atmosphere filled with dust, ash, and sadness.

Tom-Tom had dropped me on my street corner, and I happily used the short walk past the little houses to be grateful to still be alive and in the land of the living. I even welcomed the threaded tightness in my leg where the scar was, its dull pain a reminder that I continued to live. Oddly, my cheek no longer hurt, nor did my teeth ache from getting slammed by Freddy's pistol.

The surprising spring in my steps died off though when my house came into view at the end of the block. The lights were off. I tried to remember the last time I'd been home. Right before my shift when I was itching to go to New Bethlehem to see what I had missed. It felt like a lifetime ago. Despite that, I was damn sure I'd left all my lights on like always.

I skirted around to the back of the house and walked as quietly as possible up the steps. The door wasn't locked, which was something else I would never forget to do. I slowly turned the knob and slid in through the barely cracked open door. There was a piece of laminate flooring in the kitchen that had a tendency to creak under my step, I avoided it and stuck to the wall instead.

I'm not sure if it was my time in the Veil, surrounded by the absence of life, that made me so aware of its presence, but there it was inside my house – a heartbeat somewhere in the darkness and not just my own.

I held my breath and focused on that heartbeat. Somehow, I could tell it was there inside the room with me, thudding in a steady, only slightly raised rhythm while mine hammered away like a hummingbird. I looked out across the kitchen, my mind reeling at what my eyes said couldn't possibly be true. My kitchen was a tiny one, with no place to hide. The only furniture was the table, which sat there empty in a beam of moonlight streaming in through the lacy curtained window above the sink. And yet the heartbeat was there, thumping away and waiting.

I forced myself to take a deep, steadying breath. I could wait too.

I pretended nothing was amiss, that it was completely normal for me to come home to a pitch-black house despite having just sneaked into it. I dropped my keys into the dish I kept by the door, spread out my mail on the counter, and folded a dishtowel for no reason except to give my hands something to do.

I almost gave up when a distorted shadow moved out of the corner of my eye. I swung hard, channeling all my fear and anxiety into a single punch in the dark. My fist painfully made contact with something solid.

The distortion flickered and suddenly Scott was there, appearing out of thin air right in front of me.

"It's you," I breathed, stunned by his sudden appearance.

I flipped on the kitchen lights and cradled my tender knuckles against my chest. The punch hadn't phased him except for a faint redness that surfaced on his right cheek.

He was beautiful, as always, but scruffy with a thick five o'clock shadow and disheveled hair. It was the kind of disarray that only makes hot guys even hotter.

"Are they out there with you?" he practically growled.

"Who?" I blinked stupidly at him. My oblivious response only made the muscles in his jaw clench tighter in anger. Understanding dawned on me. He meant the Brethren.

"No." I narrowed my eyes at him, annoyed. "It's just me. Like it's always been."

We stood there in the kitchen in a silent standoff, neither moving. Well, this was getting us nowhere. I took a step toward the refrigerator and his fists tensed at his sides. I ignored them and opened the freezer to pull out a bag of peas.

"Here." I held out the bag. He stared at it, his jaw clenching once more.

"For that." I motioned to his red cheek, but he didn't move.

"Fine. Suit yourself." I dropped the bag on the table between us. I was afraid he was going to stay that way, like some angry unmoving statue.

The anger in his face fractured the littlest bit and I glimpsed a hint of the Scott I used to know. He relented, picking up the bag and pressing it to his cheek.

"How did you do that, by the way?" I said in regard to the whole invisible thing he did. "Is it some kind of magic trick? I've seen that same shimmer twice before, was it you? How–"

"Where have you been?" he demanded, shifting the peas around to glare accusingly at me. "It's been almost two days."

Two days? That was impossible! It felt like I'd been gone for only a few hours. God, the shifts I missed at the Piggly Wiggly... did I even have a job still? And Mortie! My breath caught in my throat. How worried he must be about me. Scott surely couldn't be right. But if, somehow, he was, then time must move differently inside the Veil. The concept was staggering. Mind-blowing. But was it really? After all, the measurement of time was pretty much irrelevant to the dead. Perhaps that was the reason my cheek no longer felt the sting of the pistol.

"One second you were right in front of me," he went on, "and in the next you were gone."

He was one to talk. Considering he had his own tendency to disappear into thin air.

"Did the Brethren take you?" Another flicker of the Scott I once knew appeared. "Are you working with them against your will?" Concern for me mixed with hope in his eyes that perhaps that narrative might be true.

"No. I'm not," I said, and it was like I'd doused that flame of hope with ice-cold water. "But before I saw you turn them all into human shish kabobs, for all I knew, you could've been with them." I crossed my arms in front of me and leaned back against the kitchen counter, waiting for at least one single explanation from him.

Confusion and that damned detachment fought for control over his beautiful features.

And then we were back to that silent standoff once again. My knuckles ached and I wanted to rub my hand over them, but I refused to budge.

Surprisingly, he did.

"Are your knuckles okay?" he asked, as if he read my mind.

"They're fine," I lied.

He handed the peas to me, and I took them, making a show that at least *I* wasn't ridiculous enough to not accept them. The tiniest hint of a smile played at the corner of his lip.

The silence fell yet again between us but at least the tension lessened. He looked over me openly and thank God that purposeful indifference wasn't there as he did.

"Who are you?" he said.

"Well for starters – *not* with the Brethren or anyone else," I said pointedly. 'I'm just me. I promise."

He nodded along, sifting his way through what appeared to be some internal debate. "Okay," he said, as if deciding to give in to that truth.

The last little bit of my own icy chill melted away. "And you?" I asked timidly.

He gave a weary sigh, running a frustrated hand across his face. "Right now, I'm wishing I could just be me too." His hand fell away and that brilliant green intensity in his eyes met mine. "You have no idea how much."

"You can be, you know?" I ventured, giving him an olive branch. "It's okay to just be you when you're with me."

A sad smile fell across his face. "Oh Louise," he shook his head. "Of course, you'd say something like that."

"It's true though."

"You know what?" Those kind green eyes of his stared back at me. "I think I believe you."

And for the moment, it was like we were on my front porch steps all over again and it amazed me how easy it was for us to escape to right back where we left off. It was as if we were both running from our world of chaos, each looking for respite in a completely normal moment.

He looked around my kitchen, taking in all my knick-knacks and mismatched art. "I can see something of you all around here, in the way you decorate, the colors you choose," he said softly. "I haven't been somewhere like this in a very long time."

I scoffed, suddenly self-conscious about every home decor decision I'd ever made. "Somewhere cluttered you mean."

He shook his head. "Somewhere that feels like a home."

I recognized that lost, hollow look in his face. I'd seen it in my own reflection staring back at me for years. It was a look that had only just started to vanish with my new life here.

"Did you run away too?" I asked, daring to venture into his real past.

"No," he said quietly, looking away from me. "No. I chose this life, foolishly."

I wanted to know more. I wanted to know all of it, but I was terrified of ruining the moment by opening up all his scars that were so clearly there. Instead, I simply nodded.

It struck me then that I had a man in my home – right here, standing beside my lace covered kitchen table. I never thought that would ever actually happen. Naturally, something had to come along and ruin the moment. That was the one rule in my universe.

I felt it – that chill I'd known all my life. It started at the kitchen's far wall and snaked across the floor before running in goosebumps up along my shoulders. I looked toward that far wall a second before the subtle blue glow appeared. I pushed off the counter I was leaning against, alarmed at the only other thing that had never been in my house before.

"What is it?" Scott said, instantly alert.

In that blue glow appeared a face and shoulders as Hank walked through my wall. He glanced nervously over his shoulder as if he was being followed. "He's found you, Lou."

CHAPTER 19

Hank's apparition stood in my kitchen. I never knew him to venture this far from his rooftop before. He shifted from one foot to the other in his overalls, nervously looking back over his shoulder.

"He's found you," he said, his voice filled with worry.

"Who found me, Hank?" I asked.

Scott's eyes momentarily darted between me and the general spot where Hank stood. I wasn't sure what he was thinking, and he didn't stay long enough for me to find out. A knife appeared in his hand. He slunk up against the other kitchen wall and pulled back the curtain over the window an inch to peek out at the backyard. Finding nothing, he darted out the door and disappeared outside.

"Who found me, Hank?" I repeated firmly.

He said nothing, still glancing over his shoulder at the empty wall.

I pulled off Scott's sweatshirt and tried not to cry. That brief chapter of my life was surely over now, and I couldn't bear to keep the reminder of it on me for another second more in case I became delusional enough to think I'd ever be able to have it again. I rifled through my coat closet searching for something else to cover my nervously shaking arms with.

The front door opened, and Scott came back inside, sheathing the knife at his side. "No one's there," he said, confused.

I pushed my arms through my corduroy jacket, feeling more like myself – the cursed girl who could never have a boyfriend. "You asked who I talked to at night in the cemetery." I didn't dare look at him, terrified of what I would see. "They're ghosts."

I didn't give him time to answer and turned back to the other man in the room. "Now please, Hank. Who is it that found me?" I pressed him again. Hank wasn't like Tom-Tom. He'd only ever been forthright with me. Him holding back was uncharacteristic to say the least.

He fidgeted, his fists clenching and unclenching at his sides. "He's getting angrier… impatient. He's found you, where your heart is."

Where my heart is? I looked at Scott. His expression was guarded though curious. I didn't even want to begin to analyze what that meant or how I'd ruined what we just shared. Where my heart is? Well, if no one was outside then…

"Mortie!" I breathed and made a run for the door.

"Louise, wait!" Scott shouted after me.

Guilt racked through me. I should've checked in on Mortie the second after being in the Veil. What was wrong with me? How could I have been so foolish?

I scrambled down the front porch steps and would've run across the yard to Mortie's if an arm hadn't clamped down around my waist, pulling me back.

Scott's hand covered my mouth, muting my protest. I struggled against him, but he kept me pinned gently against his back. "We'll go there, I promise," he breathed into my ear as he pulled us back into the shadows of my house. "But we have to be smart. I need you to trust me. Can you trust me? At least just a little?"

It was a heavy, loaded question. Trust. Did either of us have the right to have that from the other?

I wasn't sure I was capable of that with him, and yet, I remembered Alice inside the Veil and what she said about how people would help me... if I let them. I nodded and he slowly removed his hand from my mouth.

"Stay behind me the entire time," he whispered. "When I move, you move, got it?"

I nodded again.

He let go of my waist and paused for a beat as if I might still bolt. When I didn't, he nudged me into position behind him. Moonlight glinted off the two knives he held, one in each hand.

"Hang onto me."

I gripped the back of his shirt. He tapped the inside of his left wrist three times with his index and middle finger and the night around us changed, becoming distorted. He led me across the backyard.

Scott's shield was a little like being inside the Veil. We moved through the world in a sort of invisible bubble that warped and wobbled along with each step we took. Shadows were everywhere except underneath us and I wondered if anyone looking at us would see only the same shimmering effect I'd seen before.

He led us between the two yards, past the lawn chairs and wind chimes, and pushed us up against the cream-colored siding of Mortie's house. We went slowly around the perimeter, ducking down and staying close to the walls. The lights were off, and all the curtains were closed.

Much like me, Mortie was a creature of habit. While leaving the lights on at night was my thing, Mortie's was to keep his curtains open regardless of the time. He once told me that Peter liked to wake up in the morning with the sunlight warming the kitchen. After he lost him, Mortie said he couldn't bring himself to let the habit die with Peter. Closing them was something he could never bring himself to do. My fist tightened around Scott's shirt.

When we got around to the back of the house, the door was ajar, hanging by its top hinge like it'd been violently thrown open. I held back a fearful sob as Scott inched us slowly up the back steps until we stood unmoving in the kitchen, the same place where I'd made Mortie and I peanut-butter sandwiches. Except this time there was no Mortie calling out to me from his workroom, no Zelda brushing up against my shins to say hello.

The house had been ransacked. Cabinets and drawers were open, their contents overturned and strewn about, littering the floor. I blinked back the tears rapidly pooling in my eyes.

We moved to the bedroom and found it much the same as the kitchen and living room. I kept my grip on Scott's shirt as we stepped down the hallway into Mortie's workroom.

We weren't alone.

An inky black mass floated over the table, rippling over the top of it, rolling over Mortie's tools and lingering on the spot where the book had been and where it was no longer. It was the same inky black creature I'd come face to face with inside the Veil. How could it exist in the world of the living? I didn't have a clue, but knives were definitely not going to stop it.

I pulled Scott by the shirt back up against me and wrapped my arm around him, putting a calm hand against his chest in the hope he would understand my unspoken words. He did and lowered his blades. He took a step back and another, backing us silently up against the wall. Would his shimmering invisible shield, still up and distorting the world around us, work here with this thing?

The inky black creature gave up its fruitless search and poured off the table, spreading out across the floor. Its rolling mass made contact with Scott's invisible shield, brushing up against it as it rippled over the floor. I held my breath and waited for it to discover us hidden in the corner. It didn't and rolled out the threshold to the living room. I relaxed my arm and bumped into the stool next to me, making it teeter.

The black mass froze in place. The outer edge of it perked up as if it had ears. Slowly it poured back into the workroom, suddenly suspicious. The ink cloud seemed to be more aware of its perimeters this time and when its edge brushed back up against Scott's shield it flew into a rage.

Black nettles slammed into the shield, ramming up against the invisible wall over and over again until the shimmer began to crackle and weaken like the explosions I'd witnessed in the Veil. Scott raised his knives again despite how useless they would be against a creature like this, and I knew then we were in trouble.

I took my hand off his chest and held it out. The shimmering wall didn't feel all that different from the Veil as I placed my palm against it, only this bubble-like surface felt alive, like it had a living pulse to it. At my touch, sparks of blue intertwined with the invisible surface, strengthening it. Whatever weird energy I'd managed to tap into before, poured out of me now, mingling with the magic of the shield.

The sensation was something I'd felt before. Two times in fact. Once when I read from the book in this very room and another when Vick's hands came round my neck.

Except now, the sensation wasn't fleeting, it was slow and steady, and it felt insane. It was almost like I could feel the essence of Scott right there in my fingers. He gasped as if he could feel me too and from where I stood behind him, I could see tiny blue sparkling bits lighting up the veins just under the skin of his neck.

The inky creature recoiled in a screech, running from the room and out of the house like a wild animal injured by a predator. The shimmering shield disappeared, my added blue energy vanishing with it.

Scott slumped against me. "What... was... that?" He struggled to breathe. I wasn't sure if he was referring to the ink creature or me.

"Are you okay?" I asked, turning him around to look at him.

He wasn't. The color drained from his face, and he staggered against me, struggling to stay standing. He checked his own pulse, his fingers shaking against his neck as he did so. He fumbled with the leather strap holding the sheaths for his knives and pulled out a thimble sized metal case from a hidden pocket. He tried to open the lid but couldn't and handed it to me.

"The g-green one," his voice trembled. "Break it open, dissolve into w-warm water."

I clutched the metal case and pulled his arm around my shoulders, half-carrying him to the kitchen. Oh God, what had I done to him?

I grabbed one of Mortie's coffee mugs lying on the floor, discarded from the ransacked cupboards, and filled it with warm tap water. Scott clung to my side, the breath coming labored from his chest. Frantically, I flipped open the metal case. There were three pills inside. One red, one clear with glittering powder inside it, and the third, green. I took out the green one and returned the case to the hideaway in his leather strap. I broke open the pill and dumped its neon green contents into the water. A putrid smell like dirt and sulfur hit me in the face as I stirred it.

Scott took the mug from my hands and downed its contents in a single gulp. He sagged against the wall and slumped down to the floor, his arm still around my shoulder, pulling me down with him. He grabbed my hand in his shaky one and peered into my palm as he ran his fingers over my skin.

"W–what was that?" he repeated his question from before.

"I... I don't know. It's never happened before. I just sort of reached out and... I don't know. I'm so sorry. If I'd known it would do this, I never would've–"

He shook his head. "You did what needed to be done."

The color was coming back into his cheeks, and he no longer strained for breath. Whatever was in that green pill seemed to be working. He curled my fingers back into my hand and looked up, assessing me.

"They weren't wrong, were they, the Brethren?" he said quietly. A calm sort of resignation settled over him. "You're the key they've been looking for this whole time. The Blessed One."

"What? No. No, I'm not. I'm not anything," I said, but he hadn't really asked it in a question.

He pulled himself up off the floor, struggling to stand for a moment, needing to use one of Mortie's stools to keep upright. The moment he was steady, he started moving through Mortie's house looking out the windows, the strength returning to his stride a little bit with each step.

"What are you doing?" I asked, following closely after him, worried he might topple over at any minute.

"We have to get you out of here. Now," he said, adamant.

My mind reeled. Things were moving too fast. Mortie was gone. Zelda too. On top of that, I'd somehow shot blue energy out of my hand again, half on purpose and half out of instinct, nearly killing Scott in the process. Where was the book? And why was Scott looking at me like that?

"Louise, I've been hunting these people for almost two years now. Whatever you just did to that... that thing, the Brethren are going to know you did it." He scanned the house, assessing it and the situation all at the same time. "We can't stay here."

He drew back the lace curtain covering the little window at the top of the door and looked out into the front yard.

"But what about Mortie? I can't leave without–"

"*Shit,*" he breathed.

It was too late. Somehow, I knew that without looking out the window. In fact, I could hear them even from inside the house. It started out as a hum, low and unified, identical to the hum I'd heard coming from the book and the jewel. Then it became chanting. I didn't recognize the words, but I felt them, almost like their voices were pounding against the walls. I looked over Scott's shoulder and out the small window.

The house was surrounded. Somehow, in the short time I administered the green pill to Scott, they'd come. Men in ragged cloaks circled Mortie's house, torches burning in their hands.

He tapped his left wrist three times, but nothing happened. Whatever I'd done to him must've drained the shield's power to make it not work. How was that possible? He tried again but there was nothing.

"Listen to me–" he said but I didn't give him a chance to finish that sentence.

"We have to get out of here," I said to myself. The urge to freak out was building up like a pressure cooker in me, causing the breath to catch in my throat. We were cornered and it was all my fault. I didn't know how, but I'd drawn them here. There was nowhere to run, and I'd seen firsthand what these lunatics were capable of.

"Louise, listen," Scott said calmly. "There will be a break in their circle. When you see it, I want you to run. Run as fast as you can. Don't go to the store, don't go to the cemetery.

Stay away from any place you've been in the last year, do you understand? I don't know how long they've been watching you, but they'll piece together your life quick enough if they haven't already. You've run before; you can do it again."

"What about you? What are you going to do?"

He put his hand on my neck, steady and calm against my racing pulse. His thumb brushed against my jawline as he looked into my eyes. "Just run, okay?"

He kissed me, quick and hard, and then flung Mortie's front door open.

He was going to die.

Knowing this was like staring into the ribbon behind Mrs Renwick and Alice and feeling the finality inside it. He might take out maybe four or five of them but there were too many. I'd already lost Mortie to them, I'd be damned if I was about to give up Scott, too.

"No!" I screamed and grabbed onto him.

Mortie's house was gone. The yard full of Brethren was gone. There was just him in my arms as we were yanked through oblivion.

CHAPTER 20

We landed hard in Magnolia Grove Cemetery. The night air was cold, and the grass beneath us was already slick with dew. Scott groaned and rolled onto his stomach, grabbing fistfuls of wet grass to anchor himself.

"Take a deep breath," I said, holding onto him. "It takes a second to get used to." My voice was shaking. All this time I thought it was only Mrs Hammond that could do the yanking, or transporting, or whatever, but no. Somehow, I managed to do it too.

Scott rolled onto his back. "Holy shit!" he shouted, his eyes going wide as a blue halo fell across the tombstones. He reached for his knife, throwing it right into the glowing aura of Mrs Hammond's chest as she floated up to us. It went straight through, landing somewhere in the shadows behind her.

"He's a rather rude boy." Mrs Hammond hovered there in a huff with her hands on her hips.

"She – she talks!" he shouted, reaching for another knife.

"You can see her?" I saw our linked hands and pulled away my touch. His eyes darted around as if I'd switched off the nightlight lighting Mrs H up. I put my hand back on him and he scrambled back, trying to pull me behind him.

"How very rude," Mrs H said, scrunching up her nose in distaste.

He gaped at her, his arms around me, frozen in the process of trying to shield me. He looked down at our linked limbs making the same connection I had, and then back at Mrs H, unsure of the reality in front of him.

"I... I'm gonna need a minute," he said and took his hand off my arm, extinguishing Mrs H, at least from his vision. She still floated there for me, looking him up and down.

"Despite being rude, he is very handsome," Mrs H said, smoothing her dress and fluffing up her hair.

I scanned the cemetery for any sign of Tom-Tom, but from what I could tell it was just Mrs H.

Scott sat on the ground, his elbows propped up on bent knees, his head ducked down between them.

I could only imagine what he was thinking. He'd just narrowly escaped death by being ripped out of one spot in the city and dumped in another in the blink of an eye only to come face to face with a full-blown apparition. Given the circumstances, he was handling it surprisingly well, definitely better than I would be.

He stood up, took a deep, steadying breath and another, then rolled his shoulders.

"Okay," he said, raising a determined face in the general vicinity of Mrs H. "Let's try that again."

He took my hand in his and stared up at Mrs Hammond. He blinked and blinked again.

"This is Mrs Hammond," I said by way of introduction. He took her in, scanning her from her bouffant hair and string of pearls to the black strappy pumps covering her feet as they hovered in the air.

"Uh... sorry about all the –" he motioned throwing an imaginary knife, "Ma'am," he said to Mrs Hammond, which of course was exactly the kind of response she loved to hear.

With a flutter of her eyelashes, I knew she instantly forgave him about the knives. I rolled my eyes at how easily she folded under a display of basic proper manners.

"How long have you been able to... to see and talk to them?" Scott asked me, still staring wide-eyed at Mrs H.

His question wasn't all that different from the one I asked Ivan that night at the funeral home. My answer was the same he'd given me.

"All my life."

He tore his eyes away from Mrs H to look at me. The part of me that perpetually felt like a freak wanted to shirk away from this moment of reckoning, but there was no point. We were beyond that now. This was who I was, and I couldn't hide that from him any longer. I lifted my chin and faced him, ready for the worst.

"No wonder," he whispered.

"No wonder what?" I repeated. No wonder I was creepy? No wonder a cult of necromancers was after me? No wonder everything about me was a nightmare?

"No wonder you're as strong as you are," he said, taking me off guard.

Was this real? Was this happening? It was. There he stood, staring at me in open, earnest admiration. Somehow, in some un-freaking-believable way, I'd been accepted, embraced for what I truly was by a man I could easily see myself falling in love with.

Mrs Hammond politely cleared her throat, snapping me out of my daze.

The moment should've been perfect, and it very nearly was, until I felt something linger just there at the edges of my happiness – something I couldn't put my finger on but that had been nagging me since I dropped into the cemetery with Scott.

It'd been a while since I'd been here with Mrs H. Add to that the two days I didn't know I'd lost inside the Veil, according to Scott. The peace I usually felt in Magnolia Grove Cemetery wasn't there. In its place was a cold, eerie emptiness that hung over the graves and seemed to lengthen the shadows of the tombstones. Something had disturbed the cemetery in my absence. Sure, a few days ago a cult had literally ripped the place apart, causing chaos and havoc, but that wasn't it. Even Mrs H seemed a bit ruffled and on edge as her fingers flitted reassuringly for her pearls.

"Something's wrong here," I said.

"What do you mean?" Scott asked, instantly on the alert again.

"I'm not sure yet." I took his hand, wrapping my fingers around his, and started scouting the cemetery's perimeter. He stayed beside me, his eyes flicking back to Mrs H every now and then as she floated along beside us.

From the old oak tree to the arching iron front gate, everything looked exactly like I left it, minus the freshly dug graves the Brethren disturbed days ago. But even they had been tended, the rightful owners of their caskets resting back inside them with fresh mounds of dirt piled on top. Someone had even placed pretty purple and pink petunias at the base of each tombstone, likely the Women's Prayer Circle from the Lutheran church. They planted flowers on the graves twice a year and must've done an extra visit after all the news crews and police officers traipsed through the place.

It didn't make sense. Everybody was accounted for and tucked in where they should be... everybody, plus one.

She wasn't buried in the earth like all the others. It was her high heel I saw first, a red stiletto with a thin heel that must've sunk through the ground when she walked between the tombstones. I saw her leg next, the rest of her body obscured by one of the few above-ground crypts in the cemetery, an old one, nothing more than rectangular moss-covered slabs that were somehow still standing.

I knew who she was before I reached her. If someone asked me what her name was days ago when she talked to me after interviewing the police chief, I wouldn't have been able to remember. But now, I could see it, like I saw the names on Mortie's tracing paper he always brought me to try to figure out for him.

Sharon Flaherty. It was a strange enough last name to go by as a news reporter, though, and didn't roll off the tongue as well as Sharon Galloway.

Bits of her life came to me but in a disjointed way, like I'd stumbled upon broken glass shards of memories. I latched onto one of them to try to make sense of it.

Sharon liked using her mother's maiden name onscreen. She hadn't known her mother much at all, only having a few precious childhood memories to cling to. Using her last name made Sharon feel closer to her, after having lost her to a car accident when she was six.

Scott checked for a pulse, but I already knew. Sharon was dead.

"Her heart gave out," I said quietly, and placed my warm hand on her cold one as if I could give her the comfort she'd needed when she lay dying alone.

"How can you tell?" he asked, checking for injuries while trying not to disturb the body.

I couldn't explain how. It was just something I knew.

Once more, I felt the wrongness of it all.

"Something's missing," I said, staring perplexed down at her unmoving form. It didn't make any sense. It should've been just like it was with all the other corpses in Magnolia Grove Cemetery that had passed on but were buried deep beneath the ground; I should've been able to see more about her life than that fractured glimpse.

I realized then exactly what was wrong.

Sharon hadn't gone on to whatever waited for her – whatever it was that awaited each and every one of us after this life. And nor was her ghost here either.

"What happened?" I asked Mrs Hammond. Scott's hand touched my forearm, and he turned to face her, waiting to hear the answer for himself.

I expected her to twist her hankie nervously or clutch the pearls at her neck like she always did. She did neither. Instead, she floated near the crypt to descend next to Sharon's lifeless form. In a surprising gesture, her fingers brushed over the strands of hair that had fallen in front of Sharon's unseeing eyes. Her touch passed through the locks of auburn hair in a motherly motion.

"He took it… her soul," Mrs H said quietly. "He devours them."

"Who does?" Scott asked. His voice came out calm and steady and in control of the situation – an impossible situation involving a dead reporter and the only witness to her death, a ghost. I wish I was as calm. Instead, fury ripped through me, threatening to overtake me. I knew what had done this and didn't need to hear the answer, didn't expect one either considering ghosts were notorious for not being informative. Mrs Hammond surprised me once again, though, by answering him.

"The Lich." She raised a defiant chin to the night around us, daring it to attack her as she said it.

So, the inky creature had a name. I didn't know exactly who or what a Lich was, but hearing it spoken out loud, hearing it classified as something, gave it boundaries. A Lich was a tangible thing. Not a figment of my imagination. No longer a mere nightmare. And now I knew what fueled it.

I shook with terror. The Lich had been inside Mortie's home; I'd seen it crawling over his possessions, invading his workspace. What had it done to my friend? Had it devoured his soul like it had Sharon's? Would I stumble across shattered memories of his somewhere? The image of it sucking the life out of him as it must have Sharon until her heart gave out was too much to bear. How many others would come next? And how many had come before? The horror turned into a white-hot flash of anger, my vision blurring at the edges.

"Louise?" Scott's worried voice found its way through my boiling fury.

I looked toward the police station, instinct telling me that all the answers to my unspoken questions lay there, despite the dread that pooled in my stomach at the thought of walking there. "I think I know where her soul is." At least what was left of it.

Mrs Hammond stayed hovering protectively over Sharon's body. I left the cemetery, walking down the sidewalk toward the station, not even feeling my feet as they hit the pavement. My mind overflowed with anger and sadness at what I knew I would find. Scott was behind me, saying something.

"Louise, did you hear me? We can't be here," he said, his eyes scanning the currently empty police station parking lot. "What happened in New Bethlehem was probably enough to blow my cover. If the police see me now, there's a damn good chance they'll know I'm not who I say I am. Let me try to get you out of here, maybe hide you till I can figure something out. Louise?"

He reached for me. My back was to him, but I could still feel it – feel him, like a heartbeat – alive and warm behind me, his hand about to touch my shoulder.

"Don't touch me," I ordered. "Please," I quickly added in a softer voice and turned around to face him.

He held his hands up and took a step back. "Okay, I won't."

"Can you trust me?" I repeated the question he'd asked me outside of Mortie's. "Just a little?"

"Yes," he said readily, and it warmed my heart how fast he said it.

"Then whatever you do, don't touch me and don't follow me. There are some things you aren't supposed to see." *That you can't handle seeing, that the living aren't meant to see, that will hurt and terrify you till they take root deep in your heart and never leave.*

"Okay," he said. "I won't. I promise."

It wasn't long ago that I was standing on this same sidewalk watching him come out of the police station after his shift, our eyes meeting across the way. And now here we were, what felt like a lifetime later. No longer a cop, no longer just a grocery store stock girl. I didn't know what we were or what we were to each other, but he was still here. I hadn't scared him off yet.

That calculating look of his scanned the area around us until it landed on a patrol car parked outside the station. "Listen, I think I know a way I can get us out of here. If I do it though, there's no going back," he warned. "My cover will definitely be blown, but at least it'll give us a chance."

"Do what you have to do," I told him, because I was about to do the same.

He raised his wrist and tapped the inside of it. There was that same disappearing shimmer and then nothing as he went invisible again. Whatever battery that powered his shield, that I'd sucked dry earlier, seemed to be restored enough for him to do his trick.

"I won't leave you here alone. I promise. I'm not going anywhere." His words came to me from a seemingly empty sidewalk. I hung onto them, replaying them in my head as I turned my back to where he'd been. He wasn't just talking about leaving me alone outside the police station. I'd felt those eyes from that invisible wall staring at me as he'd said those words. He meant he wasn't going to leave *me*. Somehow, he guessed my worst, unspoken, fear and had given me a moment, something hopeful, to latch onto as I went to face the horror in front of me.

The horde of wisps swirled around the outside of the police station, crowding up against it like they always did. Their numbers were greater than I remembered, their pained howls somehow louder.

Stepping through their masses was like enveloping myself in their misery. Wave after wave of sorrow crashed against me, ripping apart every shred of happiness in my soul. I wanted to run away and hide forever, to cover my ears and never hear their sorrowful wails again, but I had to know, I had to see for myself the evil that had been done.

The swarm parted and there she was. She looked just like the rest, all of them identical with their shattered, fragmented auras, their blurry unrecognizable faces and sunken eye sockets. Still, somehow, I knew it was her.

"Oh, Sharon," I cried. Angry tears ran down my cheeks. "I'm sorry. I'm so sorry."

Her hand passed through mine. *He'll take more of us, Lou*, her voice whispered inside my head. And I cried harder thinking of Mortie somewhere, floating like this, his soul fractured beyond repair.

Let us rest, she begged. *Help us rest.*

Then they all begged, repeating those same words over and over. *Let us rest, help us rest.* Their desperation ate at me, turning my insides hollow at their loss, at what had been robbed from each and every one of them.

There was only one way I could think of to try and help them. I'd only ever used it on the living though – just twice so far; once with Vick at my kitchen table and again with Scott inside Mortie's house – and who knew if using it would even help the wisps or make things worse? Still, it was all I could think to try.

I held out my hand palm up and waited for that flickering blue energy to dance across my fingertips.

Nothing happened.

I clenched my fingers into a fist and relaxed them open, unsure of how to get that weird new freak power of mine to flare up and work. Every time before, I'd done it out desperation and survival.

The wisps' sunken eyes all turned to me, their heads tilting curiously at my effort.

I focused on them. After all, this wasn't about me. This was for them. Blue energy flickered at the very ends of my fingertips. I kept my thoughts on the wisps. There were too many of them though and every ounce of my breath seemed to get swallowed up by them – threatening to overwhelm me like a tidal wave of horror.

I closed them all off and centered my focus solely on Sharon.

Blue light poured out of my hand as if it had its own ghostly aura.

Sharon's wisp flickered like a flashing image on a TV screen to the real-life woman she'd been. I could hear her laughter over mango margaritas at the Mexican restaurant she went to with work friends after her shift at the news station. I could feel her insatiable need as a reporter to track down a lead in a story, and the rush she got when a source confirmed something she suspected all along.

The blue aura wrapped around my hand crackled and popped with electricity as I dug deeper trying to piece together the rest of her. I searched for every part of her – from her hopes and dreams to the love she always wanted to find but never felt like she deserved. The echoes of her were there but somehow the fullness of her eluded me. In its absence, other things began to fill in the gaps. Horror, anguish, pain flooded in and once again, it felt like the tidal wave was back and slamming into me.

I staggered a step back. The blue aura on my hand died out and darkness crept back in.

I stood amongst the wisps momentarily feeling as if I was one of them, floating there shattered, lost and broken. I couldn't take another second of it and walked back up to the sidewalk, fresh tears pouring down the streaks of already drying tears that caked my cheeks, chapping my skin.

A police cruiser pulled over next to me on the side of the street. Scott pushed open the passenger door from inside. I got in and he drove a short distance down the street before pulling into the 7-Eleven and parking by the air pump.

It was only my second time being in a cruiser, the first I'd been fighting for my life, this time, it felt like my life had been partially drained away by the wisps. The only difference between this one and Scott's was the exposed wires hanging out from the removed ignition cover.

"Are you okay?" he asked.

I wiped at the tears and managed to nod.

"Can I touch you now?"

I nodded again.

He reached across the gear shift. Hands came up to my cheeks, wiping away the tears. He pulled me to him, and I pressed my cheek against his chest.

"I wish there was something I could do to help," he murmured against my hair.

There was comfort in his arms along with the warmth and vitality of life I'd been deprived of among the wisps, and it felt a little bit like the sun shining down on me, but it still wasn't enough to heal the hurt in my heart. Mortie was missing and it seemed a part of my soul fractured like a wisp's at the thought of him lost out there somewhere.

"What do we do now?" I asked aloud the question that kept playing on repeat in my head.

"We run." He said it in a calculated tone I'd come to recognize. There was a resolved look in his eyes that said he took in all options for survival and came to only one outcome. I wondered what forged him into a man that could do something like that? What was he that he could detach from the chaos around us and compartmentalize everything down into a simple decision of living and dying?

"We find your friend, Mortie," he added, taking in my moment of my hesitation, "and we run. None of this matters." He motioned to Magnolia Grove around us. "You can start again anywhere." *With me*, his eyes so very clearly finished the rest of that sentence.

Whoa. My heart lurched at the idea. My mind raced with what that might even be like. I won't lie, it was tempting. Sixteen-year-old me would've leaped at the chance to run away from all her problems, not to mention having a guy like him running alongside her, making her feel safe. That would've been a fantasy I'd happily jumped at the chance for. But now?

I placed my hand on his arm. "That's not something I can do."

As much as I was afraid to admit it to myself, I had a purpose here. More than that, Mortie and I forged a life here. This was our home. And someone was threatening that home. I hated thinking of Sharon up there all alone in my cemetery with only Mrs Hammond to watch over her, and the wisps surrounding the station who'd been damned to their fate by that thing the Lich.

"I thought you might say that." He looked out across the empty 7-Eleven parking lot and ran a frustrated hand through his hair. "Alright, what do we do?" He asked me and I had no idea how to answer.

The calculating look came over his features again as he reassessed. "This is a stolen cop car," he said to himself. "My cover at the station is likely burned. And now the Brethren have had a taste of what you can do." That assessing look took me in as a factor and only then did it soften. "I'm not gonna lie, Louise. It feels like the shit is really hitting the fan here."

That was an understatement. His words played out again in my head, tugging at a forgotten memory. An image of Vick leaning seductively over Cliff's desk to place a wet kiss on his forehead came to mind.

"The shit is hitting the fan!" I said with a jump that startled him. I dug eagerly into the pocket of my jean skirt.

There it was, the piece of sticky paper I'd crumpled after Cliff had given it to me. Vick's note. An address was scrawled beneath the exact same words Scott just said.

"I know where to go," I said and handed him the note. "Can you take me here?"

CHAPTER 21

I wasn't sure exactly where the address was that Vick scribbled down but it took us to a side of town I rarely ventured.

Magnolia Grove was a rather small town, considerably dwarfed in size when compared to bigger cities in Indiana, like Fort Wayne or Bloomington. Still, even after a few years of living here, I really only knew my neck of the woods, which encompassed my house, the library, the Piggly Wiggly, and, of course, the three cemeteries within the city limits. Wherever the address was located, it had us riding past the liquor store and the pawn shop. Bars covered the windows in almost every building that blurred by, and graffiti covered rundown, abandoned storefronts.

Scott pulled the cruiser into the crowded parking lot of a squat, unassuming building. Its few windows were blacked out. There weren't any streetlamps, not that the parking lot needed it. A giant neon sign, the bulbs forming the silhouette of a naked woman and the words *Candied Tips* lit up the area like an airport runway. A ways off, in a plot of undeveloped land behind the building, stood a bright pink trailer with a matching pink flamingo out front.

Scott looked doubtfully at the strip club, the trailer, then down at the address scribbled on the crinkled paper. "You sure about this?"

The strip club's side door opened next to a dumpster. Blaring music and flashing lights poured out as Vick stepped outside in a fake fur coat and leopard print skirt that hugged the top of her thighs. She lit a cigarette and leaned against the outside wall.

"Vick!" I shouted and ran across the parking lot to her.

She took a long drag of her cigarette and breathed out a perfect ring of smoke. "What took you so long?" she asked, taking another puff.

"Vick, please, I–"

She ignored me and glared at Scott. "Hello, liar. Finally found out about you, did she? I'm surprised you're still around," she seethed. "Then again, women like her and me have always been suckers for the likes of you."

"At least she doesn't come away with scrapes and bruises every time she's been with me," he said to her accusingly. I bristled at the cold tone in his voice that was identical to how he had talked to me over the file with my missing person's report.

I looked from one to the other and wanted to scream in frustration. "Guys, come on," I managed instead.

She looked like she was about to rip him apart when the door behind her opened again. Music and lights poured out of the open doorway along with the smell of alcohol and cheap perfume. A very wide, very tall man with hair buzzed in a short crew cut ducked his head out the door. He looked Scott up and down through narrowing eyes.

"This guy giving you trouble, V?" he said, cracking his giant knuckles. Scott didn't pay any attention to him and kept scanning the traffic and the parking lot.

"Nothing I can't handle," she said, purposely blowing a puff of smoke toward Scott. The man bobbed his head, gave one more threatening glance at Scott then disappeared back inside.

She nodded toward the unmarked police cruiser in the parking lot. "I see you're still playing pretend cop."

"I stole it," he told her, his eyes watching the cars speeding down the highway.

"You don't say?" Her lips turned up in a wolfish smile. "Finally decided to show Lou your naughty side, did you?"

"Vick, listen," I insisted. "I need you. Mortie is–"

"No." She interrupted me with a shake of her head. "You *needed* me." She emphasized the word with a jab of her cigarette in my direction before putting it out on the cement with the toe of her stiletto.

I stared at her dumbfounded. "What do you mean?"

She nodded toward the pink trailer. I didn't wait for an explanation and took off at a run toward it.

"Here! You'll need these," she shouted, tossing me the keys. I fumbled with them, picking out the one with the pink butterfly sticker on it, and unlocked the front door.

I flung it open and nearly fainted in relief.

Sitting in an old recliner, a quilt draped over his legs with Zelda curled up on his lap, was Mortie. The TV tray next to him held an empty plastic microwave dinner container and a sleeve of store-bought cookies. He looked tired and somehow older than when I last saw him. Did the tufts of his hair seem whiter, the creases at the corners of his eyes deeper, or was that my imagination?

"You're here!" I ran across the room and threw my arms around him.

"There now, Lewis," he said, patting my wet cheeks. "What's all this?"

"Oh God, Mortie, this is all my fault. I should never–"

He rubbed my shoulders and brushed the hair away from my tear-stained face. "Hush now. I'm fine, can't you tell?"

Zelda jumped from his lap, tired of being squished between us. She gave me an affectionate headbutt hello against my leg and then made herself at home, perching on the nearby countertop.

"What about you, how are you, hmm?" He took my hands and cupped them in his palms. His eyes turned white. The ambush in New Bethlehem, the infected scar on my leg, Scott confronting me with a folder full of my past, being sucked inside the Veil... everything I'd felt in the past few days bubbled up to the surface.

"Quite a bit I see," he said quietly, the words coming out a little choked. "But you're okay. And I'm okay, right? We're made of tougher stuff than people think. Though I can say we've never had a week quite like this one before, have we?"

"You can say that again," Vick said, walking into the trailer.

"Lucky for us," Mortie went on. "Firecracker here always seems to show up right when we need her. When she knocked on my front door with a cat carrier in tow and told me Zelda and I needed to pack up and go, I knew we were about to weather quite the storm."

Vick's eyes softened at Mortie, and a genuine smile crossed her face.

I got up and hugged her. "Thank you."

She smelled like cigarette smoke and the cheap perfume from the strip club. Bits of glitter on her outfit transferred to my shirt. She was taken aback by the sudden physical contact and awkwardly patted me on the shoulder in return.

"Don't be too grateful, kid, you still owe me."

"Where's Scott?" I asked, looking behind her at the closed door.

Her genuine smile transformed into a snarl. "He said something about checking the perimeter or whatever. I told him we're safe here, but I don't think he trusts me, which is odd, since out of the two of us I'm the only one that's not a liar."

"Maybe I shouldn't have come," I said more to myself than her. Yes, I'd found Mortie but now I was potentially putting them both in danger by being here. Vick followed my train of thought.

"As long as Mortie stays here, he's safe," she said. "I promise."

It didn't escape my notice that she'd left the rest of us out of that statement. I believed her though, how could I not after everything? And now that Mortie was safely tucked into her trailer out of harm's way I felt secure enough to lend a little brain power to finally think about what needed to be done, answers I needed to find. And that first step started right here with Mortie.

"Do you have a laptop I can use?" I asked Vick.

"Sure, just give me a second to find it." She pulled Zelda into her arms and looked under the pile of stuff on the counter she'd been sleeping on.

I could always count on getting a friendly nudge or rub against my leg from the cat but with Vick, much like the way she was with Mortie, Zelda was smitten, and I had to admit it made me a tad jealous. Zelda went limp like a baby in Vick's arms, purring loud enough to be heard across the room as Vick absently scratched behind her ear while she searched for the laptop.

I wasn't sure what I'd been expecting from Vick's home exactly, but it definitely wasn't this. The trailer was basically one long tube that looked like a teenage girl's room exploded in a cloud of pink. Perfume bottles, makeup containers, and cans of hairspray crowded the few flat surfaces available. Despite that, she didn't keep a sloppy home. There was no trash or messy dishes piled up. It was more like whoever lived here was constantly running late. She had a nice flat screen TV in front of the one recliner where Mortie sat. In the kitchen, for a dining room table, she used a plastic white patio set. A stack of outfits still on their hangers draped the back of one of the chairs, on the other were crammed a mix of platform shoes and stilettos.

"Aha!" she said, lifting a stack of magazines off the table to hand me a small bubblegum-colored laptop covered in anime stickers. Again, not what I expected. I brought up the internet browser and handed it to Mortie.

"Mortie, can you access your cemetery database without your home computer?"

"Why certainly." He perked up; his fingers flew over the keyboard. He was always better at this kind of thing than me. He actually seemed to enjoy it and even had a laptop at home that was nicer than Vick's. "What are you looking for?"

"A grave in New Bethlehem Cemetery. Last name Osgood. Alice Osgood."

Vick's fingers froze mid scratch on Zelda's ear.

He turned the laptop back around when he found it and I stared at the screen. There she was. Next to her name was a picture of her gravesite. The last time I'd seen it, the tombstone had been riddled with bullets but in the picture, it was brand new and intact. More than that, the day the picture had been taken, her body was right where it was supposed to be, resting in the ground beneath it.

Alice Loreen Osgood, beloved wife.

1939–1973

Whoever filled out her information in the database had been diligent, linking to her family tree on a genealogy website, and even posting her obituary from when it ran in the newspaper. I didn't need any of that though. With her body buried under it, the picture of the tombstone itself was enough.

Before she married, Alice worked as a librarian in a small town in Nebraska. She enjoyed doing storytime with the elementary school kids during her summers there, even making felted puppets to go along with the books she read to them. Alice died of a heart defect at thirty-four. And she loved her husband so much it was staggering.

Mortie leaned over my shoulder and looked at the name etched to the right of hers, an empty slot for the date of death yet to happen.

Ivan Oliver Osgood

1934–

"Why, he's older than I am!" Mortie proclaimed, adjusting his glasses to make sure he'd read that right. "How is that possible?"

"That lying son of a bitch!" Vick growled.

I sat back and wanted to cry. Alice's love for Ivan was intense. Intense enough that it shot out of the laptop screen to pierce its way right into my heart. I thought I'd seen what their love was like during my time inside the Veil but that was nothing – just a glimpse – a mere fraction of what was between them. The last twenty-four hours had taken a toll on me emotionally, especially after my time among the wisps with Sharon. I was exhausted. My soul felt more chapped than my cheeks did, which still held dried flakes of previously fallen tears. How many tears did a person have before they were turned into nothing but an empty, hollow shell deprived of all feelings? How many heartaches and tragedies would I be forced to witness before it turned me bitter and cold? I thought of Ivan alone in his funeral home. Is that what broke him? Would it break me too?

The trailer door opened, and Scott came in. "We're really exposed here. If we stay any longer–" His eyes met mine. "What is it? What happened?" he said, rushing to my side.

"Oh, please." Vick rolled her eyes. "Calm yourself, Prince Charming, she's fine."

Mortie quirked his head curiously at Scott, scrutinizing him behind the thick glasses, and then touched my hand, his eyes turning milky white. He looked back at Alice's tombstone on the computer screen.

Tears pooled in his eyes as he felt what I'd felt – all the love they shared, the flashes of memory clinging to her tombstone, the loss that must be Ivan's as their love story ended tragically too soon.

"It's a choice," Mortie said, answering my unspoken questions. "You can let their stories drain you, eventually changing you into something hardened and numb. Or you can embrace them, giving yourself the allowance to feel all their sorrow, all their pain. You let it pass through you, accepting it. On the other side of acceptance comes compassion and understanding. And then you simply press on and keep living. But always, it starts as a choice."

"Understanding?   Compassion?"   Vick   raged, misunderstanding the moment between us. "That son of a bitch lied! He even figured out a way to lie to *me* of all people." She put a hand to her chest, dismayed. "He never said he had a wife and that she was dead. I actually believed his sob story bullshit, that shy guy 'pity me, I'm misunderstood and have to deal with ghosts' demeanor. All the while this is obviously some bullshit attempt to have those Brethren fuckers bring her back. I should've burned his damn book!" she railed.

Which led me to the second thing that needed addressing.

"Where is the book?" I'd noted its absence the second I stepped into the trailer.

"What book?" Scott asked, uneasy.

"Old ass book that raises the dead and has a cult of fanboys after it. Come on, Batman, keep up," she snapped at him.

"Where is it?" I pushed back, determined.

"Relax, kid. I took it somewhere safe but now I'm thinking I should've ripped it apart in front of Osgood's creepy old face."

Mortie cleared his throat, breaking through the back and forth.

"I don't believe we've met," he said, extending a hand to Scott. "I'm Mortimer, an old friend of Louise's."

"I'm Scott," he said, introducing himself as took the offered hand. "Glad to find you safe, sir."

Vick clamped her mouth shut, watching the two shake hands. If anyone knew the power in a single touch, it was her. I waited for Mortie to do his thing, for his eyes to change, but they didn't.

"Back to the book," she said, annoyed that Mortie beamed approvingly at Scott and that even Zelda came up to sniff his shoe, extending her chin contentedly as he reached down to pet her. "Whatever that damned thing is, it sure works as an excellent GPS. The Brethren were at Mortie's house and on my trail minutes after I'd taken him. I didn't shake 'em until I dropped it where it's at right now."

A car backfired outside in the strip club parking lot making us jump. It was nothing, just a chorus of men who had poured out of the strip club and laughed around an old mustang.

Scott peeked outside the front door, his hand going to the sheath I knew held a hidden knife. "I better check things out."

"I told you, we're safe for now," Vick said.

He ignored her and turned to me, his hand briefly touching my elbow. "We really shouldn't stay much longer."

I nodded. He was right. Any longer and I'd be putting Mortie in even more danger.

"I need that book, Vick," I said when the door shut behind him. There was no denying it was the next piece of the puzzle. Lord knows I didn't want anything to do with it, didn't even know what to do with it for that matter, but there was a reason Ivan insisted I have it and I was worried I might know now what that reason was.

Vick crossed her arms and shook her head. "The time isn't right yet."

I wasn't sure what she meant by that, but there was a ring of prophecy in her voice that I'd heard once before back at my kitchen table. What future had she seen where it *was* the right time and what would happen between now and then?

"In the meantime, we have this." Mortie took out a rolled-up old paper from his front shirt pocket. It looked different from the others I'd seen attached to the book, but I recognized where it came from all the same. The textured surface no longer looked like paper, but eerily similar to skin, a thin leaf of skin with a sickly gray pallor. The edge where it had been connected to the book's binding looked like torn flesh, ragged and uneven.

"You ripped a page from a book?" I asked Mortie. Even the words felt blasphemous on my tongue.

"More like the book shed it," he said, and held it out to me.

There was no pulse of life like before, no energy in the paper fibers woven with the flesh. It was dead, if a page could be called that. The letters or runes that made themselves visible when Mortie read from the book before weren't there, instead this page had silver inked chicken scratches engraved in it that looked like a dozen cuts.

"What's it say?"

"I have no idea. I don't think I'm the one that's meant to read it this time."

I gripped the page in my hand and said aloud what I was beginning to fear was true. "Ivan wants to bring Alice back from the dead and thinks he needs the book to do it."

And me.

I didn't say that out loud, didn't need to. Mortie and Vick knew it, I could tell by their silence that's what they were thinking. I didn't know how Ivan had found the Brethren. I didn't know how they got hold of their stupid jewel or how the Lich figured into any of it, but I knew it was him that had given them the spell they used to experiment on the dead in Magnolia Grove until he was ready to try it on Alice.

I held the page, feeling like I'd been betrayed. "Ivan's like me. He can see ghosts. He has to know what he wants is impossible. How could he desecrate the final resting places of so many?"

"By cozying up to a bunch of asshole cult fanboys who fancy themselves necromancers, that's how," Vick said, angrily.

Mortie looked back and forth between us. "Neither of you understand yet, do you?" he said in a quiet voice. "A love like Ivan and Alice's, that's once in a lifetime – if you're lucky. Do you know how far someone would go to get it back?" He touched the pocket where he kept his pocket watch. "I've had that kind of love before."

Mortie never ever asked me about Peter, whether or not I'd ever seen him. I believed there was a mutual unspoken understanding between us. He never had to ask me if Peter lingered in this world because he must've known I would have told him.

But perhaps I should've told him before. Maybe me not saying anything had left the possibility out there.

"He's not here, Mortie," I whispered, praying my words didn't hurt him. "Neither is Alice."

"I know that," he said partly to himself, absorbing the reality of it. "Really, I do. But if I truly believed I had a chance of bringing Peter back..." His voice became distant as he thought it over. "I'm not sure just how far I would go."

His words hung heavy in the trailer.

Vick threw up her hands unexpectedly and marched to the front door, pulling it open. "Yes, yes, we're coming! Don't get your panties in a wad."

Scott stood on the step outside, his hand raised to turn the doorknob.

"Do yourself a favor," she told him before he could say anything. "And go give the keys to that stolen police cruiser to Mikey inside the club, the big guy you just met. He'll get rid of it before it attracts any heat. Tell him it's a gift from V." She held up a hand to stop the protest on his lips. "I know you'd only ever do anything I said if hell froze over, but deep down you know it'll help keep her safe. Try and argue with that one, Batman," she said and slammed the door back in his brooding face.

She grinned. "God, that felt good. Now I'm going to change out of my work clothes and then we're going to go figure out what it'll take to stop Ivan from stupidly opening the gates of hell in an attempt to bring his dead wife back, okay?"

I gaped at her as she strode to the bedroom at the end of the trailer.

"I told you, that one's a firecracker," Mortie said, chuckling.

I sank down on the fuzzy pink footstool next to the recliner. For a moment, it was just the two of us and it felt like we were back in the alley between our houses, the wind chimes clinking and twirling over our heads. I wanted more than anything to be back there with him now, to eat cookies and talk about nothing except whatever was going on with Amy and Diego and when microwave dinners might go on sale again.

"I'm sorry, Mortie. I should've told you before that Peter–"

He put his fingers to my lips to silence me. "Hush now, sweetheart, you did. In your own way. You're a lot like him, you know. Peter Lewis McCullen," he said the name with a quiver in his chin. "A glass face, the both of you. I almost never need to use my gift on you. It was the same with him. Everything you feel is right there in those big slate-colored eyes."

He took out his pocket watch and opened it.

I'd seen the picture once before. It was of an incredibly handsome young man in black and white, his suit and tie a dark shade of gray. He had thick eyebrows, a curl at the front of his jet-black hair, and a smile that was crooked in the corner. Peter started out teaching mathematics at a college in Illinois before moving to Indiana and meeting Mortimer Thornbush while touring the museum. He loved listening to live jazz music and having English Breakfast tea in the mornings with a croissant smeared with plum jam. And with Mortie, for the first and only time in his life, Peter found a home he never dared let himself even imagine he could have.

"I knew he was truly gone by the sorrow in your eyes the first time you saw this picture," Mortie said, watching me. "It's a strange sorrow, laced with love, almost like you can feel a tiny fraction of the love we shared, mirrored right there in your face when you looked down at him just as you do now. I never asked you if he was here, because I knew without a doubt, in that moment, he wasn't."

Mortie reverently closed the pocket watch and returned it to its rightful place in the front pocket of his shirt, next to his heart. I wanted to tell him I knew that Peter loved him more than anything. That before he met Mortie, Peter believed he'd never find real love, and that he was scared of dying and never having someone see the real him. I wanted to tell Mortie all of that and more, because I knew, somewhere on the other side of the Veil, Peter wanted me to, but when I looked up into Mortie's eyes I realized I didn't have to. Mortie already knew.

He swallowed back tears and nodded as if reading along with my thoughts. He wrapped his arms around me and hugged me in a surprisingly tight grip.

"Why didn't you look into Scott?" I asked against his shirt.

"Aren't you listening?" he scoffed. "There's no need to use my gift when I can see what's right there in front of me, Lewis." He reached across his lap to put a finger under my chin. "I believe that boy might be falling in love with you, but I think you probably already know that, hmm?"

Could that be true?

"Lewis," Mortie went on, his bushy eyebrows drawn together in worry. "Be careful when it comes to Mr Osgood. I know you see a part of yourself in him, but don't let it distract you from his intentions. Love is powerful. People think that because love feels right and true, it must also be good. It isn't always. It can blind you, make you do things you'd never thought you would before. There's a good chance he only sees the end he wants and not what it will cost to get there."

Vick breezed back into the room wearing an oversized plaid shirt, a crop top, tennis shoes and jeans. With her hair swept up in a loose bun she looked like a trendy soccer mom and not a psychic stripper.

"Alright, let's get out of here." She planted a kiss goodbye on Mortie's head, wiped the lipstick off with her thumb and hooked her elbow through mine, pulling me toward the door.

"Wait, where are we going?" I said, hurrying to catch up. "We can't just run off. We need a plan."

"A plan is exactly what I have." She spun her car keys around her finger. "Which brings me back to you owing me."

CHAPTER 22

The neon signs in the windows were off, but I could still make out the letters in the dark. *Madam Minerva's Psychic Realm*. Smaller signs underneath that read *Tarot Cards* and *Palm & Tea Leaf Readings*. Above the front door a crystal ball was still lit up, blinking different colors inside the ball.

I shrank back and bumped into Scott walking behind me.

"What is it?" he asked, eyes darting around to look for a threat.

"Oh, come off it, kid." Vick grabbed me by the arm and hauled me onward. "She's not even a real psychic. She's a witch. And just a reminder, *I'm* a real psychic and I haven't forced you to do jack shit."

"Except this."

She rolled her eyes and knocked on the door.

"A psychic?" Scott echoed and looked down at his hand, remembering their one and only handshake.

"Sure am." She gave him a wicked smile and wriggled her fingers at him.

"Come in! The door's unlocked," a voice called out from inside.

The sound of mystical chimes rang out as we walked over the threshold. The batteries were wearing out though, so the sound came off as more electric than ethereal.

The doorway opened to a small foyer converted to a waiting room with two worn wingback chairs and a coffee table filled with New Age magazines. Vanilla incense burned in the corner, a trail of smoke rising from the last remaining inch of scented stick.

Vick led us through a curtain of pearlescent beads into a much larger room, one with a set up that I was unfortunately all too familiar with. A round table covered with a black silk tablecloth took up the center of the room. Atop it, a dark crystal ball stood propped up on a pedestal of shining bronze. It was a much finer setup than the cheap glass ball and fake gold stand my mother once used.

My steps slowed. Part of me wanted to turn back and make a run for it and maybe I would've if Scott's hand hadn't found mine and given it a reassuring squeeze.

Vick kept going to the kitchen in the next room. The rest of the house may have been packed with gaudy fortune teller decor, but the kitchen was a different story. It felt like walking into Aunt Bee's kitchen from *The Andy Griffith Show.* A checkered tablecloth covered the table with a fresh vase of daisies sitting in the middle. The cabinets were the kind with a doorless open style, displaying different pots and pans stacked in orderly fashion next to glass jars filled with canned beans, peaches, and jams. It was cozy and welcoming, and I had no doubt Mrs Hammond would've approved.

An old woman moved around the room drying and putting away dishes. Her appearance encompassed pretty much every cliche attached to the word psychic, from the half dozen bracelets jangling on her wrists and wide hoop earrings hanging from her ears to the silky shawl draped across her shoulders. Beneath all that, though, she looked like everyone's favorite grandma.

"Minnie!" Vick threw her arms around the old woman and gave her a kiss on the cheek.

"Vicky, honey, how are you?" The old woman patted her on the back before holding her away at arm's length to look her over. "You've been working too hard. Tell Little Mikey he needs to give you a night off every now and then. Surely he has other girls to take your place."

"Look who's here," Vick said, standing aside to show me off with a sweep of her arm. "I finally brought the kid."

"This is Lou? My goodness, she's young." She swished across the floor toward me. "Hello, at last, little one," she said, cupping my face in her hands. I expected to walk in and hate the woman but damned if I didn't find myself smiling back at her. "Good Lord! I can feel the power radiating off you even now. Amazing. And who's this?"

She looked at Scott standing behind me. Her smile faltered.

"Ma'am." He dipped his head in a nod.

Minnie turned to Vick with wide eyes. "Victoria," she chided. "You didn't tell me."

"Surprise," Vick said, flashing that mischievous smile again. Vick moved around the kitchen like she was at home. She opened the refrigerator and took out a box of pizza and a beer.

"Forgive me, honey," Minnie said to Scott, taking him by the arm and pulling him toward the table. "Sit down, sit down. Help yourself to some cold pizza. I made some apple dumplings earlier too that turned out pretty good." She put down plates in front of us and started scooping gooey apple dumplings on each of them, her eyes drifting back to Scott every now and then.

My own cooking skills amounted to heating up frozen microwave dinners and popping bread in the toaster. Other than the occasional casserole Mortie made for us to share, this was the first homemade thing I'd eaten in years, and it was amazing.

Minnie eased down into one of the kitchen chairs with a cup of hot tea in front of her and started to take off her clip-on earrings and bracelets.

"And how long have you lived in Magnolia Grove, honey?" she asked Scott.

He shifted uncomfortably in his seat. "Just a short time."

"You don't have to ease into it, Minnie. Officer Campbell here is the type of guy that appreciates an upfront approach."

"What's going on?" I asked, a spoonful of dumpling freezing halfway to my mouth. There was something off about all of this. "I thought you said we had to come here because you can't read my future anymore."

"We are, but there's some unfinished business we need to attend to first." Vick eyed Scott as she took a gulp of beer.

That detached cop facade came back down, guarding his features. He nudged away his plate full of dumpling and assessed Vick and Minnie across the table.

I set my spoon down and pushed away my own plate. I didn't care how sweet this little old lady seemed to be or how yummy her dumplings were. I didn't enjoy being manipulated nor did I care for the predatory look on Vick's face.

"We don't have to be here," I told Scott and started to get up. I would've been more than happy to get the hell out of there and put as much distance between me and that crystal ball I could feel sitting in the other room.

"It's okay, Louise," he said, drawing me back toward the table. "I'll play along."

"You see? He's curious." Vick grinned knowingly as she watched him. "He feels the pull of it. Don't you, Officer?"

"The pull of what?" I asked, frustrated.

"Witch's blood," Vick answered.

Minnie upended a saltshaker, dumping its contents on the checkerboard tablecloth.

"What is it that you do, Scott?" she asked. "What line of work are you in?" She made a trail through the salt granules with her index finger.

"Surveillance," came his clipped answer.

It was the question I still hadn't asked him. I knew it had something to do with the Brethren being in Magnolia Grove, that much was obvious, but I had yet to ask why and I knew part of the reason was because I was afraid of the answer.

"I take it our little cult infestation is what brought you here. The Sons of something or other," Minnie said with a wave of her hand.

"The Brethren of the Eternal Blood," he corrected her.

The old woman raised her shoulder in half a shrug, uninterested in what they chose to call themselves.

Vick stared him down, drumming her nails against the empty beer can. "He's holding something back, Minnie. You don't have to be a psychic to see that."

Minnie pushed the salt around, making circles in them and raised an eyebrow in challenge to Scott. "More than just surveillance then, hmm?"

"Surveillance and... elimination."

She peered into the mess of salt granules on the tablecloth then shuffled her hand over the pile, erasing the circles she'd made. "I'm not interested in vague explanations and half-truths, sweet boy."

He looked at me and the cop mask came off. "I'm an assassin."

My stomach twisted into a knot of betrayal. I mean, it wasn't that big of a leap to come to that conclusion. After all, I'd seen him wipe out a cemetery full of Brethren goons. It was more just hearing it out loud… spoken right out of his mouth. That somehow made it more real to me and a more serious deception.

Vick sucked in a sharp breath.

"What? Didn't you see that?" Scott said to her. "Aren't you supposed to be a psychic?"

She didn't look offended; she looked scared and shared a mutual look of fear with Minnie who held up her salt-covered fingertip as if to tell her to wait.

"And who is it you've been sent to 'eliminate?'" Minnie licked the tip of her middle finger and dipped it in the salt, keeping it still on the table as she waited for an answer.

"Not just who," he said. "But what."

"Who, goddammit!?" Vick demanded, pounding a fist against the table.

His eyes fell on me and the knot in my stomach turned to an anvil.

"He knows, Minnie!" Vick gasped, panicked.

"Knows what?" I asked, though it didn't matter what she said. It was me. He'd been sent here to kill me. I had no idea why, but the truth was right there in the handsome, pained face looking back at me.

Vick grabbed his wrist, not bothering to ask permission or wait for deceptive handshakes.

"Victoria!" Minnie chided.

"I won't let manners get in the way of protecting her." She narrowed her eyes at Scott, daring him to challenge her. He didn't. I don't know what she saw when she looked into him, but her eyes flitted briefly to me. Her grip on him got tighter the harder she looked for answers but still she came up short.

"Dammit! Nothing," she said, shoving his arm away.

"Of course not," Minnie said. "Whoever trained him was sure to have put up mental blocks in the event he ever became compromised."

"Didn't I tell you, kid?" Vick seethed. "You can't trust a single fucking one of them."

He turned away from me, staring at the dumpling on his plate, unable to look at me anymore.

So much in life is a choice, just like Mortie said. You can choose to feel all the horrible things instead of letting yourself go numb to them. You can choose to face fears before they gain power over you. And you can choose to take a risk and jump, though if I was being honest with myself, it didn't feel like too much of a risk when I knew the person I was jumping to would never let me fall.

Vick was saying something to Minnie when I spoke up.

"You're wrong about him," I said. He looked up from his plate and met my eyes. The kitchen went silent. "I trust him. I trust him with my life."

I remembered the first time I saw those green eyes staring at me like they were now, the shade perfectly matching the granny smith apples in the produce section. This man had saved my life again and again, but more than that, I knew him. I knew the very essence of him, even feeling and holding it as a tangible thing in my own hands as I'd stupidly drained his life in an attempt to save us both. How could I ever not trust him?

Vick opened her mouth in protest, but Minnie interrupted her.

"Hush now, Vicky," Minnie said, a coy smile playing at the corner of her mouth. "Don't be upset with yourself. No one's ever right a hundred percent of the time, especially when they're blinded by their own past hurts."

Minnie's finger twisted in the salt, and she picked up with her interrogation.

"The ones that sent you here, to Magnolia Grove, who are they?"

He kept quiet, his lips pressed tight.

"You've already broken their rules, honey, otherwise she wouldn't be sitting here right now, would she, hmm?" Minnie said, nodding toward me.

It was exactly what she needed to say to make his defenses fall. I wondered if she knew that all along.

"There is… an organization," he struggled to start. "One with a mission to protect the world from, well…" He shifted awkwardly in his chair. "From people like you." He nodded in the direction of Vick and Minnie though I knew by the way he said 'you' that I was part of that too.

"Freaks, you mean?" Vick practically spit. She was still fuming, throwing every ounce of her anger at him when at least a little bit should've been directed at me for going against her and trusting him.

Minnie didn't take offense. "There's people like us all over," she said with an unoffended shrug. "What makes a handful of us in a small town like Magnolia Grove any different?"

"This… organization… issues directives based on prophecies." He turned to Vick. "You're not the only fortune teller in the world."

A cold laugh bubbled up out of her throat. "A self-righteous organization centered around hunting down freaks is *powered* by freaks? Christ, the hypocrisy."

"And the prophecy that sent you to us?" Minnie's voice was urgent, her finger dancing in circles on the tablecloth as she stared right into him.

"I don't know."

"But you suspect."

"I've been tracking the Brethren of the Eternal Blood for two years. They've been around for more than ten. Sending me here means they're now capable of what they've been trying to accomplish for a decade. I've been ordered to eliminate and destroy anything–" his eyes fell on me "– *anyone* capable of making that happen."

Minnie nodded as if this all confirmed what she already knew and scooped up the salt into her palm. She turned in her seat and held her palm up to her mouth then blew. Salt danced in the air before falling in a mess on her kitchen floor. She stared at where the cloud of salt had been and then glanced over her shoulder at Scott. Her entire countenance changed, softening back into nice granny mode.

"And while you're out doing your surveillance, you use Magic." It wasn't a question, but he answered it anyway with a shrug, confused at the change in interrogation.

"The organization I… uh… work for teaches you incantations or whatever to hide your presence. They give you potions to help if you're injured, that kind of stuff," he explained. "They even embed you with an identity to help you go undercover – make it so that the right people believe you are who you say you are."

"Who the hell is 'they?'" Vick asked, exasperated, but both Minnie and Scott ignored her.

"I'd be interested to see just what sort of potions you have but I'll tell you this: the spells they taught you are all useless lies." His brows furrowed as she said it. "They are nothing but a way for you to focus your intent. You could chant any phrase, say a series of numbers, even rattle off gibberish. As long as your intent stays focused, the result will be the same."

"I don't understand," he said.

"Spells can't be cast by just anyone, you see," Minnie went on with a knowing smile.

"What are you saying?"

"Oh, honey, I think you know that already." Minnie pulled up the wrist of her sleeve, exposing pale crepe-paper thin skin and a network of blue veins working their way up her arm. "The Magic flowing in my veins is the same as the Magic in yours."

"She means you're a witch." Vick grinned maliciously, happy once more to have the upper hand.

"It's likely why they recruited you in the first place." Minnie patted his hand. "One day you and I will sit here in my kitchen, you will tell me about the people who sent you here and I will show you Magic. But for now" – she turned to me – "we have much bigger problems to deal with."

She considered me, assessing me with eyes that didn't belong to a sweet old lady but a powerful force to be reckoned with.

"One of the hardest things we must do is to look inside ourselves and see the reality of who and what we are, not simply what we wish to be," Minnie said to me, her words twisting in my gut more than Scott's revelation had. "Sometimes it's ourselves we hide from the most."

Minnie turned to Scott. "When did you realize she's what they're looking for?"

He kept silent, unwilling to answer.

"I suppose it doesn't matter," she said, yielding the point. "It only matters that your witch blood told you the truth of it and that your instincts didn't fail you."

She got up from her chair and circled around, her magic trailing her like heavy scented perfume.

"I bet you thought you could ignore it," she said to me, her tone changing, becoming almost snide. "Maybe it was easier to pretend you were some poor, cursed creature. You've been used terribly by your mother. It's a convincing narrative. Perhaps, even convincing enough to fool yourself, hmm?"

I decided I didn't like Minnie all that much. I didn't say that out loud, but she nodded as if she understood why all the same.

"You're not like the rest of us, even as unique and gifted as we are, and I think you know that," she said as if catching me in an unspoken lie. "You're an altogether different being. Death himself has bestowed you with his own powers, purposely positioning you in the realm of the living."

She reached inside her blouse and, with a practiced flick, pulled out what looked like a Tarot card. It wasn't one exactly. I'd seen my fair share of them at my mother's kitchen table. This was different. All black, not unlike the book, and frayed at the edges from being held too many times. The image was of a chasm and a skull rising up out of the fog at the base of it. Looking at it sent an uncomfortable tremor of some weird truth over my skin.

Minnie's eyes were on me, watching my reaction, and I hated that I'd given her one and not hidden it better. She nodded once more and I gritted my teeth in irritation.

She tapped a finger on the skull card. "Death has given you the ability to see lives lived of those who are dead and gone. You can speak with the damned who are trapped here amongst us. And you might even have the ability to shepherd them to what awaits by bridging the gap between this world and what's next." Her voice dropped lower, falling to a whisper, and her eyes looked at me accusingly. "Maybe even opening it wider."

She quickly went on. "To face what we're really capable of is a harsh truth to embrace. If you do not accept it, you lose your power. Others will prey on it. They will use you, mold you into what they want, make you do the things they want."

Scott came to my defense, adamant. "Louise would never do what the Brethren want of her."

Vick spoke up. "And how would you know? Are you a psychic?"

"Tell her, Vicky."

"I'm sorry, kid. He's wrong. You're the key to this whole thing." She fanned out her hands, encompassing the entire room. "And if this puritanical, hypocritical, bullshit organization of his knew exactly what you were, they would've sent more than just Batman here to get rid of you."

That tough exterior of hers fell away, exposing the genuine Vick underneath.

"I'm sorry, Lou. I didn't see it before. I didn't know what you were until you and I..." she hesitated. "Until I read for you. But even Mortie suspects the truth, he's just never told you before."

The same fear that had been in her eyes when she looked at me after the reading in my kitchen was back, and seeing it again made me angry somehow.

"Oh yeah?" I said, my voice coming out cold. "And what am I?"

She cowered, her words coming out quiet and scared and impossible to believe.

"You're more than what anyone thinks you are. You're the queen of the dead."

CHAPTER 23

"Queen of the dead?" I echoed with a scoff. "That sounds ridiculous. What does that even mean? Is this some kind of thing I inherited from my mom, like a gene that skips a generation or something 'cuz that tracks. Or, wait, is this like reincarnation? Is that a thing?" I laughed. The sound came out cold and harsh to my ears.

No one else laughed. Vick bit her bottom lip, her fear of me still there. Minnie stood taut, her fists clenched on the sides of her chair, magic radiating from her, invisible to the eye but undeniably there by the way it changed the tension in the air. Scott's hand went to the sheath at his side, ready to pull out a knife if needed.

"You can take your hand off that weapon, honey. No one here wants to hurt her," Minnie said, raising her hands up off the chair to show she meant it. "We just want to make her see."

"'Make me see?' See what?" I asked angrily. "Seeing things is part of the problem. Ghosts, wisps, poltergeists, banshees… I've seen it all, and more, through no choice of my own and that doesn't make me queen of anything, that just makes me a freak."

"The Queen of the Dead is a vessel for Death himself – a sort of hand he reaches out through here in the land of the living," Minnie explained. "You're a protector of the souls that are trapped here and a guardian to what lies beyond."

"Nope, this is stupid. I should've left," I said, shaking my head at how dumb it all sounded. "I should've turned around the second I walked through that door."

"Tell her what she must hear, Victoria."

Vick stood there, unsure. I always thought of her as older than me. Sure, just like Cliff, she had a good five to seven years on me, though she didn't really look it. Age wasn't what gave her the impression of seniority to me. It was her wisdom, how she knew all the answers that made her feel almost matronly to me. Until now. Now she looked young and scared, and it frustrated me to see her that way instead of the way I needed her to be – someone with all the answers.

"I told you before. The future is a big thing to take a gander at, with lots of moving parts and changing possibilities," Vick said to me. "There isn't a future I've seen where you don't do what they want of you. No matter how many times I've tried to find it, it's not there."

"You're wrong." The fury I'd felt when the Brethren ransacked the cemeteries came back. Maybe it never left. "I would never do what they've done – the rest they disturbed, the souls they've violated."

"I'm sorry, Lou, but I saw –"

"No." A chill crept up from my fingers into my forearms, the breath coming out cold from my lips. "Never."

Vick backed away from me. Even Minnie flinched at the change in me. What was happening? What was wrong with me? My breath caught, refusing to escape my lips in anything but short, hitched breaths as the now-familiar blue glow flickered to life in my hands.

Oh, God. Minnie... Vick... they were right. I was something else. Even Alice alluded to it in the Veil. I started to shake, the anger taking over, turning my vision a blurry blue at the edges.

A hand touched my neck, a thumb rubbing calmly against my pulse. Scott's eyes met mine and whatever was raging inside me came to a frozen halt, terrified that I might hurt him as I had before.

"You're not scared of me," I said, my voice trembling. "Even *I'm* scared of me."

His voice came out steady, soothing. "You're worried that knowing this about yourself will change things, that it might change you into something you're not."

His fingers intertwined with mine and suddenly it felt like it was just him and me, alone by the riverside, sitting on the dock talking as the water lapped up against the wood beams below us.

"I'm not sure that's how power really works. Instead of changing you, I think it only magnifies what you already are. And, Louise," he said, looking into my eyes, "you're like no one I've ever met before. The first time I saw you, you were walking out of the cemetery in the dead of night, this beautiful woman emerging from a world of sorrow, regret and forgotten memories. I thought to myself, how could someone with that much death and darkness wrapped around her emit that much light? I couldn't resist her. Not even now."

He smiled down at me and there was that hint of sunshine pouring over me again. My fear melted away. I didn't know what I was or what was happening to me but here was someone I could tether myself to in the changing storm; someone to bring me back to myself.

"There she is," he whispered, watching me. "Stronger than ever, like always."

I took a deep breath, feeling like myself once more. Vick gave Scott a begrudging nod of acceptance. Minnie's stance eased and the magic clinging to her abated.

I closed my eyes and asked Vick the question I knew I had to. "If I am what you say I am and that this future is unavoidable, then what can we do?"

Minnie answered, easing herself down into the chair, more exhausted than when we came in. "I'm afraid the answer to that is nothing, sweetie. What Vicky has seen will come to pass. It always does," she said, looking at Vick with a mixture of pity and love. "I could offer you a protection or strength charm though I'm not sure if it will be anywhere near powerful enough for the future you must face. My only hope is that now you know what you are, and what you're really capable of. And maybe somewhere in that, we'll have a chance."

Vick cleared her throat. "There is one other thing that might help. One last chance, but it's a longshot, Minn," she said, her voice timid, as if she were ashamed. "Lou has something she needs you to take a look at."

Vick slid out the page Mortie gave me that was peeking up out of my back pocket, and rolled it open on the tabletop.

Minnie sucked in a breath and scooted her chair far away from the table's edge.

"What is *that*?" she asked in a quiet voice. I started to answer but she held up a hand to silence me. "Forgive me, honey, that was more of a rhetorical question."

Clearly disturbed by its presence, she turned to Vick. "Why did you bring this into my home, Victoria?"

"I'm sorry, Minnie. Really, I am. I wouldn't if I had any other choice but you're the only one I know who might be able to read it."

Minnie stared down at the page lying on her checkered tablecloth. Its dead skin and marred surface looked out of place next to her cheery vase full of daisies.

"The empath could not read it, then." It wasn't a question, but Vick answered anyway.

"The book only showed one spell to Mortie, and then, it sort of... shed this one."

"I see," Minnie whispered.

I was glad someone did because I sure as hell didn't.

Minnie looked curiously at Scott, then at the page, then back to Scott. "Do you not feel the power it holds?"

He took a moment to consider the page on the table then shook his head. "No. Why?"

"Interesting," she mused. "Blood Magic appears to have no pull on you. Perhaps that is why your organization sent you here in the first place."

She eyed the page wearily. "Unfortunately, it does have a pull on me."

"I'm sorry, Minnie," Vick said again, dipping her head in guilt. "There's a reason it's been shed from the spine. It's a message for Lou. At least I think it is, it's hard to tell. But if there's anything in it that can help her..." Her voice trailed off. "You're the only one I know that might be able to read it," she repeated, looking guilty once again.

"What's done is done. You had no choice. I understand." She lifted Vick's head with a finger under her chin and patted her cheek. "Perhaps I still have enough power in these old bones to resist. It helps that I'm not the only witch here."

Minnie crossed her arms over her chest and studied the page from afar. "Alright then," she said, rolling up her sleeves. "In for a penny, in for a pound. Let's get started."

She rooted through her cabinets and pulled out a large cooking pot and wooden spoon. From a drawer, she took out a brown paper bag rolled down at the top and filled with tied off bunches of dried herbs.

She nodded toward the page. "Bring that cursed thing and follow me."

Minnie led us back through the house to the room with the crystal ball.

"Vicky, dear, put that silly thing aside, will you?" she said, pointing to the crystal ball. Vick took it, lifted up the draping velvet tablecloth and unceremoniously shoved the crystal ball under the table.

I shifted uncomfortably. "Couldn't we just do this in the kitchen?"

"Unfortunately, not," Minnie said as she set the pot on top of a portable hot plate at the center of the table where the stand and its crystal ball had been. "We're looking for the truth of things, you see. And with this kind of magic, we must pull that truth out of the shadows from where it hides and there is simply far too much light in the kitchen."

That didn't make a bit of sense as it was night out and the curtains were drawn in her kitchen windows, but I didn't really have a say; Vick was already shoving me into a chair at the table beside her.

"Scent is a powerful tool. In much the same way that a single smell can instantly trigger a memory, scent acts as a gateway to many things," Minnie explained to Scott as she filled the pot with water, her voice taking on an instructor's tone. "Once again, it isn't precisely what herbs or spices you use but your intent, and preference," she added, crumbling herbs with her fingers then stirring it all together with a wooden spoon. "In Magic, intent is everything."

The scent of cloves, cardamom, and orange rind rose in a cloud of steam from the pot.

"The smells of my childhood," she explained, breathing deep the citrusy Christmas-like scent. "The happiness it brings will temper the darkness in the page… at least, that's my hope."

She plucked a hair from her long braid and dropped it in the mixture. "All conjuring requires a sacrifice from the caster, even a small one such as this."

Her air of the teacher dissipated. The old woman who'd been nothing but calm and exhausted after a day's work now fidgeted, clenching and unclenching her fingers in the folds of her skirt, nervous energy brimming inside her as she looked at the page and then at the pot.

"And finally, to unlock this kind of magic, a payment is required," Minnie said, taking a deep steadying breath. "Blood." She turned to me. "Yours, sweetie."

I didn't like the sound of that. For starters, my blood had consequences. I had no clue what they were, but I'd felt some of those consequences trembling in the ground in New Bethlehem when Toby had taken my blood and smeared it over the jewel.

"I don't know if that's a good idea."

"I agree," she said readily. "But the page was created with a binding spell and I'm afraid yours is the only blood powerful enough to break through these enchantments for us to use it. Just one drop should do the trick."

Reluctantly, I offered up my hand and she pricked my index finger with a pin. She held my finger over the pot, squeezing until a drop of blood pooled out from my skin and fell into the bubbling mixture.

Nothing happened. I wasn't sure what I expected. Swirling blue energy? Electrical arcs? Cemeteries coming to life? There was nothing that dramatic, just more puffs of steam rising out of the pot as Minnie stirred in my one drop of blood. There did seem to be a notable change in the air, though, turning humid and heady with the scent of cloves. It was enough to make me a little dizzy. Vick too, apparently, as she momentarily swayed side to side but then shook it off.

"That was the easy part," Minnie said. "Scott, honey, if you wouldn't mind." She gestured to the page on the table.

He started to hand it to her and for a moment it looked like she might take it, that she wanted nothing more than to take it as she started to reach for it.

"No," she said, sharply drawing her hand back. "Don't hand it to me, put it in the pot."

Scott looked doubtfully at the water bubbling in an angry boil.

"Do it before I change my mind," she pleaded.

He did as ordered and dropped it in the pot.

The pot let out an ear-piercing scream. The corners of the page shrank in, retracting in pain. Minnie trembled and faltered where she stood. Scott caught her, holding her upright as she leaned against him.

"Blow on it," she instructed him, in a tired voice. "Like you're cooling your soup, except with the added intent of trying to calm an injured child."

He closed his eyes, focused on what she said and blew out a long breath over the rising steam. The boiling stopped. The page floated on the surface, its corners slowly unfurling. Minnie looked at it from over the rim.

"Well done," she told him. "You're a quick study."

"Can you read it?" Vick asked.

The chicken scratches were gone, turned into flowing silver curves that resembled waves instead of words.

"Yes," Minnie whispered in awe.

"And what's it say?" I asked, almost afraid to hear the answer.

She said nothing at first. Her demeanor reminded me of Ivan's back at the funeral home when he was surrounded by dead bodies.

Wonder.

Minnie was full of wonder, and I didn't like the look of it.

"They're heartbeats," she breathed.

Again, that didn't make any sense. How could you read a heartbeat in a book?

"Once you dabble in Blood Magic, it becomes, in a way, addictive. Magic comes to you easier when you call upon it, it's more pliable, and bends faster to your will. Blood Magic held quite the temptation for me in my youth. It was a way to cut corners and create stronger spells. But this page," Minnie went on, the wonder still there in her eyes as she gazed down at the page. "Is made with the purest form of Blood Magic I've ever seen. To use this type of magic, the caster must do the unspeakable." Her voice dropped to a whisper and her wonder turned to fear. "Murder... the taking of a life. The victim's lifeforce is then woven into the fibers, lending its power to the caster. Each word on this page is a life. To make an entire book with more pages like this must have required hundreds, if not thousands, of lives taken."

"Ivan called it the Book of Souls," I told her.

"An apt name, considering the cost required to create it." Minnie nodded along with her assessment. "Whoever created this book – the power required – only a sorcerer could create something like this, and the world has not seen their like for quite some time."

"Or maybe a Lich."

Minnie's head snapped up, her voice going hollow. "What did you say?"

I spoke up louder in case she hadn't heard me. "Mrs Hammond called him a Lich. What's a Lich anyway?"

Minnie gasped and grabbed tight onto Scott's arm. "Sweet goddess, we've made a mistake."

"Yes," Vick's voice coupled with another's came from across the room. "You certainly have."

Vick stepped forward, her eyes a dark gray and growing darker by the second.

"An old woman, a boy, and a whore." The Lich's voice took over Vick's until hers became a faraway echo. "And here, all this time, I was afraid of who might be helping her."

Minnie reached into the collar of her blouse and grabbed onto a cloth pouch hanging by an embossing thread. She clutched the sachet bag and raised her other hand, mumbling words I couldn't hear under her breath. Wind rushed through the room, tugging at the silver strands of Minnie's braid. The Lich inside Vick closed her eyes and breathed deep the wind swirling around the table.

"Minerva, is it? Your magic is impressive… for a witch." The Lich looked around the room, taking in the dark drapes and velvet tablecloth. "Do you sell such charms with the other lies you tell around your crystal ball, or do you save them for the customers who know what you really are?"

"You can do no harm in this home, sorcerer," Minnie's stern words reverberated through the small room.

"Harm? I have no interest in inflicting any harm here," the Lich said playfully. "Which means, I'm afraid, that beautifully woven protection spell won't be of much use against me."

Vick's body came up to the table. Gone was Vick's usual sultry stroll. Her body moved with someone else's long, elegantly poised steps as her body moved across the floor to peer into the pot. "When the whore showed you the page from my book, you felt it, didn't you Minerva?" The face that looked at her over the rim of the pot wasn't Vick's usual expression of admiration for the woman, but one with an enticingly wicked grin. "The potential, right here, begging to be used. It calls to you, I know it does, I can hear it. There's a part of you yearning to control it, to bend it to your will."

Minnie trembled and shook her head. "There is no such thing as control of Blood Magic."

"Oh, there is indeed," the Lich purred. "But it comes at a cost... such a heavy cost that only a few are willing to pay it," he said, waving a hand gracefully above the pot. "As you told the boy earlier, it also required a sacrifice from me, the caster, to make sure the spell bound itself to the page. And let's just say it was a much greater sacrifice than that lovely strand of silver hair you so willingly gave."

Vick trailed a finger over the velvet tablecloth. "In the end, when Time came to reclaim the rest of my days, there wasn't much left for her to take that wasn't already poured into the pages of this book."

Her body moved around the table to Minnie. Scott stepped forward to intervene, but Minnie held up a hand to stop him.

"The Lich will not harm me," she said, her words steady though she still trembled.

The Lich reached out and touched Minnie, Vick's fingers cupping her cheeks. "There are many gifts that come with embracing Blood Magic, Minerva. Including the ability to pass into the world between worlds so that you can hide from Time herself. Perhaps you would like to learn such gifts?" The Lich stroked her cheeks with Vick's thumbs and whispered. "Imagine, eternal youth, untouched by the passing years."

For a moment, I could see Minnie as she once was, her wheat-colored hair framing a smooth heart-shaped face.

"With me, you would be powerful enough to test the limits of magic, in all its forms, and shake off the shackles of a common witch to become the sorceress you were destined to be."

Minnie's trembling stilled. She took a deep breath and covered the hands on her face with her own. "I always wondered if I had it in me to turn down someone like you. It's very reassuring to find that kind of strength inside myself."

The Lich sneered and dropped Vick's hands.

Free of temptation, Minnie openly studied him. "You certainly are powerful for someone who fractured his soul into a book."

Bored with her now, the Lich merely shrugged and turned his attention to me. "That's what happens when you *eat*." He emphasized the last word by running a tongue along Vick's teeth.

A sickening truth hit me. Sharon. He was talking about Sharon's soul. He grinned, following along with my thoughts. "Such a young thing – that nosy reporter; so vibrant and full of life. All that energy of hers lives on in me. What better purpose could she ever have than that?"

"You'll pay for what you did to her," I breathed.

The Lich circled the table, coming toward me. Scott went in the opposite direction, his hand low at his side. The Lich ignored him, unthreatened, and focused on me.

"You're not weak like my tender-hearted Ivan, are you?" he said, tilting his head at me, taking my measure. "When I first found our mutual friend, he cowered at the ghosts that swarmed him, terrified of all he saw. Such a fragile, delicate man. But you… you're an altogether different creature aren't you, little one?"

Scott came around beside me right as the Lich stood in front of me. The Lich reached out and Scott quickly tapped the inside of his wrist. The air in front of me sizzled and popped. The Lich yanked Vick's hand back, cradling it to her body as if it'd been burned.

Scott dumped a fistful of crushed rosemary and thyme on the carpet in front of him that he'd snagged from Minnie's paper bag of herbs. A circle of flaky bits and broken stems trailed where he had walked, encompassing the table, the pot, and Vick.

"The old witch taught you something already, did she?" he said, looking at Scott for the first time. Vick's face assessed him in an angry, murderous gaze that broke into an evil, slow smile spreading over her lips.

"These women look at you and see an assassin with the blood of a witch. I see merely a boy. Terrified and afraid, tears falling down his round little cheeks as he stumbles into the living room to find the bodies of his murdered parents."

Scott went still beside me, his shoulders tense and taut, fury flaring his nostrils.

"Did you not tell our Lou your story yet? No, I suppose not. You keep that pain locked deep inside, only letting it out when it's time for a kill. Pouring all that rage and despair into whatever mission they've sent you on this time. Do you even know what war you're fighting? Does it even matter? Or is it just the kill alone that's enough for you?"

"Stop it!" I shouted.

The Lich laughed, a low chuckle. "It makes no difference, little one. For your coven of witches here has locked me in with the one thing I came for."

He went to the pot and dipped a finger into the mixture, swirling the page around until it disintegrated into a fizzle of white bubbles.

"I was disappointed when you wouldn't give your blood freely to my Brethren," he said to me. "But here it is, laid out right before me."

"No!" Minnie cried out, realizing too late what had been done.

The Lich lifted the pot and drank and drank until every last drop was gone. He rolled Vick's head back and sighed, blue energy popping at his fingertips.

His knowing eyes met mine. "An altogether different creature," he repeated. And then he was gone.

Vick collapsed onto the carpet, the empty pot falling beside her. Scott rushed into the circle and checked her for a pulse, her blue eyes staring blankly up at him.

"She's still alive," he said.

She came to with a jolt, gasping for breath.

"Vicky!" Minnie cried out. Instead of running forward, she bent over, hurriedly brushing a hand through the pile of rosemary and thyme in front of her and ran into the circle.

Vick spoke, her voice sounding far away and distant, her eyes still empty. "I – I can see... everything," she breathed. "...it hurts, Minnie."

"I'm here, honey. Focus on me," Minnie said, cradling Vick's hand in her own.

She bolted upright, gripping tight to the old woman's hand. Her eyes remained blank, but an urgency filled her shaking voice. "I – I need to go get Lou by the lake. She'll drown if I don't."

I took a step forward and rammed face first into what lingered of Scott's invisible shield. I winced as the healing bruises from the pistol whip made contact with it. It felt like walking into a sliding glass door you didn't know was there. I reached down and copied what Minnie had done and brushed away the herbs at my feet. When I stepped into the circle it felt like walking through a doorway with an invisible threshold.

I knelt beside Vick. "You already saved me from Josephine's cries, remember?"

She blinked heavily at me, her eyes trying to focus. She looked at Scott who was keeping her upright with a firm hold on her shoulder, now that her urgency had fallen away.

"You're about to go die for her outside Mortie's. Or is it in the cemetery? You keep dying for her." She rubbed her forehead and winced. "I was wrong about you. Minnie's right. I couldn't see beyond my own pain."

"Vicky, honey, listen to my voice," Minnie said, brushing the hair off her forehead. "Focus on my voice."

Vick's head lulled heavily to the side. "We're running out of time. If she doesn't destroy it… It hurts Minnie."

"Hush, child, I have you," Minnie soothed. "It'll fade."

Vick's eyelids fluttered and the blank look dissipated for a fraction of a second. "We're running out of time," she repeated. "The Lich took something from me. From you, Minn. You too, Lou." She rolled her head to look up at Scott, the blank look came back into her blue eyes. "He'll take it all from you. Everything. What you did to him just now, what you denied him, made him angry."

Confusion contorted her beautiful features. "James is going to break my heart," she said to no one in particular, her voice sounding farther and farther away. "Minnie wants me to find love, says I'll grow cold and bitter without it. What if I already am? They all break my heart, but maybe not one of them. He's different, not like others. He's bald and he has kids… they're going to become my kids," her voice rose in a panic. "I can't see into him. Dammit, why can't I?!"

"Calm down, Vick. It'll be okay," I said, trying to help, echoing the words Mortie used to calm her back in my kitchen. "Just give it some time."

She reached out to me, touching my chin. "Mortie knows Peter's going to die. Knows it before the doctors tell him but knowing it still won't stop how much it'll hurt him in the end. He's going to meet Lewis though. She'll help the pain, the loneliness. The daughter he never had but always wanted. She even has Peter's black hair and glass face."

Her words formed a lump in my throat. She stared, bewildered by my sadness.

She blinked; the emptiness momentarily gone. She grabbed onto Scott's wrist, coming back to herself. "The Book needs to be destroyed. I hid it. Only Lou can destroy it, and she has to. If she doesn't..." her voice trailed off becoming distant once more and a tear fell down her cheek. "Take her there – where the Book is and where magic isn't. He has it safe. He keeps things safe. He doesn't know it, but I think he kept Lou safe these last three years. He'll keep me safe if I let him."

She shook her head as if trying to shake off a fog.

"The Lich's power is growing," she said, fighting to hold on. "He can do things we've never seen before. He eats souls. That's how he has power. Now he's eaten a little of my time and Minnie's Magic, and Lou's..." she looked at me, her eyes pleading. "Help them rest, Lou. They only want to rest." Her words held the echo of Sharon's.

"Time's running out," Vick said again, looking around in a panic. "Hurry. Only Lou can destroy it."

"I will," I said, though I didn't have a clue as to how, but it seemed she needed to hear it. She nodded and leaned over on the table to rest her head on her arms.

"You must do as she says and quickly." Minnie instructed. "Don't worry about Vicky," she said when I started to object. "She's safe with me." Minnie took off the sachet around her neck and tucked it into my pocket where the page had been. "To give you added strength."

"Wait, Scott!" Vick pulled him back down to her, clawing at his shirt.

Surprised and a little confused by her desperation, he calmly covered her hands on his shirt. "It's going to be okay," he said, trying to reassure her.

"You have to hang on," she pleaded. "She'll find you. I promise. Just hang on a little longer. She's coming. I promise." She let go of his shirt and crumpled into Minnie's waiting arms, her voice coming out in a whisper. "Don't forget. I promise."

CHAPTER 24

We sat in Vick's Toyota in the nearly empty Piggly Wiggly parking lot. Scott took the keys out of the ignition, suspiciously eyeing an SUV that drove by and then an elderly couple walking hand in hand out of the store's front doors with a cart packed full of groceries in front of them.

"You're sure this is it?" he asked.

There was only one place – one person – that matched up with what Vick said, and that was the Piggly Wiggly. And Cliff. She'd said a lot of stuff about Cliff when she was delirious – personal, future stuff I wasn't ready to wrap my head around just yet.

"Yeah, I'm sure."

"Then take this," he said, handing me a small switchblade covered in a leather case with a single button fastened at the top to keep it closed and secure. "If anything goes south, I don't want you in there without a way to defend yourself."

I nodded and slid it into my front pocket. It was small but still bulky and I had to pull my shirt down a bit to cover it up.

We got out of the car, and he took my hand, leading the way past the cart return. A beat-up van drove by, its engine belt squealing in protest as the driver laid on the gas to make it through the yellow traffic light at the nearby intersection.

"Shouldn't we maybe – I don't know, do the wrist thing?" I asked, feeling exposed in the vast Piggly Wiggly parking lot more than I ever had before.

"I tried, just now," he said with a shake of his head. "It's not working. Our best bet is to get in, get the book, and get out as fast as we can."

The sliding doors swooshed open as we approached the front entrance and Scott's hand tightened around mine. "You know, I think she might be right. I didn't feel it before, but I kind of do now. It's like there's something about this place… something that makes it so that Magic," he paused, still not used to saying that word out loud, "is almost muted here." He scanned the area, reassessing everything around us in a new light.

Walking into the Piggly Wiggly after everything that happened was bizarre. Here, before me, was the normal world, untouched by a bloodthirsty cult, the Lich, or magic.

Marge stood at the cash register ringing up a box of wine and a pack of cigarettes for a customer. She gave me a weary wave from behind the checkout counter, tired as she neared the end of her shift. Diego worked in the produce section unloading celery while Amy leaned up against a stack of boxes packed with green bell peppers and onions. He said something and her bubbling laugh filled the air.

Seeing it all was like getting punched in the stomach. Years of running away and I'd finally made myself a home here, and now that home was in danger with everyone I loved in it at risk.

"Hey Lou, you finally came back!" Diego called out to me. "Didn't think I'd see you today. Since when do you ever call in sick? Was it 'cuz you got beat up? Those bruises look like they're healing pretty good though and whoa!" He saw my hand linked with Scott's and beamed. "I see you guys finally got past just saying 'hey' to each other, eh?"

My cheeks burned. It would've been a happy, sort of embarrassing, moment if the world wasn't ending and I had time to experience anything besides doom.

"Have you seen Cliff?" I asked him. "I'm supposed to pick up something from him."

He scanned the front and shook his head. "Last I saw he was in the backroom unloading a palette of Spaghetti-O's and Rice-A-Roni."

Amy shook her head. "Ten minutes ago, I heard him say he was going to take a smoke break," she said, her own cheeks burning as she looked sideways at Scott, her eyelashes fluttering prettily.

Marge's voice came over the loudspeaker. "Cliff to the front with a roll of receipt tape, please."

"Hey, there ya go," Diego said. "He should be up here any second."

"Cliff to the fr–" Marge's voice cut off.

Silence fell over the Piggly Wiggly. Not even the store's usual easy-listening music played out over the loudspeakers.

"What the hell?" I looked toward the checkout counter.

Marge stood completely motionless behind the register, her mouth still forming her last word into the phone's speaker. The customer in front of her hovered a hand over the conveyor belt about to add a pack of gum to their pile of groceries. They weren't the only ones frozen in place. The entire Piggly Wiggly had gone deathly still.

"What's happening?" I asked Scott.

He didn't answer.

Scott stood still as a statue beside me, his jacket frozen halfway open as he reached for the knife hidden at his waist. His attention wasn't on Marge but at the front entrance. Behind me, Diego and Amy looked perplexed staring at the same place Scott did. The sliding doors were frozen two-thirds of the way open despite no one standing in the walkway.

"Scott!" I tried to shake him out of it, but he was rock solid, not budging an inch.

Cliff ran up to the front, emerging out of the cold and flu aisle near the pharmacy on the opposite side of the registers.

"What in the hell?" he said, taking in the sight of the storefront frozen in time.

"Cliff!" I shouted, though I could've just said it in a normal voice and still be easily heard in the absolute silence.

He swiveled around at my shout. "Lou?" he said in disbelief.

The fluorescent light bulbs above us popped and fizzled then burned out.

Cliff ran over to me and waved a hand in front of Diego's unblinking face. He sized up Scott standing there frozen dressed all in black and reaching for a knife.

"Fuck, it's happening!" he said with a startled realization. He grabbed me by the upper arm and pushed me towards the back office as the overnight security lights kicked in, shrouding the Piggly Wiggly in a dim orange glow.

"What's happening?" I asked, panic rising in me.

"No time," he said. He opened the filing cabinet in the corner and pulled out a kid's purple unicorn backpack. He threw it at me and reached for a baseball bat hidden away under his desk. When I started to unzip the bag he rushed toward me, yanking the zipper closed.

"I said there's no time!" he repeated, frantically sliding the arm strap over my shoulder. He half dragged me back out of the office, one hand on my arm, the other gripping tight to the baseball bat.

Rolling black fog gushed through the sliding doors still frozen open, blue electric arcs popped inside the churning cloud like little bolts of lightning. The Brethren in their ragged robes walked out of the fog and into the store. Cliff sucked in a breath and picked up the pace, jogging us past the produce section and the still figures of Scott, Diego, and Amy.

"Wait!" I squirmed in Cliff's grip, trying to break free. "We can't leave them!"

"You have to," he said, his hand clamped around my arm refusing to budge. "She said if you go back now, it's all over – as in they're dead, you're dead, we're *all* dead."

Three Brethren swarmed the store, their tattered robes fluttering around them as they ran down the aisles after us. Already inside the store, coming from the customer service counter was Toby. He wasn't in his innocent cameraman getup this time, instead he stood out from the rest of the Brethren wearing a deep crimson robe, with a golden braided rope draped around his waist. The arm that Scott stabbed in New Bethlehem Cemetery lay in a sling secured to his chest. He lowered his hood, his eyes finding mine as Cliff pulled me down the household cleaner aisle. He took out the knife Scott reached for, flashed me a wicked grin, and plunged it into Scott's stomach.

"No!" I screamed, my voice echoing through the aisle.

The black clouds spun up around them, twisting into a cyclone right there in the produce section. Toby walked through the cyclone, dragging an unmoving Scott along with him and disappeared, leaving the three other Brethren behind to chase after us.

Cliff aimed his bat at the shelves, knocking items off and spewing them into the aisle behind us, blocking the way. I struggled to keep up as he barreled through the store, running toward the back in an evasive zigzag pattern away from our pursuers.

"I don't understand," I cried. "There can't be any magic here."

"It's not magic," Cliff said. "It's time. There's no time. It's frozen," he explained, apparently frustrated at having to spell it out for me.

He shoved me to the side when we reached the end of the paper goods aisle and grabbed hold of a display unit full of office supplies. He pulled onto it, adding his body weight to it, heaving it over until it toppled onto its side, falling on a flutter of black tattered hem.

Cliff grabbed me by the backpack's shoulder strap and took a sharp right turn at the meat counter. Pain shot through the tightly gnarled scar on my thigh at the jarring movement and I staggered along behind him in a struggle to keep my footing.

"That thing, whatever it was, it took Victoria's time," he rushed the explanation as he pulled me along with him. "And now it's using her time to get to you." He said it like it made more sense than it actually did.

We made it to the back bathrooms and then we were cut off. One of the Brethren loomed in the hallway in front of us. Black fog swirled in his eyes as his mouth twisted up into a familiar sneer.

"Mine… mine… mine," the Lich's voice laughed out of the Brethren's mouth.

Cliff swung hard. The man sidestepped but the bat caught him in the hip. He didn't wince at the pain, the unfeeling sneer still there as the Lich retained control of the man's body. Cliff grabbed the front of his cloak and pulled him in, landing a right hook in his cheek. The second Cliff's fist grabbed hold of the cloak, the fog vanished in the man's surprised eyes before the impact from the punch sent him sprawling back in a painful yelp.

I swung around the janitorial cart we used to clean the bathrooms and knocked it over, spilling ammonia and industrial-sized toilet paper rolls out across the polished concrete floors, hoping to create a barrier between us or at least block part of the way.

Cliff grabbed hold of my wrist and we were running again, down through the backroom and finally out onto the loading dock.

He scrambled with the keys trying to find the right ones before giving up and just tossing them at me. I quickly locked each deadbolt in place as he pulled a pallet jack loaded over six feet high with wooden pallets in front of the door.

"Fucking hell," he said, slumping over the pallet jack's handles, out of breath and heaving. "I believed her, but it's one thing to believe someone when they tell you the store's going to be under attack and then another when you see it play out right in front of you."

I unzipped the bag. There inside the purple folds was the book, pulsing weakly. I moved toward Cliff, holding the book closer to him. The pulse died off completely. Vick was right. Magic didn't work on Cliff. I took a step back and the faint hum returned. I closed the bag back up, pulling the zipper past the name "Charlie" stitched in dark purple thread at the top.

"You saved my life," I said to him as I stared dumbfounded down at the backpack belonging to Cliff's youngest daughter, Charlotte. "Thank you."

"Thank Victoria. I thought I was going insane believing her, but, shit," he said, looking around us at the empty loading platform. "Here we are."

"What happens next? Did she say what we need to do now? What about Diego, Amy, and Marge? We can't leave them there. And what about Scott? Did she say where they took him?"

"Hold up now," he said, trying to keep up with my rapid-fire questions. "If we can get you out of here, the store is good. I'll find a way to take care of things. As for the rest of that... I don't know. Everything she predicted up till now came from her getting a read on your boyfriend. She said something about not being able to read me. I'm sorry. She did have a message for you though I don't know how much it helps," he said. "She just said to tell you, 'Trinity.' I'm not even sure what that means."

"I do," I said, the last puzzle piece falling into place. I started to unzip the bag again to give it back to him, but he stopped me.

"Hang onto it. I got Charlie a new Disney princess backpack this school year."

He lengthened the straps and helped slide them over my shoulders. The backpack was small, but it worked. Cliff stepped away and the steady hum of the book vibrated stronger against my back. I was starting to think Vick was right. Maybe Cliff was the reason I'd been safe here all this time.

"You need to get going, kid," he said, checking his watch. "I'd offer you my Trans Am to get you where you need to go, but she said you didn't need it."

"I don't." At least I didn't think I did.

The stack of pallets shook as someone tried to force the door. Cliff gripped the baseball bat, ready to swing again.

I hesitated, unsure whether or not I should leave him, though where I was headed was sure as hell going to be a lot more dangerous than here.

"Don't worry," he said, guessing the cause of my hesitation. He smoothed his comb-over and it felt like a million years ago that I was coming back from seeing Mrs Hammond during my lunch break to find him standing here in almost the exact same spot, a cigarette dangling from his lips.

"I'll be okay," he said, striking a fatherly tone that made me want to hug him. "It'll all be okay. Now go, kiddo. You got this."

Again, I was faced with a dilemma. I knew where I needed to go but *how* to get there was the problem. Just like with the blue glow around my hands, I'd only ever transported myself and Scott out of sheer desperation and survival. I wasn't sure how to do it intentionally.

I decided to try it like I did with my moment among the wisps. I focused only on where I needed to go and the bodies buried in the ground waiting there. I squeezed my eyes tight – held onto that thought and took a step straight off the loading dock.

I stumbled backwards and opened my eyes.

Cliff was gone.

The Piggly Wiggly was gone.

There was no yanking sensation this time. Instead, it was just a single, purposeful step toward the place I needed to go, the world between here and there going by in a blur.

CHAPTER 25

There were only three cemeteries in Magnolia Grove, plus the county one, but technically that wasn't within city limits. There was Magnolia Grove Cemetery (Mrs Hammond's stomping grounds), New Bethlehem (which very well might have turned into the stomping grounds of some recently departed Brethren – rest in peace, fellas) and lastly, Trinity Cemetery. It lay nestled behind an abandoned country church with double doors, their red paint chipping, and a towering steeple missing a few bricks. I rarely ever visited, as it was usually quiet as the dirt road that led to it.

Except for tonight.

I popped out next to the dilapidated wooden fence surrounding the churchyard. Trinity Church was nothing but a dark silhouette, backlit by the light pouring out of the cemetery behind it. The church itself had a pretty, stained glass window that was broken in a few places. As a result, a family of bats managed to nestle their home into the top of the steeple. The rest of the building was in the same state of affairs, not horribly neglected but still suffering from the passage of time and lack of upkeep.

On a normal night, the few dozen rows of crumbling tombstones and crosses would be completely cloaked in darkness, difficult to see, especially since they were mostly hidden by wild overgrown grass and weeds. Tonight, though, they were bathed in the firelight of a dozen torches.

The Brethren weren't dressed in their usual ragged black robes. Tonight, they wore new cloaks like Toby's, deep red with golden ropes draped around their midsections. From their waists dangled individual shards from the jewel Scott tried to destroy, blood smeared across each jagged piece. I had a sinking feeling as to whose blood it might be.

Their red bodies moved between the rows of gravestones, using shovels to dig up tombstones and adding them to a steep mound made of stone erected at the center of the cemetery.

At the top of the pile, was a flat cement slab with an empty gurney. Behind it stood Ivan. He wore a fresh new suit and had his hair neatly combed back. He looked up and his eyes met mine from across the churchyard.

"Lou!" he called out cheerfully, seemingly unaware of how insane this all was. Here he was in a forgotten cemetery in the middle of the night, surrounded by a cult of necromancers with strings of bloodied shards hanging from their cloak-covered waists, and he called out to me as if I had just dropped by the funeral home for a chat.

I stayed at the edge of the cemetery, unwilling to step inside the stone walled perimeter that went up to my shins. There were no ghosts in Trinity Cemetery. No one haunted its forgotten place at the edge of town. And yet, the almost one hundred souls that should be resting in the church grounds were disturbed, their agitation and fear rising from within their burial plots up to me.

"Where is he?" I asked, gritting my teeth to keep my fury at bay.

"Who?" Ivan asked, looking dumbfounded, as if he had no idea the reality of what was happening around him.

It was Toby that gave me the answer. He stepped out from behind the pile of broken tombstones. The arm Scott injured with a knife was no longer in a sling and hung worthless at his side. He looked sicklier than when I saw him in the Piggly Wiggly, his pallor gray, the skin on his face flakey and his eyes desaturated. He nodded with a wicked smile toward a stone angel at the far end of the cemetery, hidden by the shadows of the pine trees. Only the angel's cherub head was visible, the rest covered in an angry swirling black cloud.

I sucked in a breath and grabbed the switchblade Scott gave me, unsure who to point it at. I wasn't a skilled fighter, or any other type of fighter for that matter, but I had stabbed one of them before – granted he was technically already dead at the time. Best case scenario, I would manage to stab one of them again, but there were too many and they would surely take me out. In fact, I wasn't sure why they hadn't already. For the moment, they remained uninterested in me, moving like unthinking drones ordered to one single task. I shrugged off the backpack, held it up by the back loop and pointed the knife at it.

The Brethren stopped working, turning in one motion toward me.

On the surface, it all looked ridiculous – me, holding a purple unicorn backpack at knifepoint – but everyone in the cemetery knew exactly what was in it. Even the Book knew what I intended, violently vibrating inside the bag like it was trying to break out of it.

"I'll destroy it," I said, directing my words to the swirling cloud around the angel. "Everything you've done here will be for nothing if you don't let him go."

Someone else might think Toby or even Ivan was in charge of this nightmare shindig, but I knew who really pulled the strings around here.

The black inky cloud that was the essence of the Lich in this world, relented to my hostage negotiating tactic and fell away from the angel to swoop his way across the cemetery toward the book. He dropped down to hover over the head of one of the cloaked Brethren along the way, sucking the life from his face before diving down to another and another, feeding on each one of them in turn, taking a little bit of their life to fuel the Lich's presence here in the land of the living.

Collapsed in a heap at the angel's stone feet, was Scott. His wrists were tied to the stone legs and his head was slumped back, unmoving.

I threw the bag down and ran to him and cut his restraints free. The front of his shirt was soaked in blood where Toby stabbed him. His hair was wet from drying sweat and his eyes, their once vibrant shade of green, were dull and staring blankly up at me.

"Scott!" I cradled him while trying to put pressure on his wound.

An image came into my mind. He was a boy, not even twelve years-old, pedaling madly on a bike with tears streaming down his face, desperate to get away from the scene inside the small house, to forget the image of his parents murdered inside.

Panic gripped me. What was happening? Why could I see this memory of his?

Another surfaced inside my mind.

He sped through a tunnel under the city on his motorcycle, his heart racing at what he'd just done. His first assignment. What had he become? Was he a killer just like the man who took his parents' lives? No. This was different, he told himself. This was to protect people like them, to prevent something like that from happening again. Still, he couldn't shake the cold, dark feeling that started to wrap itself around his heart.

No, I breathed. I tried to push out the thoughts as they came one right after the other into my head. There was only one reason why this would be happening, and I didn't want to believe it.

"Scott!" I shouted, shaking him desperately in my arms, hoping it pulled him back into the land of the living.

His eyelids fluttered and a slow breath rose in his chest.

"Louise?" he said, his voice coming out in a staggered wheeze.

"I'm here," I said through the tears, struggling to keep his head upright.

Louise. He sees her across the parking lot every time she leaves the cemetery, and it reminds him of sunshine peeking out from behind dark clouds.

My heart lurched.

Scott wants to get a little bit closer to that sunshine even though he thinks he doesn't deserve to feel it shining on him.

No, no, no, no. "Don't go," I begged him. "Stay with me."

Ivan descended his mound of gravestones and came up to me, placing a hand on my shoulder. "Do you know this man?" he asked, looking perplexed.

I violently shrugged his hand off, ignored him and focused everything I had on Scott.

"What do you need, Scott?" I begged him. "Tell me what to do to help you." There was no little pill I could crush and mix with water to bring him back from this.

He focused on me, what little green remained in his eyes was rapidly fading away. "I was wondering if you would see me… after," he whispered, struggling to breathe. "At least we'll have this… whatever this is."

He thought he was already dead. Whatever the Lich did to him was enough to convince him that he *was* dead, and soon he would be. I could feel the life in him fading, everything about him was becoming clearer in my head, just like reading a gravestone in Mortie's pictures. I pressed my face against him and sobbed.

"You care for this man?" Ivan's voice came from over my shoulder. I wanted to kill him, to cry against him, but in the end I only nodded.

He pushed me aside. His long fingers worked quickly, stitching up the wound then wrapping it in a gauze that somehow appeared in his hands. "I don't know if this will save him, but it's the best I can do. Forgive me, Lou. I didn't know what he was to you. I didn't know it was their intent to take someone you cared about."

But did that make it okay to take someone I didn't care about? What the hell was wrong with him? How far gone was he that taking a life – any life – didn't matter to him? Then it hit me. The word he used. *Intent.* I scrambled back to Scott and pushed Ivan aside.

I'd taken something from Scott before, could I do the reverse this time instead?

I took his hand in mine and gently placed them both against the wound. I was no witch but whatever energy flowed through me had mingled with the magic in him once before, so maybe I could do it again. I reached inward for that energy and intertwined it with the life he still had in him, hanging desperately onto my intent. Whatever I had in me, I willed it to him, to give him my years, my lifeforce, anything. There was no blue glow this time, but golden. Where there was a chill before, now there was only warmth. *Please, please, please,* I begged in a repeated mantra. As before, I felt something of him right there in my own hands. What I thought was his life, I realized now was his magic and it too looked fragile and diminishing like the light in his eyes. *Take a little bit of my life and give it to him,* I pleaded with it.

A shudder racked through me, draining me. My strength left me in a single breath and passed to him. His chest rose. That little spark of life in him ignited, burning stronger. I slumped against him weak, but happy. He would live. If I could get us out of here. And that was a big "if."

"It's true then, what the Lich whispers," Ivan said in awe behind me. "You aren't what we expected."

Red cloaks swarmed me. I was lifted and dragged away from Scott, my depleted strength making me too weak to fight back. Ivan no longer pitied me, instead he was excited, leading the way up to the pile of tombstones at the center of Trinity Cemetery. The inky fog poured over the cement slab, swirling over it as if waiting for something.

Charlotte's purple unicorn backpack was passed through hands until it appeared near the gurney. One of the Brethren unzipped the pack and pulled out the book, before discarding the bag between a row of tombstones that had managed to go unplucked from the ground. They propped the book open on a stack of tombstones made to serve as a makeshift pedestal.

Black clouds swirled in the air above the Book before diving into its pages and disappearing. The Book itself transformed. No longer were the pages ragged and torn, they were smooth and velvety black, the cover like new. Its drumbeat of doom returned, this time louder than ever and pouring out relentless waves of dread.

Ivan raised a hand above the book, wanting to touch the page but it snapped an electric arc at him and he drew his hand back. He looked up to me, his eyes hopeful.

"Only you can read from it, please," he pleaded. "You can bring her back, Lou. You're meant to, we both are."

I shook my head. "No, I can't. I promise you."

"I saw what you did for him, the gift you gave him." He motioned to Scott, who still lay at the angel's feet and would've appeared dead if it weren't for the subtle rise and fall of his chest, growing slowly steadier.

"It's not the same, Ivan," I said to him, wearily trying to get him to understand "He still has life in him."

Ivan shook his head, and I was reminded of a child covering their ears pretending not to hear. Just like the book, Ivan looked different than before. He seemed invigorated. The circles under his eyes were gone. He looked younger; there even seemed less gray in his hair.

"You don't know how long I've waited for this, Lou, and now it's within my reach." He nodded toward one of the cloaked Brethren waiting at the edge of the cemetery. "She's going to come back. You can bring her back. I know it," he said, determined.

It broke my heart to see such blind, desperate hope in him. There was no coming back from death and he, of all people, should've known that. I thought of what Mortie said back at Vick's trailer. Just because love felt right and true didn't mean that whatever came from it was good. And here was Ivan proving every bit of that.

Six of the Brethren entered the cemetery's stone walls, carrying a casket between them like pallbearers. I didn't need to use my gift to know who was inside. Here was the earthly shell of Alice, nowhere near her grave where she was meant to be. At one time, it had been a pretty, olive-green casket with silver handles and a band of silver around the lid, sculpted with daylilies. Now, it was a gray box of rotted wood with tarnished, corroded handles and only a hint of the daylilies visible on the trim as time and nature had long since started to reclaim it.

Ivan faltered beside me. I took advantage of the moment to try to reason with him.

"She doesn't belong here, Ivan," I said, trying to reach him. "She isn't even haunting anywhere. She's gone on. Her life was full of the love you shared. There was nothing else to keep her here."

He stuck out his chin, defiant. "You're wrong. I was enough. She wouldn't have gone on, not with me still here. She knew what I was, that somehow I would find a way to bring her back. And I will."

Shit. I'd taken it too far.

"You don't understand, Lou," he said, his eyes taking on a fiery passion I'd never seen in them before. "You've never felt it – a love like that. Very few ever do and trust me, I would know. I've seen their loss. I've seen their regret and mourning play out in front of me day after day, funeral after funeral, death after death, and not one of them had what she and I have. Not even close. A love like that is so rare, Lou."

It was eerie how much his words echoed Mortie's warning.

"The dead have haunted me for decades, serving as a reminder that she's out there somewhere, always just beyond my reach no matter how hard I search for her. I used to think that there must be a reason that we're like this," he went on, "that we have some divine purpose. And you know what I've found?" His voice became cold and detached. "There isn't. It really is a curse. So why shouldn't I just use it? Why let time steal the one powerful, unbreakable love I'd been given?" I wasn't sure if I was imagining the voice that paired along with his in an echo similar to the one in Vick's. "Why would I ever let it rob me of her when right in front of me," his eyes zeroed in on me, "is a way to get her back forever?"

He straightened his shoulders, more determined now, and motioned for the Brethren to set her casket on the empty gurney in front of us.

"Open it," he ordered.

A crowbar appeared and one of the cloaked men shoved it unceremoniously into the sealed lid.

It cracked open and three of the Brethren shoved it off, letting it fall with a heavy thud to the ground beneath the pile.

The Alice that lay inside the once-ivory folds of the casket wasn't the Alice I'd seen. The little bit of skin that still hugged her bones had been mummified and clung to a skeleton that appeared similar to a wisp with its eyeless sockets. Her coarse matted hair, dry like straw, was tied back at the nape of her neck. The wedding dress she'd been buried in, once a simple white gown with sheer long sleeves and a high empire waist, was now merely a bug-rotted, discolored remnant. A shudder ran through Ivan at the sight of her. Tears poured down his face and for a moment as we stood side by side, I was worried he might collapse against me.

Half a dozen red cloaks climbed the mound and moved in a circle around the casket. The shards draped around the Brethren's waists flickered and began to glow.

"Forgive this, Lou," Ivan said at the same time he grasped tight my hand and ran a razor across my palm in a flick of movement. I gasped at the fleeting, sharp pain and tried to yank my hand from his but his fingers were surprisingly tight around my wrist, and I was still too weak from healing Scott to fight back.

Ivan ran the razor edge against his own palm and together smeared both our bleeding hands along what remained of the trim of daylilies along the casket's edge.

He rolled back his head and let out a slow breath. Black mist rose from his lips and floated over the air until it hovered over Alice's corpse and fell like a sprinkle against her skeleton, the black droplets dissolving into her bones. A blue-white aura from the mixture of Ivan's blood with mine wrapped around the casket.

The atmosphere in Trinity Cemetery changed. The air becoming close and dense. This wasn't like reanimating Mrs Renwick; this was more than that and I knew just what sacrifice had been made to make it that much more. It came at the cost of Sharon's life and nearly Scott's, along with countless more. It desecrated hallowed ground as it robbed the peace of those resting within. And it tore at the Veil, dangerously thinning the barrier as the Lich moved in and out of it, nearly shattering the sacred space that separated this world from the next.

It had never been Mrs Renwick that was reanimated, and it wasn't Alice now. It was the Lich, and all of this was a lie, mere theater. But if Ivan knew that, it didn't matter because Alice's shell began to soften and fill out, becoming more like the Alice he knew. Supple skin layered on top of her bones, morphing her skeleton into the body of a woman with a beautiful face that was round with youth and yet still pale gray from the absence of blood. A breath filled her lungs, raising her chest. Beside me, Ivan gasped in turn, watching mesmerized at the transformation taking place before us.

Long pretty eyelashes fluttered against her cheeks and then shot open.

Black eyes stared up at the night sky.

Her body got up out of the coffin, stepping slowly over the edge as the Lich adjusted to the parameters of a new host, and a very much dead one at that. Still, his movements were poised and graceful, just like they'd been in Vick's body. The tattered remains of the wedding dress stood out in stark contrast from the body it clothed. Bits of yellowed lace dangled by hanging threads and bug-eaten fabric gaped open at the seams.

Ivan wasn't bothered by any of that and pulled her into his arms, to cry against her shoulder.

"I waited for you, my love," he said, cupping her dead face in his hands.

Eyes of swirling black ink looked up at him. "And the waiting is almost over," she said. "There's only one last step to take."

They both looked toward me.

Shit.

"This is a lie, Ivan," I tried one last time. "She's not here. This isn't her."

"Read from the book," Ivan ordered me. "Make it so her soul stays in her body permanently."

I backed away only to bump into a wall of Brethren behind me. "What you want is impossible, Ivan. The Lich is lying to you. There's no book, no spell that can bring her back from where she is now. Her soul is not here and it's not in that body." I pointed with a vehemence at Alice's occupied corpse.

He acted as if I hadn't said any of that and nodded toward Scott. "I helped heal him," he said. "But I can't promise they won't finish what they started."

And now he was threatening me. I went rigid with fury. Ivan just kept falling lower and lower.

"You have no idea how much it's hurt the *real* Alice to see how far you've gone." It was the fucking truth and my words landed as if I'd struck him. Hurt and shame flitted across his eyes but they were quickly gone, replaced by an anger that furrowed his brow.

"Try and force her if she won't do it herself," Ivan ordered the Brethren. "And if she still doesn't, kill the boy." Beside him, Alice's smile, which had always been sweet and kind, twisted up in wicked pleasure.

I tried to push through the wall of Brethren in a useless hope of bolting down the mound of tombstones but one of them grabbed me, hauling me back to dump me down in front of the book. He kept me anchored in place with a vice-like grip on the space between my neck and shoulder.

"You're pathetic, by the way," I told Ivan, but he kept still, ignoring me as he looked out at the cemetery filled with Brethren. "Every last one of you. Can't you see the Lich is using you? Feeding off you?"

None of them listened. They only stood silent, waiting.

Ivan nodded and one of the Brethren went up to Scott's fallen form, pointing a knife at his throat. He was still so weak and barely registered the threat to his life.

I stared enraged at Ivan and the Lich next to him and placed my shaking palm against the page.

The idea of reading it like any other book was wrong: that wasn't how one read from this cursed thing. Mortie did it by using his gift, it was the same with Minnie. And I'd unintentionally read from it before, when it knocked me on my ass, I just hadn't known it then. Now I could feel the meaning right there under my hand, the intent of the spells that had been forged by the souls sacrificed to make it.

The spell wasn't to bring Alice back, or any other soul that had truly passed on. The Lich never intended that. He knew it was impossible just as I did. No, it was a spell to bring the Lich himself back from the Veil, to cement his possession of Alice's body and to recover the power he'd poured into the book to stay alive all these years.

"You understand at last what needs to be done, the spell that has to be read," the Lich said through Alice's voice. Those black eyes peered knowingly into mine, guessing correctly that I'd stumbled upon the truth.

I wanted to shout that truth to Ivan, to shake him and make him see it. But he would never believe me. He'd already decided that it was *his* Alice who stood beside him and not the Lich and there was nothing I could say to take that hopeful belief away from him. My mind raced with what to do instead.

Alice's body walked over to me in two long, graceful steps. Staring into her eyes was like staring into the abyss. If it had been the real Alice, her kindness would've poured out of her, but here, there was only the hint of a sneer as the Lich looked into my face.

"Read from it." The Lich's voice, growing angry, echoed this time with Alice's and a flicker of confusion passed briefly over Ivan's face but was just as quickly dismissed.

I picked up the Book off the pedestal and hugged it to my chest.

Vick was right, I was going to do exactly what they wanted. It was the only way – the only thing I could think to do to end it. I grabbed onto Alice's cold dead arm and closed my eyes, taking us where we needed to go in one purposeful step.

We stood alone in Trinity Cemetery, the world inside the Veil devoid of warmth, of color, of life.

Alice's corpse wasn't in front of me anymore. There was only the Lich.

He wasn't just an inky fog, though it remained in his eyes. He was the Lich as he once was, back when he was a sorcerer, before he poured what remained of himself into the Book. Interestingly, I could see a little bit of Ivan in him, and I wondered just how much their time together had shaped and transformed Ivan's face. This man was taller though and wider in his shoulders, his features stronger, too, with a sharper nose and a wicked, calculating smile.

"Alone at last" he said. "And you brought us back to where we first met. How romantic." He wore old clothes, a tunic over a pair of homespun pants with a braided rope draped around his waist. Unlike Ivan, his hair was longer, reaching his shoulders and parted down the middle. "I remember the second you passed through this world on your way to your little cemetery with that horrid ghost of a woman."

He circled me, appraising me in this in-between world. "Louise Helena Cordova. In all my years, I have never before met your like. Do you know how extraordinary that is?"

"And in all those years you've taken bits and pieces from those who've passed through here," I seethed at him. "Trapping them in the land of the living, damning them for eternity, never allowing them peace. How many did it take to keep you here? Dozens? Hundreds?"

He seemed unbothered by the accusation, running a finger through the ash collected on top of a nearby tombstone. "Thousands," he purred.

I gripped tightly to the book and tried a different tactic. "How long has it been? Do you even know who you are anymore? What your name was? Or is that lost too, just like the rest of you?"

That hit a mark. His lip curled upward, and lightning bolts danced in the swirling fog in his eyes. "Enough of this," he hissed. "We're not all that different, you and I."

Every inch of me screamed out in revulsion at the idea of being anything at all like him.

His hand took mine and suddenly Trinity Cemetery disappeared and we were in my bedroom closet the year I turned six.

"No," I breathed. He ignored me.

"Look at you. Adorable little thing that you are." He pointed to the little girl curled up in the corner, her hands on her ears trying to block out the screams that only she could hear coming from her mother's television set. "Much too young and innocent to be cursed and tortured by evils that would break any adult."

"Stop," I whispered the plea, but he went on, gripping my hand tighter, the world blurring faster around us.

And now the eleven year-old version of me sat at the table in the dimly lit kitchen draped in a fake silk shawl, a crystal ball in front of me. My mother brought in the next mark through the beaded curtain – a woman whose sister had passed away, her picture handed to me with a string of pearls. My mother gripped hard onto my shoulder, digging her fingernails into my skin under the shawl to make sure I played my part.

Another blur and I was sixteen and the face in front of me was the same one on the piece of paper in Scott's file folder. The terrified teenager counted wads of bills she'd been hiding away each year until she finally had enough to run for freedom and start a new life of her own.

"You were robbed of the life you should've had," the Lich said in a pitying voice that somehow sounded more like mocking. "The love that should've been given to you."

The vision before me was now a little girl with big slate-colored eyes and midnight black hair who had a loving mother and father, parents who had been there through the years. All of it was a lie, of course, but it was a lie that made my throat tighten at what I would never have.

But I wasn't alone. Not really. Alice's words came back to me. I had Mortie, and Vick, Scott, Cliff, Diego... I had a life filled with love and family. And even though it didn't look at all like the one the Lich showed, that didn't make it any less real.

"You know nothing of life or love," I said, furious. "You forfeited love a long time ago."

"I can be all of that for you, Lou," he kept on. "With me, you will master life and death. You will never know hurt, pain, heartache."

"Is that the lie you told Ivan? Offering promises that weren't within your power to give?"

The Lich shooed away the vision. "Ivan wanted what all men want... eternity."

"No," I said, adamant. "Those would be your little cult of fan boys. Ivan only ever wanted Alice."

"And you can give him that," he said readily. This future made-up version of me brought the soul of Alice back to life and into Ivan's waiting embrace.

All of it was lies. I knew the truth. There were limits to his power and the ultimate limit was death. There was no coming back. As Alice said, that was the beauty and tragedy of life. I realized then that he knew this too. This wasn't just about bringing what remained of him into Alice's body, this was about Ivan and the Brethren and me.

"All this," my hand encompassed the many visions that had passed us by, "it's not about just restoring yourself in the land of the living, is it?" The book trembled in my arms guessing my intent. "You found someone you could control in Ivan, someone you can feed off and wield like a tool, but that's not enough for you, is it?" I turned on him, appraising what was left of the man before me. "You're alone. You want an equal at your side."

His eyes lit, becoming a slate-gray similar to mine. Long fingers like those of a piano player reached out to graze my jaw. "Yes." An actual, earnest desire softened the edges of his sharp features.

He showed me a vision of him and me, my hair long and flowing down my back, a crown upon my head. Swarms of the undead surrounded us. Even in this vision, I could feel their torment.

"Your power coupled with mine… nothing will stand in our way as we rule together." His words echoed in my ears. "There will only be you and me and a world meant to serve us."

This was the world Scott had been sent to prevent, the version of me that I must never be allowed to become.

"But I'm not your equal," I said, my hands glowing vibrant blue in this desaturated world, power coursing through my veins. I jutted out my chin in defiance. "I'm your queen."

I flipped open the book and slammed my hand against the page, reading it the only way it was meant to be read, except this time I didn't try to read the words he'd written in his blood. I read the papers and fibers themselves, reading the lives that had been stolen to make this book of his – every lost love, every broken heart filled with regret, every moment of longing, misery, and hopeless, desolate thought he'd fed off – I read it all.

The Book disintegrated into ash in my hands and what was left of the souls trapped within the pages became free at last.

The Lich recoiled. "What have you done?!"

The ash from the book hovered like a dust cloud popping with static electricity in the air between us. He grasped desperate fistfuls of it, trying to hang onto whatever power from the book lingered within, but it was useless.

It started with one speck floating toward him, moving purposely as if it almost had a mind of its own. It latched onto the back of his hand as he frantically tried to grasp at the cloud. The contact it made with his skin gave off a tiny arc of electricity. Another speck floated and latched, Another, and another. He stopped his futile attempts at holding onto the book's fading power and began swiping at the painful sparks as each particle clung to him and began to glow a familiar bright white like the ribbon I'd seen with Alice.

His arms quickly became coated in light.

"Stop them, please," he begged me, wincing at each new searing touch of a speck, as he wildly tried to shake them off.

But there was nothing I could do – or would do – and I took a step back as the space between us became flooded with specks of light.

He scraped his fingers against his skin, trying to get them off his arms, his face, but only more fixed onto him as if he were a magnet for the bursts of burning light.

I stood watching, frozen in horror, as the blinding light and its feeling of complete finality swallowed up every last inch of him, until only his panicked eyes remained, meeting mine with one final moment of desperation before even they too were covered up.

"This is no place for you now, Lou." Alice's voice came as a whispered warning in my ear.

There are things the living are not meant to see. That they cannot bear to see. I'd said those words to Scott and they echoed in my head now. "Go, now, while they reclaim what was theirs," she said.

I'd never not heeded a ghost's advice and I sure as hell wasn't going to start now. I squeezed my eyes shut and took that mentally purposeful step back into the world of the living, the Lich's screams clinging to my ears as I did.

Trinity Cemetery was ablaze with lights and chaos. Wisps poured out of the crack in the Veil. They flew, twisting and swirling like vaporous sharks circling the cemetery. Hundreds flooded the graves, hunting down the Brethren as they ran screaming between the rows of tombstones.

I ran for the stone angel and threw myself on Scott. "Close your eyes and keep them closed no matter what!" I shouted over the screams, adding my hand as a cover over his face, hoping to God it was enough.

The wisps descended on the Brethren with white-hot glowing eyes and black endless voids of howling mouths as they sucked the life and soul from each man. I watched in horror as their burning gazes seared into the eyes of the Brethren, melting them to empty, hollow sockets as skin turned to ash and the bone beneath crumbled away.

I squeezed my own eyes shut and held Scott closer to me, all the while clutching Minnie's charm tight in my fist.

Dread slammed against us in wave after wave. The anguish and fury from the wisps was so palpable it felt like a hot breath on the back of my neck as they brushed up against us.

My own powers surged to life, enshrouding us in a cold, blue glow as the wisps passed over in their frenzy to reclaim centuries worth of sorrow in a torrent. But it wasn't enough to hold up against their rage and it quickly flickered and died out.

Minnie's charm disintegrated in my fingers. I grabbed a fistful of Scott's shirt instead and buried my face in the crook of his neck as the wisps' wrath started to suck the very breath from my lungs.

And then, just like that, it was done and the cemetery fell dead silent. Still, I kept my eyes shut, listening for whatever else might be out there.

"Lou," came a voice.

An ice-cold touch covered my forearm.

"You can open your eyes now, Lou," the voice said.

My eyelids fluttered open, wet with tears from squeezing them tight. Sharon stood there, no longer the wisp I'd seen in the swarm outside the police station. Her aura wasn't like Mrs

Hammond's or Tom-Tom's. This aura was like Mrs Renwick's and Alice's. I could see a bit of her mother in her features, and she smiled as if I'd said the thought out loud.

She bent over Scott. "Something was taken from him as well."

She moved her hand over his heart, her other still touching my forearm. "I kept it safe for you," she said to him, and he shuddered as he heard her through our joined touch. There was a pulse of warmth like a sunbeam over his chest.

She let go of her hands and floated back. "Thank you, Lou." A hundred souls stood with her, their same bright auras outshining the burning torches. "Because of you, we can rest."

Then, like a light switch being flipped, they were gone.

Trinity Cemetery was empty. The Brethren were gone. The cloaks they'd come in were all that remained, the wisps having taken what was stolen from them.

I raised my hand off Scott's face. Tired, but brilliant, green eyes stared at me.

"Hey there, beautiful," he said to me, managing a weak smile.

I let out a breath and held him tight to me, feeling the living warmth he exuded. His arms enveloped me, and I pressed my face against his chest desperate to hear the heartbeat there. It thrummed against my ear, weaker than I'd like, but steady as a drum.

Not all life was gone from Trinity Cemetery. There was one more heartbeat, fading, but still there.

Ivan hunched over Alice's crumpled corpse, time quickly taking from him what the Lich managed to keep at bay all these decades. His black hair was gray now and going white. Age spots appeared on his hands and cheeks. He was dying, the life inside him slowly flickering out. I left Scott and went to him.

"Lou?" Ivan looked up at me and my heart broke for him as it had before. This was the Ivan I wished I'd known all along, the one that Alice loved more than anyone else in the world. "I've lost her again, haven't I?"

The Veil, still thin, tore a little and there was the same ribbon I'd seen before, dancing like a thread of blinding light next to the coffin. I gently lifted Ivan's hand in mine.

"She's here now though. Do you see her?"

He looked down at Alice's body in his arms and shook his head.

"She's not there." I pointed behind us. "She's here."

He followed my finger and gasped. The warmth poured over his face as Alice hovered in front of him. All the times I'd seen her before, she'd worn her librarian's outfit, the wool skirt that went to her knees and the cardigan buttoned at the top. Now she was in her wedding dress and it looked just as new as the day she got it. Her hair was longer than before, wavy and tied with a white ribbon at the nape of her neck. That sweet, soft smile of hers looked down on him.

"I've been waiting for you, my love," she said, touching a hand to his face. "I've been waiting and watching all this time."

He shuddered, taking his last breaths as if a burden was lifted from him.

"Won't you come with me?" she asked him, reaching out a hand for him.

His eyes looked at me one last time. "Thank you, Lou," he said.

The hand in mine went lifeless as he took hers.

EPILOGUE

I rolled up my work apron and shoved it into my locker.

"...and Amy says 'what do you mean she's pretty?' but, Lou, she straight up asked me if I thought Liddy Biederman was pretty or not. And she totally is. How else am I supposed to answer that?"

I half-listened to Diego as he kept on, nodding as I grabbed the few bags of groceries I picked up right before clocking out of work. It was a rare early out for me. I covered half of Marge's shift so she could go to her podiatrist appointment and now I was free for the rest of the night.

"Sounds like you're overthinking it to me," I told him. "I doubt she's as mad as you say she is."

"Lou, aren't you listening?" Diego groaned, frustrated at my lack of good advice. "She turned beet-red and stomped off. It's so not good. And it's all 'cuz of Liddy Biederman who – granted – is *really* hot, but she's got the personality of a mop. Amy's gonna break up with me. I know it."

No doubt he was right and no doubt they'd be getting back together the next day.

"Maybe buy her some flowers?" I ventured. "Daisies are on sale in Floral."

"Flowers?" He scrunched up his nose. "That's old school, Lou."

Well, it was the best he was going to get out of me. "Good luck, pal. I'm off."

He gave another defeated sigh and went back to putting sale stickers on tuna fish cans.

I headed for the back door and passed Cliff's office. There was a blur of pink skirt and a shuffle of plaid shirt as Cliff quickly righted himself from what clearly had been a kiss from Vick. It left him turning a shade of burning red that matched the lipstick smeared across his mouth.

"I'm out," I told them, trying my damndest to pretend I hadn't seen any of it.

"Thanks again for covering for Marge," Cliff said, unable to meet my eyes. Next to him, Vick grinned, wolfishly, probably proud of the flustered state she'd put him in.

"Sure thing."

"Have fun at the cemetery tonight," Vick said in a mockingly sweet tone, wiggling her eyebrows as she leaned up against the desk to be closer to Cliff. "Maybe instead of your usual PG-rated walk among the tombstones, get dangerous and take a blanket," she said with a wink. "Of course, I'm talking picnic. Unless your mind went somewhere more... fun. Just a thought."

It was my turn to blush. "See ya guys," I said before she could make it any worse.

The sun was still in the sky when I stepped outside. Despite that, there was a definite chill in the air at the quickly approaching autumn. It wasn't often I saw the sun after work, and I took a second to drink it in before setting my groceries in the basket up front on my bike.

I rode past Osgood Funeral Home, no longer afraid of what might be waiting for me there. I expected my heart to give a lurch at the tragedy of Ivan's life but there was only peace.

Ever since the wisps departed Magnolia Grove, taking back what the Lich took from them, more and more ghosts seem to be popping back up around town. Even in the daylight there were one or two walking on the sidewalk, new ones that curiously looked my way.

A corporate-run chain of funeral homes purchased the house and had already replaced the sign out front with an unassumingly generic "Sunrise Funeral Home." They'd uprooted the day lilies which did cause a pang of sadness for me, only because Alice had loved them so.

I peddled on for home as the sun inched its way closer to the horizon.

I turned down my driveway, propped the bike up against the carport post and headed to Mortie's. Even though the sun was out, he'd already turned the porch light on for me. I hopped up the steps and gave my customary three knocks before letting myself in.

Zelda meowed at me as she got up from her perch in front of the window, arching her back in a perfect "Halloween cat" pose.

"It's me," I called out to Mortie working in the back. I dumped the groceries on the counter and got to work making sandwiches, packing a few extra for later. I added chips to Mortie's sandwich and went to the back room.

Instead of book-restoring materials and tools, there were a few charcoal tracings from his own recent cemetery crawls spread out across the work table.

"What do you make of this one, Lewis?" he asked as he sat down on the stool to eat his sandwich.

He had a picture of the tombstone that matched the charcoal tracing pulled up on his laptop screen. It was probably one of the worst degraded grave markers I'd ever seen. All that remained on the moss-covered stone was a lonesome little 'e' at the edge.

My time inside the Veil had changed me. I wasn't sure just how, but something was different every time I used my cursed gifts. Before, I would've only seen so much about the life connected to that little 'e.' But now... Now I saw everything... I saw that person in their entirety in my head, like a friend I'd known my whole life.

Madeline.

Her husband made the stone himself, pouring his grieving heart out into each letter he etched into that stone. He didn't put her last name on there. It was Stewart but he always told her, no matter what her last name was, even when she took on his, that she was always Madeline – a name that barely contained all that she was.

She was a sweet looking, short slip of a woman with light brown hair always unbound and running free across her shoulders instead of pulled back the way most married women wore it. Ed happily tethered himself to her wild nature, indulging all her whims and curiosities, just happy taking a front seat to the surprising, unassumingly fierce woman that she was.

"Madeline Stewart. 1803–1870. And you thought Vick was a firecracker." I laughed thinking about Madeline's clever grin and the extreme delight she took in her husband's wittiness.

Mortie had a look of surprise on his face at the unexpected happiness I felt. Usually talking about these sorts of things came with a certain measure of sadness and loss at time that never seemed enough. Instead, a fraction of Madeline was with me, and it was impossible not to feel her bright burning pleasure. I could easily imagine how Ed must have felt all the time being near that naturally radiating happiness.

"She loved to smile and laugh, and her husband made sure that happened every day," I told him.

Mortie beamed. And part of me felt Madeline beaming back even now, more than a hundred years later, that her and Ed's happiness still lingered in the world.

I hopped off the stool and gave Mortie a kiss on the cheek.

"Speaking of someone who gives you smiles," Mortie said. "Tell Scott that security job at the museum is his if he wants it."

A warm blush spread on my cheeks and I couldn't help beaming at Mortie. "I will."

I took off for a quick stop at my house to pick up a jacket just in case it got even colder when the sun went down. I started to head back out when I hesitated on my way past the couch. I thought about what Vick said and impulsively grabbed the throw blanket folded over the back of the couch, wadding it up under my arm before I could think twice about it. Hey, who knew, maybe it'd get even colder than I thought it might.

I peddled fast to the cemetery, feeling already behind schedule and wanting to soak up every minute I could of my free time with him.

He was already there when I turned my bike onto the gravel parking lot, walking slowly along the back row of graves. My stomach fluttered like it always did at the sight of him.

His face lit up when he saw me walk through the gate and the fluttering in my stomach turned to full-on flipping.

"Hey," I said with a silly grin I couldn't hold back. I felt a bit of Madeline's essence still clinging to me, as if she was there alongside me, grinning at the pure pleasure I felt.

"I have to say, I hope Marge is okay and everything, but I sure like seeing you when there's still a little bit of sunshine out."

I blushed under the open appraisal in his eyes. "Something to eat?" I offered up the peanut butter sandwiches I'd made at Mortie's.

"Goodness gracious, you can't be serious. Peanut butter, Lou?" Mrs Hammond's voice admonished. "A proper picnic would have fried chicken, potato salad... there's not even deviled eggs," she finished with a mournful *tsk* as she floated alongside us as we made our way to the oak tree in the back and spread out the blanket.

Luckily, Scott didn't seem as put off by the sandwiches. We polished them off as we chatted about the most completely normal, mundane things, both of us of drinking in the moment being just a boy and girl on a date.

He lay back on the blanket and pulled me down with him into the crook of his arm, the other tucked behind his head for a pillow.

I thought I heard a happy, dainty lady-like sigh escape Mrs Hammond's lips and saw a small blond head peek out from the angel statue to smile at me.

"Listening to the wind as it rustles through the cemetery grass right before twilight," Scott said, echoing my words from our first date. He nestled me closer. "You know, you might be onto something there."